*The* **ABC***'s of Languages and Linguistics*

# The ABC's of
# Languages and Linguistics

### by
## Jacob Ornstein, Ph.D.
*Institute of Languages and Linguistics*
*Georgetown University*
*Washington, D.C.*

### and

## William W. Gage, Ph.D.
*Center for Applied Linguistics*
*Washington, D.C.*

# Chilton Books

*A Division of Chilton Company*
*Publishers*
*Philadelphia and New York*

*Dedicated to Jan who helped make this work possible.*

# Preface

The aim in writing this book has been to provide a store of basic information about languages and linguistics. Linguistics, the objective study of language phenomena, has only recently come to play a major role in the language field. A report by a group of prominent linguists assessing the current state of the profession contains the comment that, "Most of the popular books dealing with language have had little or nothing to do with linguistics." The need to redress this imbalance was a major incentive toward producing the present volume.

A few notes on the content of the various chapters would not be amiss here. The fourth chapter is particularly concerned with the growing influence of linguistic science. Two further chapters address themselves to the core subject matter of linguistics: "How We Sound" (Ch. 5) and "The Structure of Language" (Ch. 6). Other chapters touch upon what professional linguists would call "related topics": "How the Earth Dweller Writes" (Ch. 7), "A Glance at Some Other Communication Systems" (Ch. 8), and "What Do You Mean—Semantics?" (Ch. 9). Moreover, the first chapter is largely devoted to the clearing away of false preconceptions, one of the major tasks of modern linguistics in the language field.

Several chapters concern themselves with subjects that linguists are often questioned about by non-specialists: "The Beginnings of Language" (Ch. 2), the family relationships among languages in "A Tour of Babel" (Ch. 3), and measures for expediting communication across language boundaries in "The Dream of a World Language" (Ch. 11).

Two other major topics are discussed in the book. One of these is the socio-linguistic theme of languages and politics, treated in "Languages and Riot Squads" (Ch. 10), representing an area in which language problems impinge upon the citizen. The other area of principal importance is the pressing need for Americans to communicate with people whose language is not English. The last three chapters are devoted to this problem and the efforts being made to overcome it.

The authors hope that they have succeeded at least to a modest degree in communicating what is going on in their fields, both to the interested layman and to the language teacher and specialist.

# *Acknowledgments*

First of all, the authors wish to express their gratitude to Dr. Robert J. DiPietro, Assistant Professor of Applied Linguistics, Institute of Languages and Linguistics, Georgetown University, who was kind enough to read the entire manuscript and provide useful suggestions. Their appreciation also goes to the following persons who read various parts of the work and furnished constructive comments: Dr. Charles A. Ferguson, Director of the Center for Applied Linguistics; Mr. J. C. Thompson and Mr. Ray Rackley; and Dr. John J. Gumperz, University of California at Berkeley. It is impossible to mention by name all the other individuals who in one way or another were of assistance to the authors in writing the present work. They desire, however, to make known the valuable part played by Miss Eloise Smith, who typed the manuscript in its various stages with patience and enthusiasm.

# Contents

# Chapter 1

# Language and Myths about Language

## The Importance of Speech

Probably one of the first things you did this morning was talk to somebody. What's so remarkable about that? Most of the other two and one-half billion people in the world did the same thing. But suppose a dog awoke one morning and started talking! It would make the front page of every newspaper in the world.

We are so used to talking and hearing other people talk that we forget what a marvelous accomplishment human speech is. Only when we consider the plight of *not* being able to talk may we fully appreciate its importance.

Consider a deaf-mute or an aphasia victim, a person, that is, who suddenly loses the ability to talk. He may still understand what is said and even communicate in writing; but such a person is as badly handicapped as one with the most distressing physical impairment. He needs institutional care in the same way as any cripple, or special training, at least, to enable him to carry on in the outside world.

One of the authors communicated with an aphasia victim recently, who could say almost nothing, and even said the reverse of what he meant—an intended "No" coming out "Yes," and vice versa. The man was a wealthy Florida realtor, yet one day he wrote: "Believe me, I'd give all my property and savings if I could only talk again."

By contrast, reading and writing—marks on paper that stand for speech sounds—are much less important. In fact, half the people on earth, even in this modern and advanced day, are illiterate or unable to read and write. Many of the world's languages, probably a large majority, have no writing system at all.

So although literacy is a tremendous advantage in human society, it is by no means essential. That is, you can still get along without being able to read or write. "Readers and writers, I can buy by the yard," says a New York City garment district tycoon.

Of course, this does not change the fact that illiteracy is one of the world's great social and educational problems. The point is that illiteracy does not incapacitate humans in the same way that aphasia does. People who cannot read or write may still get along quite well in our society, and even become successful. The speechless man is a hospital case until he is cured or rehabilitated.

There is a well-known story in the Bible that reflects the importance of language in human society. According to the Old Testament mankind spoke only one language until Nimrod began to build a tower that was to reach heaven. "And the Lord said, 'Behold, they are one people, and they have all one language, and this is only the beginning of what they will do; and nothing that they propose to do will now be impossible for them. Come, let us go down, and there confuse their language, that they may not understand one another's speech.' "

Some scholars attribute the source of this legend to the many languages of the slaves who were gathered together to build the famous "hanging gardens" of Babylon. The name

2

"Babel" is said to be a variation of the word "Babylon," rather than the Hebrew *balal,* meaning "to confuse."

Some people believe there is nothing men couldn't do if they really understood each other's speech. Utopia requires far more than that, no doubt, but it is true that a shared tongue tends to unite people, while different languages divide them. If you have ever lived in an environment where you didn't understand the language, you know from your personal experience how welcome a few words of your native speech can sound. Even in the strange accents of strangers, our native tongue seems lovely to us, and we have a fellow-feeling for those who speak as we do.

George Bernard Shaw said that England and America are two countries separated by the same language. The wit of this remark results, partly, from the way it clashes with our conviction that the same language really unites people. A New York psychiatrist's experience corroborates this. By learning the jargon of emotionally disturbed hotrodders, he was able to communicate with them by discussing drag racing and other "tribal customs."

The story of the Tower of Babel shows how using different languages divides people. An even sharper distinction is that between users and non-users of language. This very ability to use language is one of the chief differences between man and the lower animals. The difference between language and animal cries is truly basic. It is brought out by the traditional linguistic definition: A language is a structured system of vocal symbols by which a social group cooperates. Animals may have social groups, and may cooperate by a system of vocal sounds. A recent study of porpoises indicates that this may go much further than we ever imagined in complexity. But the key words are "structured" and "symbols." An animal's alarm call does not "stand for" the idea of danger in anything like the same way that the word "tree" symbolizes everything from a small dogwood to a towering sequoia. Even clearer is the structural nature of language. Human speech is "put together." Words are affected by the other words that surround them in

3

speech. Some words have no separate meaning. "With" or "and," for instance, do not stand for any idea by themselves. They are just the mortar that unites other words into a structural unit. Animal communication shows nothing like this.

## The Unexpected Intricacies of Other People's Languages

At a party recently a linguist was asked whether people like the Eskimos had a real language or whether they just communicated through gestures and grunts. The gentlemen who asked this question, a well-educated person with a master's degree, was truly amazed when he learned that the Eskimos not only have a real language but that it is very complex in structure from our point of view. Then the linguist completely overwhelmed the linguistically-naive guest by writing for him a single word in Eskimo which is equivalent to an entire sentence in English or any European tongue. It was *A:slisa-ut-iss ar-si-niarpu-ba,* which simply means "I am looking for something suitable for a fishline."

There is probably no subject about which there are so many errors and downright misinformation as that of language —even among persons of higher education. One of the most widespread of these is that the language of technologically under-developed or primitive peoples must be very simple and crude. The fact of the matter is that from the standpoint of the speaker of English or a European tongue the languages of such groups often contain difficulties and subtleties which do not exist in our own.

Although English speakers may think it is unusual that certain languages have gender for verbs, much stranger things may be found. In the Nahuatl (Modern Aztec) of northern Mexico, for example, it is necessary in certain verbal forms to express whether the purpose of the action affects an animate being or an inanimate object. In English we say "I *see* the women" and "I *see* the house" and the verb does not change. In Nahuatl, however, in using the verb "to eat" with the root *cua,* the Aztec speaker makes sure to prefix *tla* to indicate that he is not eating a human being. It has been pointed out that

4

this distinction appears most clearly in such words as *tetlazohtlani*, "one who loves (people)," as contrasted with *tlatlazohtlani*, "one who loves (things)."

In Hupa, an Indian language of northern California, nouns as well as verbs have tenses. Thus one finds the following distinctions:

> xonta—house (now existing)
> xontate—house which will exist in the future
> xontaneen—house which formerly existed

Even the speakers of many so-called primitive languages are convinced that their native speech has no grammar but feel that the users just make it up as it comes into their heads. They do, of course, having been trained since infancy to all of its ins and outs. When one of us tries to learn such a tongue he is, however, usually confronted by a system with some bewildering intricacies. There may be the necessity for distinguishing between objects which are in sight and those which aren't, as in southern Paiute where *ma avaaniaak'a a* means "He will give something visible to someone in sight."

There is the possibility of having different verb forms not only to show whether the principal object involved is an agent or something acted on—as with active and passive voice in some familiar languages—but in addition, as in many Philippine languages, to show that it is the instrument or that it is the beneficiary of an action. Thus in Maranao

| | |
|---|---|
| *somombali so mama sa sapi ko gelat*<br>(Emphasis on *so mama*, "the man") | "The man slaughters the cow with a knife." |
| or | |
| *isomabali o mama so gelat ko sapi*<br>(Emphasis on *so gelat*, "a knife") | "With a knife, the man slaughters the cow." |
| *begen ian reka* | "He'll give it to you."<br>(give–something he to–you) |
| *began ka ian* | "You he'll give it to."<br>(give–for someone you he) |

Different verb forms may be used to indicate who does what when relating an incident. In English our use of *he, she, it,* and

5

*they* is often ambiguous: "When Tom went hunting with Harry, he shot a moose." Who shot a moose? In Cree when the "party of the first part," "of the second part," and sometimes "of the third part" are indicated, one says:

| | |
|---|---|
| wāpamēw | A saw B |
| wāpamik | B saw A |
| wāpamēyiwa | B saw C |

Returning to Eskimo, which was thought to be so primitive by the aforementioned dinner guest, we ought to point out that indeed its structure appears formidable to one acquainted with only Indo-European patterns. It is what is known as a polysynthetic, which means that entire sentences are incorporated into a single word. Each element of the word carries meaning but does not have an independent existence. We see immediately that the traditional parts of speech of Latin or English grammar become inadequate or actually misleading in describing such a tongue. For example, "Do you think he really intends to go to look after it?" can be expressed in Eskimo by the word: *Takusar-iartor-uma-faluar-nerp-a.*

This brings us to the misconception that all languages can be analyzed as one would analyze a European tongue such as Latin, Greek, or French. The American school of scientific linguists has done a great deal to break down this fallacy, thanks to the field work it has done in such remote areas as Africa, the Marshall Islands, and North and South American reservations. Each language is in a way an island, an entity unto itself, and must be approached as such. Distinctions which are important in one language or group of languages may be insignificant or entirely lacking in another. For example, in Hungarian and the Uralic tongues for the most part, gender, which is so important in the Romance languages and German, does not matter. This is carried so far that no separate words exist for *he* and *she*, both of which are expressed by *Ő*. Within a sentence, however, it becomes clear that one is talking about a female, either of the human or animal species. While the Romance languages as well

6

as English make subtle distinctions in past tenses, such as "I looked," "I was looking," "I did look," or "I had looked," Chinese has basically only one form for the verb, as *kan,* "look, looked, will look, is looking," etc. However, suffixes may be added to the verbs to indicate various aspects, as *kanle,* "had looked, have looked, will have looked." This parallels the English perfect, which may be found in past, present, or future, though the English speaker, including many who have written grammars of Chinese, is inclined to feel that *-le* equates with the English past tense. There are many other aspects in Chinese.

It is interesting, even fascinating, to observe the distinctions that some languages make, while in others they are non-existent. One of the commonest of these is between a "we" which includes "you" and a "we but not you," as in the Maranao tongue:

| *Inclusive* | *Exclusive* |
|-------------|-------------|
| tano | kami |

To give just another example of linguistic variety, the Turkish language makes a strict distinction between personally observed and hearsay or attested past. For instance, to express the sentence, "His daughter was very beautiful," one of the two following forms must be used:

| *Hearsay* | *Attested* |
|-----------|------------|
| Kız çok güzel imiş | Kız çok güzel idi |

In the first example *imiş* is used because the speaker does not know the statement to be a fact since he has no personal knowledge of it; while in the second *idi* is employed because he has personally verified that the young lady in question was beautiful.

In Basque, a non-Indo-European language spoken in the Spanish and French Pyrenees, the verb "has" affixes to indicate the subject, object, recipient, and the sex of the person addressed. In Japanese the terms of Indo-European grammar do not work too well either. In that language, for instance, *shiro* by itself stands for "white." Add the ending *katta* and you get *shirokatta* —"it was white," or literally, "it whited."

While it is impossible to delve deeply into the formal linguistics in a work of this scope, let us note—just to satisfy the

7

curiosity of those with special thirst for knowledge—what sort of terminology the modern scientific linguist uses. Instead of using the traditional parts of speech whether they fit or not, he arranges the grammatical elements into form classes. Thus the Japanese words like *shiroi* are classified not as adjectives but into a particular form class, with explanations of both their adjectival, verbal, and other uses.

## Other Misconceptions

One reason why we often assume that other peoples must express their thoughts the way it is done in English, German, or other European languages is that for centuries we have been under the influence of the classical traditions. This means that it was the custom to regard Greek and Latin as ideal languages and to speak of other tongues in the same terms until this was changed by the advent in the twentieth century of the American school of scientific linguistics.[1]

Another widespread misconception is that other peoples must necessarily express a given thought as we do. That this is far from the case is, of course, reflected in the very term *idiom* which comes from the Greek word *idios* meaning individual (and from which the word *idiot* is also derived). No two languages in the world express all concepts and thoughts in exactly the same way. We say in English "I am hungry," but in French it is *"J'ai faim"*—which is more literally "I have hunger." All European languages have some way of saying "How are you?" but Burmese has no such expression and one must employ instead one of five or six levels of politeness. We say "I feel sorry for you," but Japanese renders this thought by *O kinodoku desu* or literally "It's a poison for your soul."

Information about the real world is organized according to the linguistic patterns of a given speech community in ways which are to a great extent arbitrary and not according to the canons of logic. All grammars contain a great deal that goes

[1] For the reader who wishes to acquire some basic books on linguistics, written in language which is not too involved, a list has been included at the end of this work.

contrary to what we would regard as the sensible way of organizing things, and it is a mistake to think that any language is particularly logical or that the more exotic languages are as a whole less logical than the more familiar ones.

This divergence in patterns of expression is the reason that so many feel that every tongue has its own soul or spirit which means something beyond mere vocabulary and grammar. This is why no matter how well-done a translation may be, something will always be lost from the original because every language is inextricably interwoven with the peculiar culture of its speakers. As Dr. W. R. Parker of Indiana University has remarked, when in Goethe's *Faust* Dr. Faustus stops addressing Margaret by the formal *Sie* (for "you") and uses the intimate *du,* there is nothing in English which can convey this subtle yet significant change in tone. Here again the individual who in learning a tongue goes beyond its basic everyday expressions and becomes acquainted with its nuances and fine distinctions is in the best position to analyze what makes its speakers tick linguistically—and to a large extent, psychologically.

Still another type of myth is the one regarding the superiority and inferiority of languages. There is in fact a tremendous body of folklore built up about most tongues. Regarding French there is the legend that it possesses special attributes which enable it to express thoughts more clearly than in any other language. There is even a saying in French, *Ce qui n'est pas clair, n'est pas français:* "What is not clear, is not French." Nationalistic Germans have attributed to their language mystic qualities which supposedly give it special powers of vigorous expression. About Italian there exist many beliefs regarding its sonority and musicality. Incidentally, in this vein the Spanish emperor Charles V once said that English was the language to speak with merchants, German with soldiers, French with women, Italian with friends, and Spanish with God!

These beliefs have no basis in scientific linguistic fact any more than the assertions that any given language is prettier than another. Like the beauty of a painting or that of a woman, the charm of any tongue lies solely in the eyes—or ears—of the

9

beholder. One often hears that German is not as beautiful as Spanish or Italian because it is guttural, and in the aesthetic judgment of some people gutturalness sounds harsh. From the scientific linguistic viewpoint this judgment is meaningless and a linguist would merely say that German has more guttural sounds than English, French, or Italian, or in more technical phraseology, that German has a high number of sounds produced with the velum, the flap of flesh which hangs down at the back of the mouth and which cuts off the breath stream between the oral and nasal cavity. Yet to many speakers of Semitic languages, gutturalness is not only not a defect but is a positive virtue. In Israel to speak Hebrew with a markedly guttural pronunciation is considered very chic. Arabic has an unusually high number of guttural sounds but few persons who claim this as their mother tongue would consider it one iota less beautiful than, let's say, French or English.

It is equally false to believe that the sounds of a particular language are in themselves easy or difficult. The degree of difficulty is dependent on the language background with which we start, and there are probably no sounds that the speakers of some language would not have trouble with. Incidentally, children of, say, a year and a half old, who have not yet mastered their own language, often make use of many sounds that the adults of their speech communities would class as extremely difficult. Learning the sounds of a first language is in part a process of learning to avoid sounds that don't belong to it.

At the root of many linguistic misconceptions is the undeniable fact that many people regard language as static and inflexible rather than something dynamic and ever-changing. It is common to hear statements to the effect that a certain language is incapable of expressing the concepts of modern society. This is a fallacy, and from the evidence of linguistic science there does not appear to be any tongue which cannot be harnessed to serve any verbal communication need. The fact that languages may express concepts through different patterns does not alter this principle at all. When Wycliffe was told that English was too "rude" for the Scriptures to appear in, he retorted, "It is not so rude as they are false liars."

It is, however, undeniable that the Wichita language of the Oklahoma Indian tribe of 500 souls is not in its present state suitable for discussing nuclear physics or celestial navigation. But this is primarily because the speakers of Wichita have never had to cope with such problems using their native language. If, however, the roles of Wichita and English were reversed, it might be English which would lack specialized terminology and expressions.

We do not know the details of the origin of speech. But we do know that languages have an organic existence, and that they develop according to the needs of the community employing them. The more technologically advanced the speakers are, the more equipped the language will be to cope with science, technology, and the concepts of an industrialized society. Conversely, the languages of such advanced nations as America, Germany, and France may and often do lack numerous concepts and nuances referring to the phenomena of nature and to pursuits like herding, hunting, and fishing, which are elaborately present in many tongues of people of a more primitive culture. Berber has a far richer vocabulary for discussing camels and livestock and their care than has Danish or Italian. Hopi is apparently far better equipped to deal with descriptions of vibratory phenomena than is any European language.

There are languages in existence in which there is no way of saying *stereophonic playback recorder* or *atomic warhead*. But this does not mean that the speakers of these languages could not coin such expressions. The coining of new terms—and this important fact is often not realized—is part of the organic development of any living language in a dynamically growing society. For example, the reason why the ancient Greek Homer had no word for motorcar is simply because he did not have such a vehicle to convey him through the hills and dales of his homeland. The modern Greeks, however, have coined a word for this useful vehicle terming it *autokinito,* composed of *auto* (self) and *kinito* (moving thing). That, after all, is the way the term *automobile,* used in most European languages, was conceived and constructed. But tastes vary in languages and although Czech, for example, uses the word *automobil,* Polish has preferred to express the same concept by the word *samochod,* composed of the elements *samo* (self) and *chod* (moving).

The Thai language was not equipped until a few years ago with words for most modern innovations. There was a tradition in Thailand of using Sanskrit roots in technical vocabulary much as we make use of Greek (astronomy, epiglottis, etc.). With modernization the Thais have avidly set about the business of coining new words, even to the extent of having contests for the best word made up to express some new western-derived concept. Preferably the new words should include Sanskrit elements already used in Thai and, ideally, should have some resemblance in sound to the term used in European languages.

The growth and development of languages presents still other opportunities for myth-building. It has been difficult for people to realize that every language is in a constant state of flux and is at any period moving in new directions usually considered to be corrupt and decadent by the purists. The constant mutability of language is obscured because of the tendency to think in terms of the standardized written form of a language. People felt that Latin was still the same thing the whole of the time that spoken Latin was becoming transformed into French, Spanish, Italian, and the other modern Romance languages. Beliefs in immunity to change on the part of any living language are totally without foundation. To this class we must consign all allegations that any language known within the span of recorded history is not really at all close to the original language of the first days of human speech. (We have more to say on this subject in the next chapter.) Another perennial favorite that crops up here is the story that somewhere—usually in the mountains of Kentucky —the natives still speak "pure Elizabethan English."

Many of the most persistent myths about language occur in the field of the relation of speech to writing. Commonly people feel that a language which has never been written is not really a language at all. In fact an unwritten language can have all the other attributes of any language and can even have a rich literature, although necessarily a literature limited to what is handed down by oral tradition. In the case of languages which have been written for centuries people often feel that the writing represents the real language and the spoken form only a pale and probably corrupted reflection of it. Scientific linguists, while understanding the great importance of the written form and recognizing the many ways in which writing and speech interact with each other, are nevertheless forced to maintain the view that speaking is the basic symbol-using activity of mankind and that writing is a superstructure built upon it.

Fact, fancy, and even prejudice exist about languages just as they do about individuals and nations. While some of these beliefs are romantic and many appeal to the imagination, it would seem to be far better to know more about the true nature of language as a branch of the behavioral sciences than to perpetuate old wives' tales about it. We propose in the following chapters to take a look at what human speech is and what general principles apply to its function and use in the world around us. We can enjoy this excursion all the more if we get rid of our misconceptions before embarking upon it. Even if we find that we cannot easily discuss the bullish and bearish fluctuations of Wall Street ticker tapes in fluent Eskimo, it may turn out that for the fine points of under-ice fishing that language may be superior to English and French combined.

# Chapter 2

# The Beginnings of Language

*The Problem of the Origin of Speech*

Just how did language get started? Although numerous theories have been suggested and scholars have argued heatedly over the question, nobody really knows. Elusive and frustrating though this question may be, man will probably continue to be intrigued by it for some time to come. Perhaps writers of mystery stories, with their uncanny ability to find solutions, might be able to help us in this.

According to Genesis man was created in the image of God and speech was one of his attributes. It says, "And out of the ground the Lord God formed every beast of the field, and every fowl of the air, and brought them unto Adam to see what he would call them; and whatsoever Adam called every creature, that was the name thereof. And Adam gave names to all cattle, and to the fowl of the air, and to every beast of the field."

This, of course, still does not tell us when and how man began to speak or in what sort of language. Both linguists and non-linguists alike love to speculate on the origin of language. In the March 27, 1960, *New York Times* Book Review Section, literary critic J. Donald Adams suggested that, "It is indeed hard to rid ourselves of the idea that the desire to name things lies at the root of language." This means that those who love a mystery have a fertile field in the problem of how language originated. Most of the books and articles written about language origins contain more fantasy than fact.

At what stage in his development did man begin to speak? How rapidly did he pass from pre-speech to something recognizable as language? Did it take centuries—millennia—from the time he could say, "I'm hungry," until he worked himself up to such profundities as, "Woman, bring me my knotty pine club"?

Perhaps you have wondered what language Adam and Eve spoke. We know that the Bible was first written in Hebrew, but the Old Testament Hebrews were late-comers in man's history on earth (from the archeological viewpoint). The story of Genesis must refer to a much more primitive period than the Hebrew Commonwealth.

Many people of the western world believed until quite recently that Hebrew was man's first language, from which all other languages were derived. There actually is, however, no reason for thinking that Hebrew even remotely resembles the first tongue of man and it can be proved by the principles of linguistic science that most of the languages of man do not come from Hebrew. Moreover, as most readers of the Bible know, the Old Testament does not mention specifically *which* tongue was spoken by Adam and Eve. As late as the seventeenth century a Swedish philologist claimed that in the Garden of Eden God spoke Swedish, Adam Danish, and the serpent French. It should be recalled, however, that according to Genesis only one language was spoken until the Lord, by way of punishing men for building the Tower of Babel, caused them to speak a multiplicity of tongues. Also there is no implication in the story that *any* of the post-Babel languages was particularly close to the original.

Attempts to trace all languages back to a common ancestor have not produced any convincing conclusions. The eighteenth century Russian empress Catherine the Great wrote to Benjamin Franklin inquiring about how American Indian tongues showed their relationship to Hebrew. As late as 1934 at a Turkish linguistic congress someone even seriously argued that Turkish is at the root of all languages—all words being derived from *gunes,* the Turkish word for sun, the first object to attract man's attention and demand a name.

By now we know that the origin of language is so far back in time that all attempts to deduce what actual elements of original languages are found in any known language are bound to fail. The time span is so great that we cannot now determine even whether there was a single language from which all present languages were descended or whether there might have been several original languages. The descendants of speakers of a single language will alter their speech so much that in a few thousand years the connection between separate languages stemming from a single original source would become untraceable without other pieces of evidence connecting them. Our present knowledge is sufficient to make us sure that we are dealing with a considerably longer period than a few thousand years when we try to trace language back to its very beginnings. As Max Mueller said a hundred years ago, and in a deeper sense than he meant it, "It is quite clear that we have no means of solving the problem of the origin of language *historically."*

If those brave men and women or their predecessors who first set foot on earth had been able to leave us phonograph or tape recordings of their speech, we feel confident that linguistic experts would have little trouble describing it. Unfortunately, however, about all we have to go on for any information about the linguistic past are inscriptions on objects and artifacts, and these are from a relatively late period in man's annals. The written documents which have come down to us both in the Occident and the Orient, mostly dating from 5,000 B.C. at the earliest, represent from the historical viewpoint a fairly recent time considering the millennia that civilization has been known to exist. The British linguist Lois H. Gray wrote in 1939, "If we are unable to affirm that the earliest men could speak (except in the sense that animals and birds can speak), no skeletal remains thus far found show any evidence that they could not. Anthropology throws no light on the problem."

One thing we do know: although animals and birds can be taught to perform certain feats and even to utter individual words, man is the only terrestrial being who is able to accomplish the act of speaking; that is, to make the complex sequence of organized noises adding up to definite meanings. Just what the things are that man can do we will mention in more detail later on. The appearance of language in the universe, at least on our planet, is thus clearly no less recent than the appearance of man himself.

## Various Theories

But let's get back to the subject of how language might have got started. There are indeed about as many theories attempting to explain this as there have been theorists. Almost all of the theories are, furthermore, of the armchair investigation type to an almost incredible degree. And one fact that militates against accepting any of them is that many of our more imaginative readers could sit down and make up one in the course of an afternoon that would sound just as plausible.

The ancient Greek philosophers, much given to speculation, theorized considerably about language. Socrates added his bit as recorded in the *Cratylus* of Plato. During the course of the dialogue Socrates notes that in Greek the sound *r* often appears in words denoting motion and *l* in those referring to smoothness. (Note in English: *run, river, ripple, ride, race, rise.*) He concludes that onomatopoeia, or the imitation of the sounds of actions, was the basis of the origin of language and the reason why the "correct" name was found for things.

The eighteenth-century German philosopher Leibnitz represented the view that all languages came from a proto-speech. In the next century Darwin advanced the hypothesis that speech originated from "mouth pantomime," by which he meant that the vocal organs unconsciously imitated gestures performed by the hands. Even as recently as 1962, one of the two speakers who dealt with this field at the meeting of the American Anthropological Association presented ideas which followed this general tack.

Numerous other theories have been proposed; many of them have been accorded picturesque names neatly cataloguing them according to the type of words they envision as forming the first stratum of speech. One of these was what the German scholar Max Mueller christened the "bow-wow" theory, according to which language arose in imitation of the sounds of nature, such as the babbling of a brook, the murmur of the wind, and so on. Since a dog barks, for example, and says "bow-wow," man referred to him as a bow-wow. This view, however, does not hold water, since the same noise is often interpreted differently by different people. In imitating a rooster, for instance, English speakers say "cock-a-doodle-doo," the Spanish and French "cocorico," and the Chinese "wang-wang." Most of our so-called onomatopoeic words are made according to the patterns of our own particular language system, and some borderline cases which aren't are just as clearly transmitted as part of our cultural heritage.

There is also the "ding-dong" theory which tries to establish a mystical and difficult-to-fathom relationship between sound and meaning. The name refers to the idea that the primeval term for an object could represent any noise associable with it, includes ones made by hitting it, blowing on it, or the like.

The "ta-ta" theory holds, somewhat in line with Darwin, that languages originated from verbal imitation of bodily movements and gestures, gesticulating with the mouth and tongue, so to speak.

It is difficult not to smile a little when we examine still other theories. The "yo-he-ho" theory argues that language arose as exclamatory utterances brought about by intense physical effort. When used as communication they presumably meant such things as "Heave on that rock," etc. And finally, the "pooh-pooh" theory maintains that language first consisted of exclamations prompted by such emotions as fear, pleasure, pain, and the like. Present-day examples in this classification, like the

18

onomatopoeic words, turn out to be mostly rather closely bound to a particular language.

Surprisingly enough, even the renowned linguist Otto Jespersen formulated a theory of original speech. Realizing that our reconstructions of earlier stages of language merely scratch the surface of the whole long period of human speech, he nevertheless felt that we could work our way back by observing general tendencies and directions of development. In his work on language history he was greatly impressed by the breaking-down processes that we can find whenever we have evidence of an earlier and a later stage of a language. Therefore, he imagined the earliest speech was vastly less broken down and by no means simple, as most other theories had taught.

"We must imagine primitive language as consisting (chiefly at least) of very long words, full of difficult sounds, and sung rather than spoken.

"*The evolution of language shows a progressive tendency from inseparable conglomerations to freely and regularly combinable short elements.*"

Obviously no term in our broken-down modern idiom could be complicated enough to do justice to such an awesomely jawbreaking protean stage, although some of the ideas might get across if we called it the "Rumpel-stiltskin" theory.

The most flagrant lapse of this great linguistic scholar was once again the failure to take account of the time span. Human speech has been around too long for this theory to be true. If, in general, breaking-down processes went on faster than building-up processes, rather than being pretty much in balance in a sort of steady state, language would have ceased long ago when the last speaker could say nothing but "Uh." Languages for most of human history must have been in broad general character pretty much like languages as we now find them.

A few years ago Dr. D. S. Diamond, an English lawyer and sociologist, wrote a book titled *The History and Origin of Language* in which he tried to prove that the first words were brief interjections something like the first distinctive utterances of infants. At first these words were made as calls for assistance accompanied by gestures designed to illustrate the sort of help desired, such as to cut, break, or crush something. Then Diamond seeks evidence in a vast variety of languages, including Hebrew and the African tongues, to support him. But, intriguing as it may be, his involved theory represents, to a large extent, sheer speculation.

G. Revesz, late Professor of Psychology at the University of Amsterdam, in his book *The Origins and Prehistory of Language*,[1] feels that human speech developed through various stages we may find in animal noises. The ultimate root is to be found in *contact sounds* which merely serve to help identify members of the same species to each other and promote a sort of togetherness. Real communication begins with the *cry* which is specific to some internal state of the animal, so that the others know it is frightened, angry, hungry, hurt, or what not, and can act accordingly. A cry does not need to be anything we would consider a deliberate message, and even when it is, it is always addressed "to whom it may concern." The last stage of pre-speech believed by Revesz to be limited to the most highly developed mammals such as cats, dogs, and monkeys, is the *call;* this is a sound addressed to one particular other individual. It was specialization in the development of calls that is assumed to have led to the *word,* which in its first unrecoverable rudimentary stage of *imperative language* was most nearly analogous to the imperatives (commands) and vocatives (names called out) of later fully functioning human speech. So far as we know this formulation has not yet been given a nickname and we would suggest calling it the "Hey, you!" theory.

One type of behavior relevant to his theory, which Revesz apparently ignores, is to be found in the actions of animals in establishing and maintaining dominance relationships. Many gregarious animals have ways of communicating messages which we might render as "I'm tougher than you are"; "No, you aren't either"; or "Okay, okay, but you needn't be so huffy about it." These forms of behavior are directed to a single other individual

[1] New York: Philosophical Library, 1956.

and in some cases they are in part vocal, thereby fitting Revesz' definition of calls. Thus it would appear that calls are more widespread among animals than he gives them credit for being.

We are tempted at this point to stop and develop a brand new "Say 'Uncle'" theory of the origin of language but, as we indicated before, take a good imagination and a rainy afternoon and the reader could come up with a more plausible one of his own.

An obvious thought is that we ought at least to try to find a way of synthesizing, out of the pieces of all the laboriously elaborated theories that have been offered, the beginnings of a reasonable explanation. We do not have to delve very deeply, however, to see that the proposals are so disparate as to be virtually unconnectible. It is hard to imagine how more than one of such a scattered lot could have a glimmer of the truth.

All of this adds up to the conclusion, paraphrasing the German philosopher, "that we only know that we don't know." We cannot reconstruct any vestige of original language; we cannot even extrapolate back from recent trends as Jespersen tried to do. The beginnings are too far lost in the mists of antiquity. Neither can we recapture glimpses of something like the original situation from observing children. Infants learning to speak do not go through the linguistic history of the race all over again. They are immersed in a world of talking from the beginning. Well before they use anything we would call words, influences of the language they hear can be detected in their babbling. Gradually they develop closer and closer approximations of the speech to which they are exposed, often working their way towards the same language, incidentally, by very different paths.

People have suggested and even tried carrying out experiments with children to see whether, if left to their own resources, they would develop languages of their own. We must perhaps grant that what would happen would no doubt be interesting to know, and it could at least make a good science fiction plot to have a Mad Linguist abducting babes for his origin-of-language researches. But, besides being "impossible, unnatural, and illegal to try the experiment," as Max Mueller put it, it would not really be relevant to how language began. Neither such experimental subjects nor the feral children who are supposed to have grown up among animals would reflect a social community which certainly already had pre-language vocal communication at the very least as well-developed as that of the gibbons.

When we resort to pure speculation, trying to discover principles that would necessarily apply to the origin of language we have an intriguing parlor game, but very disappointing scientific results, considering all the brainpower that has been lavished upon it.

## Some Basic Principles

Then, will we never know any more about it than we do now? For all the bleakness of the outlook depicted so far in this chapter, we eventually may. There are certain lines of inquiry which offer hope of leading towards a solution. One of them is the study of animal behavior, a developing discipline getting to be known as ethology. Revesz can be regarded as having in some ways made a step in the right direction in endeavoring to see what was there before speech. What we particularly need along these lines is a careful look at the social behavior of chimpanzees and gorillas in the wild, and such work is really just beginning. It has gone far enough, even so, to show that many of the things we thought we knew about the anthropoids just aren't so. Eventually such investigation could establish some sort of base line for the type of communicative system on top of which human speech must have developed. Many previous theories really seem to have set for themselves the unpromising task of trying to explain the development of language in an ape-man less socially advanced than modern apes.

The other inviting approach involves looking more closely into what are the fundamental characteristics of human language as contrasted with animal communication. In the past it has often been taken for granted that we knew what these were. Today's linguistics, in giving us a better understanding of human language workings, has helped also to clarify the real distinctiveness of human language. Charles F. Hockett in the chapter of his *Course in Modern Linguistics* called "Man's Place in Nature" has pointed out a set of essential features which included the following.

DISPLACEMENT. This is the ability to use a communicative device in the absence of the original stimulus. While this has been found in bee communication, in the wiggling called dances performed on the honeycomb by the workers returning to the hive from a source of nectar, we have as yet no evidence for such a capacity among apes or other mammals. Thus, one of the things we have to include in a theory of the origin of language is how man's ancestors came to be able to convey not only messages like "Watch out for that leopard!" but also "Watch out for leopards when you cross that open place near the river; I saw one there this morning."

PRODUCTIVITY. This is the ability to make up new messages readily rather than having to stick exclusively to an already existing repertoire.

DUALITY. This characteristic is manifested in human speech by the existence of a vast number of words all spoken by using only a rather small number of sounds. Duality is essentially a concept of linguistics, and some explanation of the two different levels on which language operates will be given in Chapters 5 and 6. Suffice it to say for present purposes that in most animal communication a particular type of noise is usually associated with only one particular type of meaning. We might add that the two-level organization in which meaningful units (like words) are made up of various combinations of units not meaningful in themselves (like sounds or, in writing, letters) seems in the present state of our knowledge probably the most salient property of human language. In fact, if we met intelligent Martians many of our linguists would probably decide to call their system of communication language if it showed duality even though it might operate by controlled emission of heat.

CULTURAL TRANSMISSION. Language is not instinctive but is part of the learned behavior of human beings.

Such a start at formulating with greater specificity what we are really trying to explain when we make up theories of the origin of language ought to help to direct speculation along more fruitful channels. It appears promising that a paper at the 1962 meeting of the American Anthropological Association dealt in terms of these essential features we have just outlined; its author considered what effects in the direction of achieving these characteristics might be expected to follow upon a large increase in the number of distinct signals used for communication in a pre-language social group.

Perhaps it is more rewarding for our purposes to look at languages as they are today, rather than losing much sleep over a question, the answer to which may always be largely sealed to us.

# Chapter 3

# A Tour of Babel

## Mapping Languages

A linguistic map of the world would have over three thousand different languages. Africa south of the Sahara has no less than eight hundred. This number refers to full-fledged languages only. Counting even the major dialects has proved to be an impossible task. No one can say how many dialects there are in Africa.

A big part of the problem of counting languages lies in deciding what is a language and what is a dialect. Take the speech of Florence and that of Palermo. These are every bit as different as the dialects of Lisbon and Madrid. Why then do we say that Florentines and people from Palermo speak the same language but that Spanish and Portuguese are two languages? The answer is usually political. The schoolchild in Palermo does not learn to write the dialect he speaks. He learns a standard Italian based on the dialect of Florence. This is because the central government of his country has made an arbitrary standard of that dialect. Portugal, of course, has been politically separate from Spain since the Middle Ages. In school the people of each country learn to read and write the dialect of the capital. Portuguese learn a standard language based on the dialect of Lisbon, but the Spanish children learn a form of the dialect of Madrid. Since they learn to write two different standard "languages," we list Portuguese separately from Spanish. The man from Palermo may speak a language almost as different from standard Italian as Portuguese is from Spanish. But because he writes the same way as the Florentine or Roman we say Italians all speak the same language.

The standardization of a dialect into a "separate language" also happened in Norway. When Norway was part of Denmark through the Napoleonic Wars the Norwegians were thought of as speaking a dialect of Danish. Nobody wrote Norwegian any more than anybody today writes Texan or Canadian. When Norwegians wrote their own language, they wrote standard Danish, just as today Texans or Canadians write English. After the separation from Denmark, a new Norwegian written language was developed based on the western Scandinavian dialect spoken in Norway. So now we say that Norwegian and Danish are different languages, though native speakers, each speaking his own dialect, understand each other reasonably well.

A true linguistic map would have to be drawn more in shades of color than in patches. The dialects of Spain and Portugal would blend into each other in some places with little pronounced difference along the political boundary. Of course, centuries of writing the languages differently have had an effect, but the Spanish and Portuguese spoken on either side of the border of Spain and Portugal are much more similar than most people realize. Seas and uninhabitable mountains would make breaks in the color gradation. More pronounced differences would occur where languages of different groups border on each other. The colors on either side of the linguistic boundary between French and the Germanic languages would be quite different. But the boundary itself would be very complex, with areas like Belgium and Alsace where both languages exist side by side.

The same linguistic map would show a few isolated blobs of highly contrasting colors. The Basque language of the western Pyrenees bears no relation to its nearest neighbors, or apparently to any other language whatsoever. Another such blob of isolated color would appear in the Caucasus. Here Georgian and the other Caucasian languages form another linguistic island.

This brings up another point of interest. Soviet linguists claim a connection between these two groups. They place Basque and Caucasian languages together in an Ibero-Caucasian unit. Most other linguists question this conclusion. It is, however, practically impossible to make a categorical statement that one given Language A is totally unconnected to an apparently unrelated Language B. After millennia of separate development, all evidences of relationship may disappear. This is the line of reasoning advanced by those who claim that all languages are derived from one original source (monogenesis). Those who favor the opposite theory of polygenesis have no way to prove their point. All they can say is that the present evidence for monogenesis is not personally convincing to them. In the same way, those of us who question the Ibero-Caucasian link can only say that the evidence we now have does not convince us. Tomorrow may bring fully convincing evidence on this or any other point of language relationships.

A true linguistic map such as we have been proposing is, of course, really an impossibility. For one thing finer and finer distinctions in dialect can be drawn until we come down to finding small differences even among members of a single family. For this reason linguists have had to recognize the concept of an *idiolect,* the speech system of a single individual.

On a more gross scale, the map is impossible because of *bilingualism,* the use of two different languages by the same people, which is a common phenomenon in various parts of the world. A good example is Paraguay where a major part of the population speaks both Spanish and the American Indian language, Guaraní.

Another complicating situation is a sort of "bi-dialectism" which linguists are coming to refer to as *diglossia.* In this case two different forms of what can be recognized easily as in some

27

sense the same languages are used by the same people for different purposes. Switzerland can serve as an excellent illustration of this point. A form of standard German is taught in the schools and generally used for most cultural and intellectual purposes, but the Swiss dialects maintain their position as the general media for ordinary communication.

## Our Language's Family: Indo-European

Suppose you were on a quiz program. The payoff question is: "To what language family does English belong?" You could ring the bell and win the prize by answering, "English is a Germanic language in the Indo-European language family." The basis for this statement lies in similarities that can be traced between the many languages of the family. Take two languages as different as Polish and Spanish. A random sentence ("His mother is old," for example) at first shows more differences than similarities. Here it is in the two languages:

| | |
|---|---|
| Spanish: | Su madre es vieja. |
| Polish: | Jego matka jest stara. |

Neither speaker would understand the sentence in the other language, but there are some deep-lying similarities nevertheless. In the first place, the word order is the same, and it is the same as the one we find in English. (Other languages may take from one to six words for the same sentence, and a large proportion of the possible combinations of word order will turn up in some language or other.) Furthermore, the words for "mother" show some similarity and the words for "is" share the element "es." At first glance "vieja" and "stara" seem completely different, and they do come from different roots. But both must be in the feminine singular form (to agree with the feminine singular "mother") and in both cases the feminine singular sign is the -a ending. Not as different as they look, are they?

Word similarities trace the relationship between languages far apart in geography. Take the words for "mother" and "three" for example.

28

| Greek | Latin | German | English | Norwegian | Gaelic (Erse) |
|---|---|---|---|---|---|
| *mater* | *mater* | *Mutter* | *mother* | *mor (moder)* | *mathair* |
| *treis* | *tres* | *drei* | *three* | *tre* | |

| Russian | Lithuanian | Albanian | Armenian | Sanskrit | Persian |
|---|---|---|---|---|---|
| *mat* | *motina* | *(noma)* | *mair* | *matr* | *mader* |
| *tri* | *tris* | *tre* | *(erek)* | *tri* | *(se)* |

The Albanian word for "mother" does not belong in the same group as the rest, and the Armenian and Persian words for "three," though related to the others, show no obvious similarities. Overall, however, the similarities are much more impressive than the differences. There are thousands of other words as well that show further similarities between the languages of the Indo-European group.

These similarities can be traced to the fact that all the Indo-European languages probably came from a single tongue, which is therefore called "Proto-Indo-European," or P.I.E. for short. (Don't call it "pie"; say each letter separately, "P-I-E.") Language detectives, who call themselves philologists, have followed two lines of investigation into P.I.E. From studies of the recorded Indo-European languages, by a process known as reconstruction, they deduce what the forms of the original language must have been like. In some cases this is pretty obvious—for instance, since the apparently related words for *mother* all begin with an *m*, an *m* is reconstructed as having stood at the beginning of the word in Proto-Indo-European. Some reconstructions of the original forms involve considerably more ingenuity to produce simple, sensible ways of explaining how the original forms could develop into the forms actually found in recorded languages.

The ancient Indian Sanskrit, preserved as a religious language, is the closest relic of P.I.E. Of living idioms, Lithuanian in many respects comes nearest. It is geographically close to the probable birthplace of P.I.E., and it has developed in the relative isolation of the primeval Baltic forests.

This brings up the second line of reasoning about P.I.E. Where did it originate? Scholars do not agree entirely as to what pieces of evidence are to be given most weight in answering this question. The general picture we get from the words we can establish by reconstruction as existing in the original language would lead us to imagine a group living mostly near, but not on, the open steppe country of eastern Europe. Nearness to open country is suggested by the reconstructibility of words for *horse* and *wheel* and *spoke,* implying the use of carts if not chariots. The fair number of tree names which reasonably solid evidence would ascribe to the vocabulary of the speakers of P.I.E. inclines us toward assigning these people to a forested region. The most significant tree for locating them is the *beech*. We can confidently associate this meaning with a Proto-Indo-European word whose derivation from a verb meaning *eat* indicates that gathering beechnuts provided these tribes with at least some part of their diet. From this fact we can eliminate from consideration as the original home of this speech all of Europe north and east of the Königsburg-Odessa line.

The only additional reconstructible item which can give us any other such clear line on a map is the word for *salmon*. Here, there is not quite as general agreement about the evidence. This reconstructed word is the one which in a modern form was borrowed into English as *lox*. If the original word in P.I.E. meant the Atlantic salmon, this would tie the Proto-Indo-European speakers down to the valleys of the Vistula, the Oder, the Elbe and conceivably the Weser. (Any place farther west can be eliminated on other grounds, including rather clear archeological evidence.) One of the languages which has preserved the word, however, is Ossetic, an Iranian language of the Caucasus. Therefore, some proponents of a homeland in that region can argue that the Caspian species of salmon was originally designated by the word. This suggestion of a primeval sojourn in the area of transition from the steppe to the forested northern Caucasus must be considered as a possible alternative theory to the steppe to forested northern Carpathian zone that would probably receive more votes among experts in this field at the best present guess.

From this origin Indo-European spread until it stretched from Iceland in the west to its eastern limit where the Brahmaputra River pushes up between Burma and Tibet. If we include more recent conquests, Indo-European languages cover the entire New World and large parts of Africa as well as Australia and the Pacific Islands. Just in the last decades it has started to ebb as new nations are born in formerly dependent areas.

The remainder of this chapter will be devoted to a guided tour of Babel. This will be in part a listing of the languages and groups within the Indo-European family and in part a sketch of the other language families and the areas they cover. If that sort of tourism does not appeal to you, feel free to skip ahead and we will meet you again at the beginning of Chapter 4.

## The Various Indo-European Languages

Indo-European divides into eastern and western groups. The eastern group includes the languages of India and Persia, the Baltic and Slavic languages, and two groups now found only in one isolated language each: Armenian and Albanian.

Western Indo-European starts with the Hellenic group whose only modern representative is Greek. It includes as well the Italic languages (represented by the Romance group and several dead languages of Italy), the Germanic group, and the Celtic. An extinct language called Tocharian, once spoken in central Asia, belonged—strangely enough—to the western group. The Hittites, a people mentioned in the Bible, once ruled an empire centered in what is now eastern Turkey. The inscriptions they left give us only an imperfect picture of their language but it was obviously related to Indo-European. Some scholars feel it may have become separated from the parent Indo-European stock before divisions within the stock, such as into the eastern and western groups, were relevant.

An accurate chart of all these languages is shown under "Indo-European" in Webster's Dictionary and goes into far more detail than is practical here. A few points are worth mentioning. The largest language in the Indic or Indo-Aryan branch of Indo-European is Hindustani, which in two somewhat different standard forms is the principal official language of two of the heavily populated countries of the world—India and Pakistan. Pakistan uses a form of this language which is called Urdu and has a great many more words borrowed from Persian and Arabic than does the Hindi used in India. Two other Indo-Aryan tongues of the sub-continent are spoken by large numbers of people and embody long established and flourishing literary traditions; these two are Marathi with over thirty million speakers in the Bombay region, and Bengali, the language of East Pakistan and the Calcutta area in India. The latter, with probably seventy-five million, is ninth largest in number of speakers among the languages of the world. Singhalese, the major language of Ceylon, is another important Indic language. Besides the large number of languages spoken throughout India, the Indic group includes the language of the gypsies (Romany) and Sanskrit. The latter is the Hindu classical language. As we said above, it is probably the closest we can come to Proto-Indo-European in a recorded language. A grammar of Sanskrit, written over 2,000 years ago by a man named Panini, gives surprisingly modern insights into the structure of the language.

The Iranian language group includes Persian, Pashto of Afghanistan, and Kurdish, a language whose speakers are divided among Iran, Afghanistan, Turkey, and the USSR. Minor members of the family include the Ossetic language spoken in the northern Caucasus—which we have already had cause to mention —and the languages of various tribes of the Pamir plateau which only recently have begun to be studied by Soviet linguists.

The Slavic (Russian, Polish, Czech, etc.) and Baltic (Lettish and Lithuanian) languages also belong to the eastern division of Indo-European. These languages use either of two different alphabets. The difference traces back to the time the Slavic peoples were Christianized. The missionaries from Rome brought with them the Latin alphabet—the same one that came to England. The modifications in each case were slight, so Polish, Czech, and the other languages that use the Roman letters look fairly familiar to us. The use of this alphabet still characterizes the countries whose people are principally Roman Catholic or Protestant. There were other missionaries in the area from the earliest times—those from the Byzantine church. One of these, St. Cyril from Macedonia, gave his name to the Cyrillic alphabet.

He is said to have been the first to adapt the Greek alphabet to the writing of Slavic languages. Like the Roman alphabet in this area, the Cyrillic alphabet is associated with a church, in this case the Eastern Orthodox Church. Russian and Bulgarian use the Cyrillic alphabet and in these countries the influence of the Eastern Orthodox Church is strongest. Serbian and Croatian are just dialects of a single language. The principal reason for listing them separately is that Croatian is written in Roman letters and Serbian in Cyrillic. Again the difference in alphabets reflects the difference between the Catholic Croatians and the Eastern Orthodox Serbs.

Turning to the western group, we have the Romance languages which are all descendants of Latin. As the Latin-speaking Roman Empire fell apart, the speech of the various areas differentiated. The major modern descendants of Latin are French, Spanish, Portuguese, Italian, and Rumanian. There are half a dozen or so less important Romance languages including Romansch, which is the fourth official language of Switzerland, even though it is spoken by less than a hundred thousand Swiss.

The Celtic group is struggling to hold its own. The whole Celtic-speaking world was overrun by speakers of Germanic and Romance tongues and the Celtic languages began to fade away. Now that Ireland is self-governing, great efforts are being made to promote the use of Irish Gaelic, but in the other Celtic areas the speakers are fewer every year. Cornish has died out, and improved communications are spreading the use of English and French where Scots Gaelic, Welsh, Manx, and Breton once flourished.

Lastly we have the Germanic tongues. These include the Scandinavian, extinct Gothic, and the German-Dutch group. Both English and Yiddish belong in the latter group. The relationship is disguised in both cases. Yiddish has a great many Slavic and other loan words and is written in the Hebrew alphabet. It is, however, basically a Germanic language.

English has several distinguishing characteristics. It has simplified itself more than most other Indo-European tongues by dropping much of the inflection that characterized P.I.E. Its vocabulary is unusually complex as a result of the Norman Conquest of 1066. Sir Walter Scott in *Ivanhoe* has the jester point out that domestic animals use their Anglo-Saxon names when in the field (cow, calf, pig, sheep) but are served up to the Norman overlord as beef, veal, pork, and mutton—words borrowed from Norman French. This double vocabulary goes much further than most of us realize. Usually the Germanic word is considered more direct, or even vulgar, and the word of Romance derivation is more refined. This starts with the well-known but unprintable four-letter, Anglo-Saxon words with their acceptable, Romance-derived alternates and goes through such other pairs as sweat–perspire, brave–valorous, think–cogitate, and literally myriads of others. Its final claim to fame is that English is second to none as a second language. More than any other language in the world, people learn English in addition to their native speech.

## The Other Language Families

Leaving the Indo-European, only one other language family covers anything like the same land area. This is the Altaic group which includes Turkish and extends past the Altai mountains of Central Asia. Just how far it goes is still under investigation, though it is clear it goes far enough to include the Yakut of northern Siberia. Almost all experts include Mongol and Manchu dialects, but the status of Korean and Japanese is not clear. Some include both the latter tongues in the Altaic group; some include only Korean; others group them separately as an unrelated family; and still others put both outside the Altaic family and furthermore separate them from each other, leaving three distinct divisions. Many, but by no means all, linguists see a connection between the Finno-Ugric group (Finnish, Hungarian, Estonian) and the Altaic group. It is probably best to wait for further investigations before taking a definite position on these questions. The connection between all these languages would be based on their spread from a central Asian source with the expansion of the nomadic tribes.

In the Middle East the principal language family is the Semitic. The largest group included is Arabic, spreading from Arabia northward into Iraq, Jordan, Syria and west across the whole top of Africa. In addition, it is the liturgical language of Islam and, as such, reaches far south into Africa and east and north into Asia and nearby Europe. Other Semitic languages are Hebrew and Amharic. The latter is the official language of Ethiopia spoken by Coptic Christians claiming descent from one of the ten lost tribes of Israel. Hebrew is basically the language of the Old Testament. It has more recently been modernized by the linguistic architects of Israel and is now the official tongue of the modern Hebrew state.

Semitic languages take their name from Shem, the second son of Noah. Shem's brother Ham gave his name to the Hamitic languages, which seem to be distantly related to the Semitic. Hamitic languages border the great deserts of Africa. They are spoken by the Berbers and Tuaregs of northwest Africa and the Sahara. Hausa, Galla, and Somali in Ethiopia and Somalia of east Africa continue the spread of this family to Africa's opposite coast. Semitic and Hamitic are grouped together by linguists in one larger family called Afro-Asiatic.

If we were to draw a line east and slanting a bit down on the map all the way across Africa from the point where the western coast makes its right-angle bend to the south, we would have approximately demarcated the northern limit of the vast Bantu family of languages. Most of the languages of western Africa south of the Sahara are now believed to be related, and Bantu is grouped among them in the Niger-Congo family which is among the more extensive language families of the world. Sandwiched between the Niger-Congo and the Afro-Asiatic languages are many others. In a belt from the eastern Sahara stretching south and east as far as Tanganyika are found several families, such as the Nilotic languages, whose possible relationships are not yet thoroughly explored.

A peculiar feature of certain south African languages is their use of click consonants. We hear some of these clicks in the sound of a kiss, the deprecating sound usually spelled *tsk-tsk*, and the sound used to start a horse or a mule moving. The very fact that we can't spell these sounds shows how foreign they are to Indo-European speech. Clicks are found in some of the southern Bantu languages, the best known of which is Zulu, but historical study has shown that these sounds did not originally exist in any Bantu languages but were imported from another family—the Bushman or Khoisan group of languages spoken by the earlier inhabitants of the region.

Afrikaans is a dialect of Dutch derived from the immigrants who helped settle South Africa. This makes it a transplanted Indo-European language. Its use is being furthered by the present government of the Republic of South Africa.

Starting at Madagascar, a language family of the Islanders, the Austronesian family, spreads through Indonesia, the Philippines, Maori of New Zealand, all the islands of Micronesia, and on east to Hawaii, Easter Island, and Tahiti. Javanese, with over 40 million speakers, is the largest member of the family. This language group reaches the mainland only in Malayan and scattered hill tribes of southeast Asia. There are still some hundred thousand aboriginal Formosans in the eastern half of the island of Taiwan whose languages belong to this group.

The last major language family of the Old World is the Sino-Tibetan. This includes the Chinese language family. It is customary to speak of the several dialects of the Chinese language, probably because there is a common writing system that speakers of any kind of Chinese can use. It would be more accurate to speak of separate Chinese languages. The speaker from Peking can understand a speaker from Canton no better than a Frenchman understands the average Italian.

The Northern Chinese or Mandarin language is spoken by two-thirds of China which gives it the most speakers of any language in the world. The most closely related language to Mandarin of the other groups is the Wu language of Shanghai, Wenchow, and the surrounding region. Cantonese is the major south-China language, spoken throughout the densely populated Canton region, including the British-controlled island of Hong

Kong. Its use extends west as far as the island of Hainan. Also it is a major language among the overseas Chinese—including most of the Chinese in the continental United States. The coastal languages between Cantonese and Wu in Fukien and eastern Kuangtung provinces are referred to as Min. It is linguistically most reasonable to regard these as belonging to two languages. The more important is spoken in the region of the cities of Amoy and Swatow and by most of the native Chinese of the island of Formosa. Together with Cantonese, it is spoken in the cities of all the countries around the South China Sea. The other Min language is spoken in the districts about the city of Foochow. The two inland Chinese languages are called Hakka and Hsiang and are found principally in Kiangsi and Hunan provinces respectively. Hakka is also the language of the earliest Chinese settlers of Formosa, mostly now confined to rural districts, and is the major Chinese language spoken in the Hawaiian Islands. How speakers of such different languages can communicate in writing is a secret we will share with you in the chapter on how speech is recorded in visible signs. Even Japanese, whose speech is as far from Chinese as either of them is from English, can use this same system of characters for writing.

Besides the Chinese language group, the Sino-Tibetan family includes languages of Tibet and southeast Asia. Burmese is probably the most important. These are generally tone languages like Chinese. What sounds to us like the same word said four different ways—the high, low, rising, or falling tones—can have meanings as different as "to meow like a kitten," "secret," "uncooked rice," and "honey." All four of these words in Mandarin Chinese sound to an English speaker like our pronoun "me."

The Dravidian language family was in India before the invasion of Indo-Europeans and many Dravidian languages are still spoken in south India. Four of these—Tamil, Telugu, Kannada and Malayalam—have speakers whose numbers run to eight figures. There are more isolated families in Asia, too. Cambodian is the only widely spoken language in the Mon-Khmer family. Vietnamese is thought by some scholars to be a remote relative even though it is a tone language while Cambodian and languages closely related to it are not. This question, like so many others mentioned in this chapter, must still be considered unsettled.

The Australian aborigines and the Papuans of New Guinea all live in the general area of Austronesian languages; however, none of their languages are Austronesian. Some people classify the Hyperborean languages of northern Siberia with the Eskimo languages of North America. Others feel that these, the Eskimo, and even some other American Indian languages should be grouped with the Ural-Altaic.

Whether or not such groupings can be substantiated, the languages of the New World are divided into hundreds of families and even more individual tongues sometimes classed as Amerindian. Some of these were widespread; more than half the area of North and South America was covered by only sixteen of the groups. Even today the Quechua language of Peru, which was once one principal language of the vast Inca empire, is still spoken by a few million people. Other South American Indian languages which continue to be important are Aymará, used in parts of Peru and Bolivia, and Guaraní, spoken together with Spanish by most Paraguayans. At least a hundred thousand Araucanians in Chile still maintain their ancient tongue, and Goajiro (Wahiro) in Colombia and Venezuela may have even more speakers than that. The Mayan languages of Yucatan and Guatemala and the Nahuatl or Aztec languages of Mexico continue to be used by sizable groups.

In the United States and Canada there are no native American languages spoken by groups anywhere as large as those we have mentioned farther south. At least three, though, show a considerable measure of vitality. The largest of these is Navajo, spoken by over 50,000. At least 40,000 Cree are the principal human population of the vast stretches of muskeg extending both east and west from the bottom of Hudson Bay. South of them, and likewise covering a belt stretching half the distance across the continent, there are probably as many speakers of

38

Ojibway. Other Amerindian groups are represented by the isolated languages of single, small tribes. The relationships between the groups are very confused. Some of them have a whole English sentence expressed in one word. In others each word is essentially a single syllable. This multiplicity of tongues made problems for the Indians themselves. If a man traveled out of his own tribal area, he was likely to find that the local inhabitants could not understand a word he said. The nomadic Indians of the great plains of North America had a solution for this problem. They developed a gesture language with a sign of the hands standing for each word.

This tour of the world's languages has been necessarily very sketchy. The subject is just too great for proper presentation in a few pages. More detailed treatment can be carried out and has been completed in several areas. Linguistic atlases of parts of Europe and the United States have been prepared. These are immense projects tracing hundreds and thousands of dialect variations. Thus, each study must decide just how deep to push its differences and distinctions, and a quick sketch like the present one pays for its speed with many rough and indistinct outlines.

## A List of Languages

We will conclude this brief and sketchy survey by giving a list of the 273 languages which were considered of sufficient importance or interest for Americans for files of information about them to be kept at the Center for Applied Linguistics of the Modern Language Association of America in Washington, D.C. Many of the languages also go by other names. Decisions as to whether we are dealing in some cases with two separate languages or two variants of one and the same language are often difficult, as the reader has been warned earlier in this chapter. The figures are intended to represent the number of persons to whom the language is the main medium of communication; the paucity of accurate surveys makes these little more than educated guesses, subject to constant revision.

| | | | MILLIONS OF |
|---|---|---|---|
| NAME OF LANGUAGE | WHERE SPOKEN | FAMILY | SPEAKERS |
| Achinese | Sumatra | Malayo-Polynesian | 1 |
| Achooli-Luo | Uganda, Sudan | Nilotic (Chari-Nile) | .8 |
| Afrikaans | South Africa | Germanic (Indo-European) | 4 |
| Albanian | Albania, Yugoslavia, Italy, Greece | Albanian (Indo-European) | 2 |
| Akan (Twi-Fante) | Ghana | Guinean (Niger-Congo) | 3 |
| Amharic | Ethiopia | Semitic (Afro-Asiatic) | 6 |
| Amoy | Fukien and Kwantung (China), Formosa, Thailand | Chinese (Sino-Tibetan) | 25 |
| Anyi-Baule | Ivory Coast, Ghana | Guinean (Niger-Congo) | 1 |
| Arabic | Northern Africa, Near East | Semitic (Afro-Asiatic) | 80 |
| Araucanian | Chile | | .2 |
| Armenian | Armenia (USSR), Near East | Armenian (Indo-European) | 3 |
| Assamese | Assam (India) | Indic (Indo-European) | 6 |
| Avar | Caucasus (USSR) | Northeast Caucasic | .3 |
| Awadhi (Eastern Hindi) | Uttar Pradesh (India) | Indic (Indo-European) | 22 |
| Aymará | Bolivia, Peru | Kičua-Aymará | 1 |
| Azerbaijani | Iran, Soviet Azerbaidzhan | Turkic (Altaic) | 7 |
| Balante | Portuguese Guinea | West Atlantic (Niger-Congo) | .2 |
| Balinese | Bali, Lombok (Indonesia) | Malayo-Polynesian | 2 |
| Baluchi | West Pakistan, Iran, Afghanistan | Iranian (Indo-European) | 2 |

| Name of Language | Where Spoken | Family | Millions of Speakers |
|---|---|---|---|
| Bamilike | Cameroun | Bantu (Niger-Congo) | .5 |
| Bashkir | Bashkir ASSR* (USSR) | Turkic (Altaic) | .6 |
| Basque | Spain, France | | .8 |
| Batak | Sumatra | Malayo-Polynesian | 2 |
| Belu | Timor | Malayo-Polynesian | .5 |
| iciBemba | Northern Rhodesia | Bantu (Niger-Congo) | .8 |
| Benga | Spanish Guinea | Bantu (Niger-Congo) | .2 |
| Bengali | West Bengal (India), East Pakistan | Indic (Indo-European) | 75 |
| Bhojpuri | Bihar and Uttar Pradesh (India) | Indic (Indo-European) | 20 |
| Bini (Edo) | Central Region of Nigeria | Guinean (Niger-Congo) | .5 |
| Bodo | Assam (India) | Tibeto-Burman (Sino-Tibetan) | .2 |
| Breton | NW France | Keltic (Indo-European) | 1 |
| Bulgarian | Bulgaria | Slavic (Indo-European) | 7 |
| Buginese-Makassarese | Celebes, Borneo | Malayo-Polynesian | 4 |
| Buriat | Buriat ASSR* (Siberia, USSR) | Mongol (Altaic) | .2 |
| Burmese | Burma | Tibeto-Burman (Sino-Tibetan) | 15 |
| Byelorussian | Byelorussia (USSR) | Slavic (Indo-European) | 7 |
| Cakchikel | Guatemala | Mayan | .4 |
| Cambodian | Cambodia, Thailand, Vietnam | Mon-Khmer | 3 |

\* ASSR—Autonomous Soviet Socialist Republic, a second level administrative unit, coming under a Union Republic. Each one is inhabited by a large ethnic minority.

| Name of Language | Where Spoken | Family | Millions of Speakers |
|---|---|---|---|
| Caribbean French Creole | Haiti, Lesser Antilles | Romance (Indo-European) | 5 |
| Cantonese | South China, Overseas China | Chinese (Sino-Tibetan) | 45 |
| Catalan | NE Spain, Balearic Islands, Sardinia, France, Andorra | Romance (Indo-European) | 5 |
| kiChagga | Tanganyika | Bantu (Niger-Congo) | .3 |
| Chechen | Caucasus (USSR) | North-Central Caucasic | .4 |
| Cheremis | Mari ASSR* (USSR) | Finnic (Uralic) | .5 |
| Cherokee | Oklahoma, North Carolina | Iroquoisan | .01 |
| Chocktaw | Oklahoma, Mississippi | Muskogean | .01 |
| Chuvash | Chuvash ASSR* (USSR) | Turkic (Altaic) | 1 |
| Circassian | Caucasus (USSR), Lebanon | Northwest Caucasic | .3 |
| ciCokwe | Angola | Bantu (Niger-Congo) | .6 |
| Cree-Montagnais | Canada, U.S. | Algonquian | .04 |
| Creek | Oklahoma, Florida, Alabama | Muskogean | .01 |
| Crioulo (W. African Portuguese Creole) | | Romance (Indo-European) | .2 |
| Czech | Czechoslovakia | Slavic (Indo-European) | 10 |
| Danish | Denmark | Germanic (Indo-European) | 5 |
| Dinka | Sudan | Nilotic (Chari-Nile) | .5 |

| Name of Language | Where Spoken | Family | Millions of Speakers |
|---|---|---|---|
| Duala | Cameroun | Bantu (Niger-Congo) | .3 |
| Dutch-Flemish | Netherlands, Belgium | Germanic (Indo-European) | 17 |
| Efik | Eastern Region of Nigeria | Central (Niger-Congo) | 1 |
| English | North America, British Isles, Australia | Germanic (Indo-European) | 260 |
| Cameroun English | Fernando Po, Cameroun | Germanic (Indo-European) | .1 |
| Eskimo | Greenland, Canada, Alaska | Esquimo-Aleut | .04 |
| Eskimo (South Alaskan) | Alaska, Siberia | Esquimo-Aleut | .01 |
| Estonian | Estonia | Finnic (Uralic) | 1 |
| Ewe-Fon | Dahomey, Togo, Ghana | Guinean (Niger-Congo) | 2 |
| Fang-Bulu | Cameroun, Gabon, Congo (Brazzaville) | Bantu (Niger-Congo) | 2 |
| Fijian | Fiji | Melanesian (Malayo-Polynesian) | .1 |
| Finnish | Finland, USSR | Finnic (Uralic) | 4 |
| Foochow | Fukien (China) | Chinese (Sino-Tibetan) | 20 |
| French | France, Belgium, Canada, Switzerland, U.S. | Romance (Indo-European) | 55 |
| Frisian | Netherlands, Germany | Germanic (Indo-European) | .4 |
| Fulani | Nigeria, Cameroun, Guinea | West Atlantic (Niger-Congo) | 6 |
| Gã | Ghana | Guinean (Niger-Congo) | .2 |

| Name of Language | Where Spoken | Family | Millions of Speakers |
|---|---|---|---|
| Gaelic | Ireland, Scotland, Isle of Man | Keltic (Indo-European) | .5 |
| Galla | Ethiopia, Kenya | Cushitic (Afro-Asiatic) | 5 |
| luGanda | Uganda | Bantu (Niger-Congo) | 2 |
| Garo | Assam (India) | Tibeto-Burman (Sino-Tibetan) | .3 |
| Georgian | Georgia (USSR) | Kartvelian | 3 |
| German | Germany, Austria, Switzerland, U.S., USSR | Germanic (Indo-European) | 85 |
| Goajiro | Colombia, Venezuela | Arawak | .4 |
| kiGogo | Tanganyika | Bantu (Niger-Congo) | .3 |
| Gondi | Andhra Pradesh (India) | Dravidian | 1 |
| Greek | Greece, Cyprus, Turkey | Hellenic (Indo-European) | 10 |
| Guaraní | Paraguay | Tupi-Guaraní | 1 |
| Gujerati | Gujerat (India), Bombay | Indic (Indo-European) | 20 |
| Gurage | Ethiopia | Semitic (Afro-Asiatic) | .3 |
| Hakka | Kiangsi (China), Formosa, Hawaii, Overseas Chinese | Chinese (Sino-Tibetan) | 17 |
| Hausa | Northern Region of Nigeria, Niger, Cameroun | Chad (Afro-Asiatic) | 10 |
| ruHaya | Tanganyika | Bantu (Niger-Congo) | .3 |

| Name of Language | Where Spoken | Family | Millions of Speakers |
|---|---|---|---|
| Hebrew | Israel | Semitic (Afro-Asiatic) | 1 |
| Hindi-Urdu | India, Pakistan, Mauritius | Indic (Indo-European) | 160 |
| Hsiang | Hunan (China) | Chinese (Sino-Tibetan) | 5 |
| Hungarian | Hungary, Rumania, United States Czechoslovakia | Ugric (Uralic) | 12 |
| Iban | Borneo | Malayo-Polynesian | .2 |
| Ibanag | NE Luzon (Philippines) | Malayo-Polynesian | .3 |
| Icelandic | Iceland | Germanic (Indo-European) | .2 |
| Igbo | Eastern Region of Nigeria | Guinean (Niger-Congo) | 5 |
| Ila | Northern Rhodesia | Bantu (Niger-Congo) | .2 |
| Ilocano | NW Luzon (Philippines) | Malayo-Polynesian | 3 |
| Indonesian-Malay | Indonesia, Malaya, Sarawak | Malayo-Polynesian | 10 |
| Italian | Italy, U.S., Brazil, North Africa | Romance (Indo-European) | 50 |
| Japanese | Japan, Hawaii | Japanese | 95 |
| Javanese | Java | Malayo-Polynesian | 45 |
| Kabre | Togo | Voltaic (Niger-Congo) | .3 |
| Kabyle | Algeria | Berber (Afro-Asiatic) | 1 |
| Kachin | Burma, Yunnan | Tibeto-Burman (Sino-Tibetan) | .5 |
| kiKamba | Kenya | Bantu (Niger-Congo) | .6 |
| Kannada | Mysore (India) | Dravidian | 18 |

| Name of Language | Where Spoken | Family | Millions of Speakers |
|---|---|---|---|
| Kanuri | Northern Region of Nigeria, Chad, Niger | Central Saharan | 2 |
| Kashmiri | Kashmir (India-Pakistan) | Indic (Indo-European) | 3 |
| Kavirondo | Kenya | Bantu (Niger-Congo) | .6 |
| Kazakh | Kazakhstan (USSR) | Turkic (Altaic) | 4 |
| Khalkha | Outer Mongolia, China | Mongol (Altaic) | 1 |
| Khasi | Assam (India) | Mon-Khmer | .3 |
| Kirgiz | Kirgizia (USSR) | Turkic (Altaic) | 1 |
| Kissi | Liberia, Guinea, Sierra Leone | West Atlantic (Niger-Congo) | .8 |
| Kololo | Northern Rhodesia | Bantu (Niger-Congo) | .3 |
| kiKongo | Congo, Angola | Bantu (Niger-Congo) | 1 |
| Korean | Korea, Japan, Hawaii | (Altaic?) | 33 |
| Kpelle | Liberia, Guinea | Mande (Niger-Congo) | .5 |
| Krio (Sierra Leone English) | | Germanic (Indo-European) | .5 |
| Kru-Bassa | Liberia, Ivory Coast | Guinean (Niger-Congo) | .7 |
| Kurdish | Iraq, Iran, Turkey, USSR | Iranian (Indo-European) | 5 |
| Kurukh | Madhya Pradesh and Orissa (India) | Dravidian | 1 |
| kiKuyu | Kenya | Bantu (Niger-Congo) | 1 |
| Lahnda | West Pakistan, Punjab (India) | Indic (Indo-European) | 9 |

46

| Name of Language | Where Spoken | Family | Millions of Speakers |
|---|---|---|---|
| Lamba | Northern Rhodesia, Katanga (Congo) | Bantu (Niger-Congo) | .2 |
| Latvian | Latvia | Baltic (Indo-European) | 2 |
| Lisu | Szechwan and Yunnan (China) | Tibeto-Burman (Sino-Tibetan) | .3 |
| Lithuanian | Lithuania | Baltic (Indo-European) | 3 |
| Lolo | Szechwan and Yunnan (China) | Tibeto-Burman (Sino-Tibetan) | 3 |
| chiLuba | Congo | Bantu (Niger-Congo) | 3 |
| Lugbara | Congo, Uganda | Bantu (Niger-Congo) | .3 |
| Macedonian | Yugoslavia, Bulgaria, Greece | Slavic (Indo-European) | 1 |
| Madurese | Java, Madura | Malayo-Polynesian | 7 |
| Magahi | Bihar and West Bengal (India) | Indic (Indo-European) | 6 |
| Maithili | Bihar (India) | Indic (Indo-European) | 10 |
| iMakua | Mozambique | Bantu (Niger-Congo) | 1 |
| Malagasy | Malagasy Rep. (Madagascar) | Malayo-Polynesian | 5 |
| Malayalam | Kerala (India), Maldive Isls. | Dravidian | 16 |
| Mam | Guatemala | Mayan | .1 |
| Mandarin | China, Formosa | Chinese (Sino-Tibetan) | 460 |
| Mandingo (Bambara) | Mali, Guinea, Ivory Coast | Mande (Niger-Congo) | 3 |
| Manipuri (Meithei) | Manipur Territory (Assam, India), Burma | Tibeto-Burman (Sino-Tibetan) | .3 |

| Name of Language | Where Spoken | Family | Millions of Speakers |
|---|---|---|---|
| Marathi | Maharashtra (India) | Indic (Indo-European) | 32 |
| Masai | Kenya, Tanganyika | Nilotic (Chari-Nile) | .2 |
| Mazatec | Mexico | Otomanguean | .06 |
| kiMbundu | Angola | Bantu (Niger-Congo) | 1 |
| uMbundu | Angola | Bantu (Niger-Congo) | 2 |
| Menangkabao | Sumatra | Malayo-Polynesian | 3 |
| Mende | Sierre Leone | Mande (Niger-Congo) | 1 |
| Miao | Southern China, Tonkin, Laos | Miao-Yao (Sino-Tibetan?) | 3 |
| Minahasa-Gorontalo | Celebes | Malayo-Polynesian | .8 |
| Mixtec | Mexico | Otomanguean | .1 |
| Mon | Thailand, Burma | Mon-Khmer | .3 |
| loMongo-Nkundo | Congo | Bantu (Niger-Congo) | .5 |
| Mordvin | Mordvin ASSR* (USSR) | Finnic (Uralic) | 1 |
| Mossi (Moré) | Upper Volta, Mali, Ivory Coast | Voltaic (Niger-Congo) | 2 |
| kinyaMwezi-kiSukuma | Tanganyika | Bantu (Niger-Congo) | 2 |
| Naga | Naga Territory (Assam, India), Burma | Tibeto-Burman (Sino-Tibetan) | .4 |
| Nahuatl | Mexico, El Salvador | Uto-Aztecan | .4 |
| Nandi | Kenya | Nilotic (Chari-Nile) | .4 |
| Navaho | Southwestern U.S. | Athabascan (Na-Dené) | .08 |

| NAME OF LANGUAGE | WHERE SPOKEN | FAMILY | MILLIONS OF SPEAKERS |
|---|---|---|---|
| Nepali | Nepal, Uttar Pradesh (India) | Indic (Indo-European) | 5 |
| Newari | Nepal | Tibeto-Burman (Sino-Tibetan) | .4 |
| liNgala | Congo (Brazzaville and Leopoldville) | Bantu (Niger-Congo) | 1 |
| Nguru | Malawi | Bantu (Niger-Congo) | .4 |
| Norwegian | Norway | Germanic (Indo-European) | 4 |
| Nubian | Sudan | Nubian (Chari-Nile) | .9 |
| Nuer | Sudan | Nilotic (Chari-Nile) | .5 |
| Nupe | Northern Region of Nigeria | Guinean (Niger-Congo) | .3 |
| chiNyanja | Malawi, Mozambique, Southern Rhodesia | Bantu (Niger-Congo) | 1 |
| luNyoro | Uganda | Bantu (Niger-Congo) | .7 |
| Ojibway | Canada | Algonquian | .04 |
| Oriya | Orissa (India) | Indic (Indo-European) | 15 |
| Ossetic | Caucasus (USSR) | Iranian (Indo-European) | .4 |
| Otomi | Mexico | Otomanguean | .09 |
| Pampanga | South Central Luzon (Philippines) | Malayo-Polynesian | .8 |
| Pangasinan | South Central Luzon (Philippines) | Malayo-Polynesian | .8 |
| Papago | U.S., Mexico | Uto-Aztecan | .01 |

49

| Name of Language | Where Spoken | Family | Millions of Speakers |
|---|---|---|---|
| Papiamento | Netherlands Antilles | Romance (Indo-European) | .2 |
| Pashtu | Afghanistan, Pakistan | Iranian (Indo-European) | 13 |
| siPedi | South Africa | Bantu (Niger-Congo) | .7 |
| Persian-Tajik | Iran, Afghanistan, Tadzhikstan (USSR) | Iranian (Indo-European) | 17 |
| Polish | Poland, U.S. | Slavic (Indo-European) | 33 |
| Polynesian | New Zealand, Polynesia | Malayo-Polynesian | .3 |
| Portuguese | Brazil, Portugal, Spain | Romance (Indo-European) | 75 |
| Provençal | Southern France | Romance (Indo-European) | 6 |
| Punjabi | Punjab (India), West Pakistan | Indic (Indo-European) | 30 |
| Pwo | Burma | Karen (Sino-Tibetan?) | .5 |
| Quechua | Peru, Bolivia, Ecuador | Kičua-Aymará | 5 |
| Quekchi | Guatemala | Mayan | .3 |
| Quiche | Guatemala | Mayan | .4 |
| Rajasthani | Rajasthan (India) | Indic (Indo-European) | 14 |
| Rif | Morocco | Berber (Afro-Asiatic) | 1 |
| Romansch | Graubünden (Switzerland) | Romance (Indo-European) | .1 |
| kinyaRuanda | Rwanda, Congo, Tanganyika | Bantu (Niger-Congo) | 5 |
| Rumanian | Rumania, USSR | Romance (Indo-European) | 18 |
| kiRundi | Congo, Burundi, Tanganyika | Bantu (Niger-Congo) | 2 |

| Name of Language | Where Spoken | Family | Millions of Speakers |
|---|---|---|---|
| Russian | USSR | Slavic (Indo-European) | 125 |
| Ryukyu | Ryukyu Islands | Japanese | .5 |
| Sadang | Celebes | Malayo-Polynesian | .5 |
| Sango-Ngbandi | Central African Republic, Congo, Cameroun | Adamawa-Eastern (Niger-Congo) | 1 |
| Santali | West Bengal and Bihar (India) | Munda | 2 |
| Sardinian | Sardinia | Romance (Indo-European) | .9 |
| Sasak | Lombok (Indonesia) | Malayo-Polynesian | .3 |
| Senari | Ivory Coast | Voltaic (Niger-Congo) | .4 |
| Serbo-Croatian | Yugoslavia | Slavic (Indo-European) | 13 |
| Serer | Senegal | West-Atlantic (Niger-Congo) | .4 |
| Sgaw | Burma, Thailand | Karen (Sino-Tibetan?) | .6 |
| Shan | Burma, Thailand, Yunnan | Tai | 2 |
| Shilha | Morocco | Berber (Afro-Asiatic) | 1 |
| Shona | Southern Rhodesia, Mozambique | Bantu (Niger-Congo) | 2 |
| Sindhi | West Pakistan | Indic (Indo-European) | 5 |
| Sinhalese | Ceylon, Maldive Islands | Indic (Indo-European) | 7 |
| Sioux | Dakotas | Siouxan | .01 |
| Slovak | Czechoslovakia | Slavic (Indo-European) | 4 |

| Name of Language | Where Spoken | Family | Millions of Speakers |
|---|---|---|---|
| Slovene | Yugoslavia | Slavic (Indo-European) | 2 |
| Somali | Somalia, Ethiopia, Kenya | Cushitic (Afro-Asiatic) | 3 |
| Songhai | Mali, Niger | Songhai | .4 |
| seSotho | South Africa, Basutoland | Bantu (Niger-Congo) | 1 |
| Spanish | Latin America, Spain | Romance (Indo-European) | 140 |
| Sundanese | Java | Malayo-Polynesian | 13 |
| Suppire | Mali | Voltaic (Niger-Congo) | .3 |
| Susu | Guinea | Mande (Niger-Congo) | .3 |
| kiSwahili | Tanganyika, Congo, Kenya, Zanzibar | Bantu (Niger-Congo) | 13 |
| Swedish | Sweden, Finland | Germanic (Indo-European) | 9 |
| Tagalog | Philippines | Malayo-Polynesian | 5 |
| Tai (Eastern) | Kwangsi (China), Tonkin | Tai | 3 |
| Tai (Northern) | South-Central China | Tai | 4 |
| Tamil | Madras (India), Ceylon, Malaya | Dravidian | 37 |
| Tarascan | Mexico | Tarascan | .06 |
| Tatar | USSR | Turkic (Altaic) | 5 |
| kiTeke | Congo (Brazzaville and Leopoldville) | Bantu (Niger-Congo) | .3 |
| Telugu | Andhra Pradesh (India) | Dravidian | 40 |
| Temne | Sierra Leone | West Atlantic (Niger-Congo) | .6 |

52

| Name of Language | Where Spoken | Family | Millions of Speakers |
|---|---|---|---|
| Teso | Uganda, Kenya | Nilotic (Chari-Nile) | .6 |
| Thai-Lao | Thailand, Laos | Tai | 18 |
| Thonga | Mozambique, Northern Rhodesia | Bantu (Niger-Congo) | 1 |
| Tibetan | Tibet, Nepal | Tibeto-Burman (Sino-Tibetan) | 6 |
| Tigre | Eritrea | Semitic (Afro-Asiatic) | .3 |
| Tigrinya | Ethiopia, Eritrea | Semitic (Afro-Asiatic) | .5 |
| Tiv | Northern Region of Nigeria | Central (Niger-Congo) | .7 |
| Totonac | Mexico | Zoque-Maya | .06 |
| shiTswa | Mozambique | Bantu (Niger-Congo) | .5 |
| seTswana | South Africa, Bechuanaland | Bantu (Niger-Congo) | 1 |
| Tuareg | Niger, Algeria, Mali | Berber (Afro-Asiatic) | .3 |
| Tulu | Mysore (India) | Dravidian | .8 |
| chiTumbaka | Malawi | Bantu (Niger-Congo) | .2 |
| Turkish | Turkey, Cyprus | Turkic (Altaic) | 25 |
| Turkmen | Turkmenistan (USSR), Iran, Afghanistan | Turkic (Altaic) | 1 |
| Tzeltal | Mexico | Mayan | .04 |
| Tzotzil | Mexico | Mayan | .05 |
| Uigur | Sinkiang (China), USSR | Turkic (Altaic) | 4 |
| Ukrainian | USSR, U.S., Canada | Slavic (Indo-European) | 35 |
| Uzbek | Uzbekstan and Tadzhikstan (USSR), Afghanistan | Turkic (Altaic) | 6 |

| Name of Language | Where Spoken | Family | Millions of Speakers |
|---|---|---|---|
| Vai | Liberia | Mande (Niger-Congo) | .3 |
| chiVenda | South Africa | Bantu (Niger-Congo) | .4 |
| Vicol | SE Luzon (Philippines) | Malayo-Polynesian | 2 |
| Vietnamese | Vietnam, Laos, Thailand, Cambodia, New Caledonia, Paris | | 25 |
| Visayan | Central Philippines | Malayo-Polynesian | 8 |
| Votyak | Udmurt ASSR* (USSR) | Finnic (Uralic) | .6 |
| Welsh | Wales | Keltic (Indo-European) | .9 |
| Wolof | Senegal, Gambia | West Atlantic (Niger-Congo) | .8 |
| Wu | Chekiang (China) | Chinese (Sino-Tibetan) | 50 |
| Yakut | Yakut ASSR* (Siberia, USSR) | Turkic (Altaic) | .2 |
| kiYao | Malawi | Bantu (Niger-Congo) | .4 |
| Yiddish | U.S., Israel, USSR, Latin America | Germanic (Indo-European) | 3 |
| Yoruba | Western and Northern Regions of Nigeria, Dahomey | Guinean (Niger-Congo) | 5 |
| Yucatec | Mexico, Guatemala | Mayan | .3 |
| Zande | Congo, Central African Republic, Sudan | Adamawa-Eastern (Niger-Congo) | .7 |

| Name of Language | Where Spoken | Family | Millions of Speakers |
|---|---|---|---|
| Isthmus Zapotec | Mexico | Otomanguean | .08 |
| isiZulu-isiXhosa | South Africa, S. Rhodesia, Malawi, Swaziland | Bantu (Niger-Congo) | 8 |
| Zyrian | Komi ASSR* (USSR) | Finnic (Uralic) | .4 |

# Chapter 4

# America's Least Known Revolution

### The New Linguistics

Several years ago, two young instructors at a western university resigned for ideological differences—about language theory. The world took little note because linguistics qualifies as one of the least known fields on America's intellectual scene today. Most people refer it to the learning of languages, considering a linguist to be someone who knows several foreign tongues —polyglot headwaiters and tourist guides included. And yet, although it is not commonly realized, linguistics has by now become a fast-moving discipline, closely bound with mathematics, acoustic physics, the social sciences, and even international political issues. Moreover, during the past thirty years it has witnessed a full-scale revolt that is by no means over. "The science of linguistics and its revolutionary implications are unknown to all but a very few people," states Robert A. Hall, Jr., of Cornell.

Until quite recently philology reigned supreme, including in its best nineteenth-century tradition, the history of language, literary criticism, and even the study of folklore. With the exception of phonetics, which was well developed, language study was oriented toward the written word and tended to look backward, being more concerned with how languages "got that way" than with how they are spoken, read, and written today. In our colleges, departments of "language and literature" were the general rule with literature dominating. Public school instructors sallied forth to classroom assignments armed with a modicum of language skill, some courses in literature, and a fair amount of training in "how to teach."

It was the "grammar-translation" approach or "reading method" that held sway, particularly after the 1929 Coleman Report. This report concluded that, as long as American youngsters took only two years of a foreign tongue, about all that could be done was to give them some ability in reading it. Of all academic subjects, language was the most static, joining science and mathematics in the role of step-children to the reigning queen—social studies. Some language specialists, feeling rejected and under-valued in their own society, identified with foreign culture, finding themselves more at home in Paris, Berlin, Rome, or Madrid than in Chicago or Atlanta. A few of them carried this so far that they became "more French than the French," and appeared completely alienated from the American grass-roots.

While many thus sought inspiration in the libraries and cafés of European capitals, a small but dedicated group was at work in the 1920's and 1930's planting the seeds of the revolt which was to shake the very underpinnings of the language field. The standard-bearer of this group was Leonard Bloomfield, for many years at the University of Chicago and later at Yale. Dissatisfied with the traditionalism of the existing professional organizations and despairing of them as a forum for new ideas, he helped found the Linguistic Society of America in 1925. Together with his followers, he began the attack on "mentalistic" subjective interpretations, and hammered away against the centuries-old confusion between writing—the graphic symbolization of what man utters—and speech—what he actually says. Of the two things it was above all speech that intrigued them.

Contrary to the image pictured by some of the young Turks among his disciples, Bloomfield did not arrive like a linguistic Moses from Mt. Sinai with a newly revealed set of theories. He knew traditional philology well and was able to tap the findings of many gifted predecessors. The earliest of these was the Hindu grammarian Panini, who, as early as the third century B.C. had written an amazingly scientific description of the sounds and structure of Sanskrit, the ancient religious language of India. Not until the nineteenth century, however, were Western scholars exposed to the descriptive methods of Panini. Another trend in linguistics began when the German-trained anthropologist Franz Boas emigrated to America in 1886 and fell under the spell of our indigenous languages. His work on languages spoken by Indians of British Columbia set a new standard in the description of aboriginal tongues, and his Introduction to the *Handbook of American Indian Languages,* recently reprinted by Georgetown University, still remains a landmark in the history of scientific language description. American-educated Edward Sapir followed the course charted by Boas, contributing his own studies of Indian tongues. The most extensive of these was the description of *The Southern Paiute Language.* Sapir is more noted for his general works on linguistic subjects. One of these, the book titled simply *Language,* although written a quarter of a century ago, still enjoys a paper-back sale today.

While unsung and unheralded specialists went about their thankless task of giving language-resistant young Americans a smattering of the West European tongues, the Bloomfieldians, although obliged to make a living in the same manner, spent as much time as possible describing the off-beat languages of the world. Bloomfield himself described Tagalog, now one of the official languages of the Philippines. Just recently his important linguistic study, *The Menomini Language,* a grammar of an American Indian idiom of the Algonquian family, has finally reached publication. Other scholars attacked such widely divergent tongues as Melanesian Pidgin English and Hungarian.

To the uninitiated, including tradition-minded language teachers, a look at a new linguist's description or "structural

58

analysis" of a language comes as a good deal of a shock. This is due both to the radically different approach and the new terminology employed. Although we will go into more detail in the next chapter, some explanation is useful here. Basic to the new linguistics is the *phoneme*. This may be loosely described as a unit of sound which, despite its variant forms or *allophones*, is always felt to be the same by a native speaker. In English an example is the consonant *p*, which in initial position, for example in the word *pill*, is pronounced with a strong puff of air. On the other hand, when it follows *s*, as in *spill*, almost no release of air follows the *p*. In spite of this and other variations, *p* is considered one and only one phoneme. Intonation, pause, and stress, the so-called "supra segmental" phonemes of the "melody of speech," all too often neglected, also receive careful attention. Linguists like to give such examples as "the lighthouse keeper's daughter" and "the light housekeeper's daughter" which when spoken are distinguished by the degree of stress—that is loudness or prominence—on the element "light" or "house."

Grammar is also analyzed in different terms. The basic concept here is the *morpheme*, which may be considered the minimum meaningful feature of structure. This, again, will be treated more amply in Chapter 6.

It should be emphasized that it is not the use of new terminology but rather their special way of regarding language that distinguishes the Bloomfieldian school. The principle is that a language should be analyzed and studied as it is rather than as normative grammarians think it ought to be. The new linguists believe in teaching the standard speech of educated persons, but they also consider the "ungrammatical" speech of substandard speakers, low-prestige dialects, and "pidgins" as proper grist for their mill. Traditionalists are often shocked by the "vulgar" expressions included in materials prepared by the Bloomfieldians. An example of this is "Hey, Mack," which appears in at least one text prepared for teaching English as a second language. In truth this reflects merely the linguists' desire to teach the actual speech forms that native users of a language are likely to employ in a given situation.

The new linguists, moreover, are "hardware-oriented," making much use in their research and teaching of such electronic equipment as tape recorders and sound spectrographs. Experimentation is going on with their cooperation to develop artificial speech tracts, and all sorts of "dream" gadgets. A number of ambitious projects are today in progress, including ones underwritten by large corporations such as General Dynamics, the Bunker-Ramo Corporation, and the Rand Corporation.

## Effects on Language Teaching

It is easy to understand why traditionalists, schooled in the familiar precepts of old-line philology, have often recoiled from both the términology and the approach of the innovators. "Their concentration on relationships has brought linguistics close to mathematics, further offending venerable colleagues who view linguistics as a plot to dehumanize the study of language," declares W. P. Lehmann of the University of Texas.

Much of the resentment is caused by still another factor. A sizable proportion of traditionalists have in effect come to feel that the innovators have tried to discredit their suitability and effectiveness in teaching languages—thus hitting them at the very source of their bread-and-butter.

And here we come to one of the most important developments in our story. As long as the new linguists stuck to such remote tongues as Menomini or Potawatomi, nobody but a small circle of *cognoscenti* cared or noticed very much. But then history took a hand. World War II broke out and the Intensive Language Program was set up under the Army Specialized Training Program (ASTP) to provide GI's with desperately needed skills in over fifty languages, ranging from German to Burmese. For most of these there existed no tradition of teaching in America, much less usable texts. This gave the new linguists who controlled the program a magnificent opportunity to put their theories into practice. Let it be recalled that Bloomfield had held a highly unflattering view of language teaching practices in this country. Here are his words: "The large part of the work in high schools and colleges that has been devoted to study includes an appalling waste of effort. Not one pupil in a hundred learns to speak and understand, or even to read a foreign language."

It was not long before the results being achieved in the war-time emergency programs came to the attention of the general public. The press and other news media reported that a new and miraculous method of teaching languages had been discovered by the Armed Forces. A great hue and cry was raised. Irate parents demanded why centuries of teaching had failed to yield this amazing approach.

Typical of the reactions was a letter received by the dean of a midwestern college: "My son William took French for two years at your college and can't say two words in it, but Robert, my younger boy, studied it in the Army and was able to speak fluently after only two months. Why don't the schools learn from the Army?"

Ironically enough, the "approach" applied by the Armed Forces was in reality that of the Bloomfieldian linguists who sometimes were professors in the very colleges that received criticisms of this sort.

The results obtained—which were by no means uniform—were due not only to the soundness of the techniques employed but also to the full-time nature of the effort, to small classes, and to the compelling motivation of hope for a better military assignment (quite often unfulfilled, as many students of Chinese were yanked out of training in mid-course and sent to France, and vice versa—no ASTP learner ever actually received the much-coveted commission!)

The field of language instruction has, however, never been the same since the ASTP. While changes come very slowly in the schools, the definite trend has been to adopt the "Method" in government teaching programs and in the academic world.

Just what does the new approach mean in concrete terms? (Many, if not most, of its features have been employed in one form or another before.)

1. Stress upon speaking and understanding, with reading and writing as later stages. This orientation has come to be called "audio-lingual" or "new key" teaching.

2. The endeavor to have text materials based upon the "structural analysis" of a language carried out by a scientific linguist.

3. Intensiveness of training. In full-time programs, such as those at the State Department's Foreign Service Institute, Army Language School, and Yale's Institute of Far Eastern Languages, there are usually at least four "contact" hours with the instructor, with the remainder of the time spent in preparation and in listening to records or tapes. At Cornell's Division of Modern Languages, the number of class and tape-listening hours are double or triple those of a traditional course.

4. Classes small enough to insure frequent participation by all the students and observation by the teacher of their difficulties. As usually implemented, this has been carried to the extent of having class sizes ranging from two to eight.

5. Two-way division of instruction. A native speaker provides drill, while a linguist administers the class and instructs it in the theoretical knowledge of the structure of the language. One of his greatest contributions can be the contrasting of the structure of the "target" language with that of the learner's native tongue. In the ideal use of this method, of course, the same person might serve as both the technically trained linguist and the native-speaking informant. For the forseeable future, unfortunately, such a combination of skills is far too rare to be widely utilized in the classroom situation.

A trend which has accompanied this pedagogical reorientation has been the increasing utilization of electronic equipment, especially magnetic-tape recorders used in soundproof booths under the supervision of a technician. This gadgetry has brought the term "language laboratory" into educational parlance. Such an installation by no means takes the place of a teacher; it merely reinforces his work.

It would be sheer hypocrisy to view the linguistic controversy only from the vantage point of Ivy-League-type ivory towers. To the overwhelming majority of America's classroom teachers the specifications noted above sound like sheer luxury. They are faced with the necessity of instructing oversized classes with up to eighty students, meeting for three to five hours weekly. Under such conditions, with no modern technological assistance, the individual learner is lucky to recite ten or fifteen minutes in an entire week. Language laboratories are only a partial solution since they actually take a great deal of the instructor's time if they are to be "cranked in" to class work. Current research is proceeding towards yet more mechanization, including the adaptation of "programmed learning" and so-called "teaching machines" to the presentation of carefully organized step-by-step materials for language instruction. Such automated teaching courses of a pioneering sort exist in various subjects including elementary linguistics. The student moving at his own pace is aware at every point whether the answers checked off by him are correct and he does not go on until he has thoroughly mastered each segment of learning. Rather than floundering as he may in traditional courses, the learner knows at every point just where he stands. Even marginal application of such techniques to language teaching is a long way off, and tremendous developmental problems lie in the way of any full-scale materials. To quote what we would consider an understatement from Fred M. Hechinger, Education Editor of the *New York Times,* in the April 9, 1963, supplement on education: "Experts now believe that more intensive collaboration between the psychologists and the subject-matter experts will be necessary before a sufficient supply of first rate programmed materials can be designed." Teaching machines are promising but still in the experimental stage. Sound films made specially for language teaching require considerable expenditure. Movie films with a magnetic-recording sound track involve equipment and techniques beyond the scope of most language programs. Television-tape facilities, now entering the realm of discussion, seem even more like a pipe-dream for most teaching situations.

It is little wonder then that in many language classrooms little or nothing has changed. Dr. Don Bigelow of the U.S. Office of Education, who in 1961 completed a country-wide survey of language and area centers, told a professional conference that, despite a great deal of pious talk about new methods in our colleges, traditional practices are still the general rule. Symptomatic of the thinking of a large segment of the profession was a candid remark made to him by a respected member of the teaching fraternity, "For goodness sake, let's not talk about the 'new key.' Under present conditions it's hard enough to teach in the old one!"

And yet, gimmick-minded Americans are still in some danger of believing that in some way the hard work required to gain a working command of a foreign language can be drastically reduced. The overhauling of language teaching is a major undertaking, and general realization of this fact would be one step towards improving the situation. Administrative changes, such as earlier starts for language programs, are clearly necessary. The psychologically best-founded methods for language teaching need to be determined and applied. Technological development of teaching aids that reduce rather than increase the complications for the ordinary language teacher should be pushed forward. Structural linguists have certainly set some fires in this field, and their objective approach to language behavior must serve as a background for all forward-looking ventures relating to language study.

As Alfred S. Hayes of the Center for Applied Linguistics has phrased it recently, linguistics or psychology or other disciplines will not provide any pills to cure our language-teaching difficulties but can furnish us a spyglass through which we can see our problems in perspective.

## Other Repercussions

The *Sturm und Drang* period of the linguistic revolt is not yet over, although the Bloomfield school is becoming rather firmly entrenched as the representative American brand of linguistics. The situation now is such that no one would think of receiving an advanced degree in the field without considerable exposure to it. In recent years several other approaches have also

64

claimed attention.[1] Interestingly enough, American linguistics is being studied more and more abroad. A committee of linguists reporting on the state of the profession has recently asserted that in this field other nations "look far more extensively to us for leadership than they ever have before." Even behind the Iron Curtain a great deal of interest has been exhibited in American linguistics. A few years ago the Moscow Foreign Languages Publishing House translated into Russian H. A. Gleason's *Introduction to Descriptive Linguistics,* one of the key works on the subject. A recent issue of *Inostrannye Yazyki v Shkole (Foreign Languages in the School)* carried a long and mostly favorable article on the Bloomfield school.

Lest a hint of chauvinism appear to have crept in, let it be pointed out that much of the type of scientific investigation that needs to be done to improve language teaching is currently being carried on in Europe, particularly in practical studies of exactly how a language is used in ordinary communicative situations. Direct experimentation with different variables in language-learning has also been pursued more actively there than in this country.

Now that the Bloomfieldian linguists have made their mark in the realm of foreign languages, they have, with typical missionary-like fervor begun to threaten a larger target—the gigantic edifice of English teaching. Although the new linguists are almost fully in control of the teaching of English as a second language, they are as yet poorly represented in public school and college English teaching, despite the efforts of Professors Fries, Trager, Smith, and Marckwardt. Nevertheless, a growing number of English departments are looking into Bloomfieldism or already have one "new linguist" teaching in their midst.

As for classical languages, Waldo Sweet at the University of Michigan has pioneered in the application of the "new key" principles to Latin teaching. Courses in these techniques are

[1] These are principally the "transformation theory" of M.I.T.'s Noam Chomsky, the "tagmemic theory" of Michigan's Kenneth L. Pike, and the "distinctive features" approach of Harvard's Roman Jakobson.

regularly offered at Michigan's Summer Linguistic Institute where many teachers go for "re-tooling" purposes.

The general public still shows resistance to the acceptance of linguistic notions. This may well be due to lack of acquaintance with modern linguistic principles. The furor created by the publication of Webster's Third International Dictionary illustrates this to some extent. Although structural linguists had little direct connection with this monumental lexicographic enterprise, they were rather widely castigated for some of its allegedly subversive leanings. The editors did adhere to the linguists' principle of describing whatever they actually found, whether or not it conformed to what had previously been considered standard. This was an attitude many vocal reviewers could hardly scorn enough.

The lumping of various types of usage together without any distinguishing labels may have been a premature venture. The inadequacy of the previous designations such as *colloquial* or *slang* had become obvious from the linguistic point of view. However, truly adequate research in this field is just beginning, principally in the Survey of English Usage under Professor Randolph Quirk at University College in London. Whether the jury-rigged system of previous editions should have been abandoned as worse than nothing is a debatable question, but most of the criticism of this point in the press was pathetically ill-informed as far as any understanding of the linguistic principles involved was concerned.

These are, in broad strokes, the main facts about America's linguistic revolt which is changing the face of both language research and study. Whatever else one may think about the Bloomfieldians, it must be admitted that they have been vigorous, productive, influential, and articulate. They have not only challenged our traditional way of thinking about language, but have been prominent in a number of applied fields, such as English as a second language, mechanical translation, and automated teaching.

Everything considered, the new linguistics, even if it cannot claim to provide all the answers, promises to continue to furnish new insight into the estimated three to six thousand languages of modern Babel. As only a fraction of them have been scientifically studied, plenty of new frontiers invite the linguist's attention.

Meanwhile, the linguistic controversy still rages. Some of the acrimony of the early post-World War II days is subsiding; reason is winning over emotion, yet there should be no illusions about the slowness of change. One young scholar voiced typical dissatisfaction with the rate of progress when he complained recently, "I can tell you of several universities where some of the old guard will have to die off before the linguist can get a foothold." At the same time, however, one is inclined to agree with linguist Archibald Hill of the University of Texas who argued recently that, "It is unthinkable that the enormous task of unlocking the language barrier will not be one in which teacher and investigator cooperate in friendly fashion."

# Chapter 5

# How We Sound

## Making Sounds

If you have ever admired the ability of pet parrots or parakeets to say, "Polly wants a cracker," or "I am hungry," you may have thought them very clever birds. A trip to the zoo makes you wonder, too, whether the sounds emitted by animals mean that they also speak. Yet in spite of claims by researchers who insist they have carried on "elementary" conversations with chimpanzees, dolphins, various types of fowls, and what not, there is no conclusive evidence that any members of the animal kingdom have any method of communication comparable to that of human beings. That they are capable of vocal responses cannot be denied.

Talking and thinking remain processes of which only man appears capable. Apparently there is no human action which is quite so complicated and which requires so much coordination. Unfortunately, however, even the most highly educated Americans are so linguistically naive that they are ignorant of the rudimentary facts of speech. In our public schools not even a single semester is devoted to the study of general language, instruction in phonology or sound systems, and basic notions of the structure of languages.

The study of phonology is that aspect of linguistics which

68

is closest to the physical sciences since it involves actual physiological organs and the acoustic effects they produce. An examination of some of the research in this field reveals that it can become as complex as biochemistry and similar studies. But for all that, the essential features of phonology or any other "ology" are such that they can be presented in a manner that will be within the grasp of any intelligent reader. The first fact to remember is that speech sounds are nothing but organized noises, as several linguists have aptly put it. Breath is expelled from the lungs through the larynx into the oral cavity or mouth, from which it is emitted. The manner in which it is emitted or released determines what sort of sounds will be heard. There may be a point of greatest constriction in the air passage; and what effects take place at this point—such as interruption, friction, and the like—help determine the nature of the sounds which come forth.

The principal organs of speech have additional and more biologically basic functions over and above producing speech, such as breathing, eating, drinking, and coughing. Proceeding from bottom to top there are the lungs and bronchial tubes and then the throat, including the larynx, or in popular terminology the "Adam's apple." Farther up there is the uvula (Latin for "little grape" because that is what is looked like to the Romans) which is the soft, pointed, and movable organ at the rear of the palate. The palate or roof of the mouth is divided into the rear portion known as the velum or "soft palate," and the front portion, which has bone underneath, known as the "hard palate." Finally there are the tongue, teeth, and lips. The most mobile of all these components is the tongue, which plays the largest role in determining the manner in which a puff of air will emerge as sound.

How does this work? You decide that you want to say the word "too." You push breath into the oral cavity and, as you slightly open your lips, your tongue touches the ridge of your gums behind your upper teeth and when it moves back down a bit to release the air, *t* emerges. A split second afterwards, in fact merged with that sound, comes the sound of *u* (oo), during

69

which the lips are kept slightly parted and are also protruded and rounded. As the air is pushed out, the back of the tongue is raised quite high toward the soft palate. If you don't realize that you do all this, it does not mean that you do not speak English well, any more than the failure to know the principles of internal combustion motors makes poor drivers of automobiles.

What we have described is one illustration of the basic principle upon which speech sounds are built. One should know that there are basically two kinds of sound: vowels and consonants. In the production of vowels only the tongue and lips play a major part. As the tongue is raised or lowered, pulled back or pushed forward, and as the lips are rounded or not, different vowels emerge.

### Types of Sounds

To produce consonants there is at least partial blocking; the stream of breath is interfered with. This can be done in four basically different ways, which we will discuss in turn. If, in addition, the vocal cords of the larynx are made to vibrate, the accompanying sounds are called voiced consonants while if there is no vibration they are termed voiceless. For the first group of sounds the breath may be completely stopped for a moment at some point in the oral cavity; such sounds are called explosives, or stops.

Let's take a look at the stops in English.

| TERMINOLOGY | POINT OF ARTICULATION | | VOICED | VOICELESS | SAMPLE WORDS |
|---|---|---|---|---|---|
| Dental | Tongue tip touching gums behind upper front teeth | $\{$ $t$ $d$ | x | x | tot dad |
| Bilabial | Both lips | $\{$ $p$ $b$ | x | x | pop Bob |
| Velar (guttural) | Soft palate (back of roof of mouth) | $\{$ $k$ $g$ | x | x | kick gag |

If the air is released through a narrow aperture—and not stopped suddenly as is the case with *b, p, t,* or *d*—the second type of consonant sound, called a spirant or fricative, is the result.

Again here the point at which the narrowing is made determines the type of sound which will come out. Here are the possibilities in English.

## SPIRANTS

| TERMINOLOGY | POINT OF ARTICULATION | | VOICED | VOICE-LESS | SAMPLE WORDS |
|---|---|---|---|---|---|
| (unrounded) Labiodental | Lower lip against upper teeth | { f | | x | fife |
| | | v | x | | verve |
| Interdental | Tongue between upper and lower teeth | { th | | x | thin |
| | | dh | [1]x | | then |
| Dental-alveolar | Tongue against ridge of gums | { s | | x | Sis |
| | | z | x | | zone |
| Palatal | Front surface of tongue and front part of roof of mouth (hard palate) | { sh | | x | shine |
| | | zh | x | | vision |

The third type of consonant sounds, the smooth continuants, are those which are without any noticeable friction noise, but in which there is some interference with the sound. Either the tongue or the lips are in the way enough to modify the output to a great extent.

## SMOOTH CONTINUANTS

| TERMINOLOGY | POINT OF ARTICULATION | | SAMPLE WORDS |
|---|---|---|---|
| (rounded) Labial | Lips are protruded and pursed | w | wow |
| Lateral | Tongue touches palate but sides are open | l | lull |
| Retroflex | Tongue is bunched, and usually the tip bent up, so that only a central passage is left open | r | roar |

[1] The sound (spelled th) in those, or either.

If the mouth is closed off completely at some point but the nasal passage is open, the result is a nasal consonant. The point where the closure in the mouth is made determines which type of nasal sound is produced.

## NASALS

| TERMINOLOGY | POINT OF ARTICULATION | | SAMPLE WORDS |
|---|---|---|---|
| Bilabial | Both lips | $m$ | Mom |
| Dental | Tongue tip against gums behind upper teeth | $n$ | nine |
| Velar | Soft palate | $ng^2$ | wing |

One important speech organ is the glottis, the space between the cords of the larynx or Adam's apple. From the linguistic point of view the chief functions of the larynx reside in the glottis. When the vocal cords are relaxed, breath passes freely between them, through the glottis, and no sound is produced. When the cords are held tense, with closing the glottis and forcing air through the space between them, they are set in vibration. Sounds which are produced in this manner are called voiced. Those with the vocal cords lax and glottis open are called voiceless. One may check on whether a sound is voiced or not simply by touching the Adam's apple and feeling the vibrations, absent in voiceless sounds.

All the vowels are voiced while the consonants vary. The glottis itself is the place of formation of a voiceless explosive produced by vocal cords exactly as $p$ is formed by the lips. The glottis, i.e., the space between the cords, is closed and is released with a sudden explosion, the effect resembling a very weak cough. Heard before initial vowels when the speaker hesitates or says "uh-uh" for "no," it is a distinct sound that can be part of a word in Danish—/hun/"her" (*hun*) but/hun?/"dog" (*hund*). Other glottal or laryngeal sounds are the English *h* as in *how,* and the voiced *h* in *ahoy.*

A vowel may be defined as a sound produced by passage of air through the oral cavity without appreciable stoppage or

² The sound (spelled *ng* or *n* before *k*) in si*ng*ing or si*n*k.

72

obstruction. The quality of the vowel is chiefly determined by which part of the tongue is most raised and to what height and the position of the lips. When the front part of the tongue is raised toward the palate, the resulting sounds are called front vowels. In using symbols to represent the vowels we are forced to depart further from the rather erratic spelling system of English than in the case of consonants.

## FRONT VOWELS

æ  (the vowel of *sat*)    the front part of the tongue is slightly raised

e  (the vowel of *set*)    the front part of the tongue is raised about half way

i  (the vowel of *sit*)    the front part of the tongue is raised fairly close to the roof of the mouth

In English when the back part of the tongue is raised for back vowels there is always also rounding of the lips.

## BACK VOWELS

ɔ  (the vowel of *sought*)    the back part of the tongue is slightly raised and the lips slightly rounded

ʊ  (the vowel of *pork*)[3]    the back part of the tongue is raised halfway and the lips moderately rounded

u  (the vowel of *soot*)    the back part of the tongue is close to the soft palate and the lips are considerably rounded

The third possibility is for the middle part of the tongue to be closest to the roof of the mouth.

## CENTRAL VOWELS

a  (the vowel of *psalm*)    the tongue is almost flat
ʌ  (the vowel of *cut*)    the middle of the tongue is raised about halfway

English central vowels, like front ones, are unrounded.

In English vowels are divided into front, middle, and back. The back vowels are rounded and the front vowels are not. In

[3] Some Americans have in fact the same vowels in *sought* and *pork*.

such languages as German and French, for instance, there are different types of vowels. The peculiarity of these mixed vowels, or umlauted vowels as they are called in German, is that they are rounded as are the back vowels but they are pronounced with the front part of the tongue raised, thus:

ü  is pronounced with tongue raised as if to pronounce *i*
(quite high) but with rounded lips
ö  is pronounced with tongue raised as for *e* but with lips rounded

It is equally possible to have vowels pronounced with the back of the tongue raised but with lips not rounded. Such, for example, are the Vietnamese *u'* and *o'*.

Since thick books have been written about the sounds of only one language or some specialized feature of it, we cannot here pretend to cover or exhaust the subject. But anyone who might develop a yen for phonology can find a happy hunting ground of just about every variety of sound. For example, one may find in French, Portuguese, and Polish not only oral vowels but nasalized vowels in which the air is released through the nose. For all the English consonants except *h,* the blocking of the air occurs somewhere in the mouth. Other languages have sounds where friction noise is caused by constrictions in the throat; such for example are the Arabic ḥa ʕ and ʕayn Ɛ .

Sounds can be produced by simultaneous blocking at two points. Such for example is the single sound at the beginning of the name of the Kpelle language spoken in Liberia and Guinea. At the beginning of this word the back of the tongue is closed against the soft palate as for English *k,* while at the same time the lips are also closed as for English *p.* When it is the glottis which is closed at the same time as another blockage and the air trapped above the glottis forced out, we have the ejective or emphatic consonants *p!, t!, k!* found in many American Indian languages. (*p!* is the sound people often make to imitate a cork popping out of a bottle.) The so-called implosive stops (ɓ ,ɗ) of many African languages similarly involve double blockage. For them the glottis is not so tightly closed and a little air passes up through it so that the vocal cords vibrate making these voiced sounds. The Adam's apple moves down and the throat is expanded so that when the upper blockage by the lips ($\beta$) or tongue ($\boldsymbol{d}$') is opened, air moves inward at the front of the mouth. (Implosive $\boldsymbol{g}$', a sound we sometimes use to imitate frogs, works the same way.)

Another example of a sound made in two places at once, so to speak, is the whistled *w* found in Twi, a major language of Ghana in West Africa. The *w* in the name of the language is an example of this sound. (To whistle it is necessary, of course, both to have your tongue in the right place and your lips in the right position.)

Often considered the strangest of all sounds used to make up words in human speech are the clicks found in the Bushman languages of South Africa and also in neighboring Bantu languages such as Zulu and Xhosa. These make use of the air space between two blocks, one of which is at the back of the mouth. Air is sucked in past the block made by the front of the tongue. (The name Xhosa begins with one of these sounds. We use clicks although not as speech sounds. A lateral click is used to start horses and an alveolar tongue tip click to express disapproval—this is the sound often represented by *tsk-tsk*. The usual name for an ingressive bilabial click is a kiss.)

*Studying Sounds*

It has seemed perhaps in what we have said that many languages use rather un-language-like sounds. Please remember that some of our English sounds impress the speakers of many other languages in much the same way. It is just a question of what one is used to. The *th* sound of *thin* can impress the uninitiated as suitable for nothing except imitating a leak in an inner tube, and the *wh* sound in *which* (used by those English speakers who make a difference between *which* and *witch*) may seem naturally designed only for blowing out candles.

Sounds and the act of hearing involve acoustic physics. Altogether the business of making sounds is about as complex a business as there is and the theoretical questions arising, as one can see from technical linguistic literature, are about as involved as, say, nuclear physics.

To permit scholars to study speech sounds in a manner which

was impossible before, some remarkable electronic devices have been developed, particularly the highly sensitive spectrograph. Any sort of sound fed into a spectrograph produces a picture called a spectrogram which reveals duration or length of the sound as well as its frequencies and intensity. With this in hand the acousticians can study and interpret the minute features of sounds and they have already contributed detailed descriptions of sounds in a number of languages which have either confirmed or exploded theories held previously. Also we might mention here that electronic devices which simulate the sounds of human speech are being developed and this *speech synthesis,* too, can serve as a check on phonetic theories.

Since there is a rather poor correlation between pronunciation and the way words are written, it has been found convenient to devise a special alphabet to help indicate the nature of sounds without depending upon the conventional writing system of any particular tongue. The best known of these is the alphabet of the International Phonetic Association which is widely used. Here are the major distinct types of sounds which a phonetician would observe in standard average American pronunciation as they would be written in the IPA transcription:

| | | | |
|---|---|---|---|
| p | s*p*y | ɫ | hu*ll* |
| pʻ | *p*ie | r | th*r*ee |
| b | *b*uy | ɹ | *r*ye |
| t | s*t*y | ɹ̥ | *p*ry |
| tʻ | *t*ie | j | *y*aw |
| d | *d*ie | ç | *h*ue |
| ɾ | a*t*om | tʃ | *ch*ar |
| k | s*k*y | dʒ | *j*ar |
| kʻ | *c*ow | i: | m*ee*t |
| g | *g*uy | i | cit*y* |
| k˕ | s*k*i | I | m*i*tt |
| kʻ˕ | *k*ey | ɛ | m*e*t |
| g˕ | *g*ear | æ | m*a*t |
| m | *m*y | u: | b*oo*t |
| n | *n*igh | u | Andr*ew* |
| ŋ | you*ng* | U | f*oo*t |
| f | *f*ie | o | p*o*rk |
| v | *v*ie | ɔ: | c*au*ght |

| s | _s_igh | ɑ | m_o_ck |
|---|---|---|---|
| z | _z_oo | ɜ | m_u_tt |
| ş | t_r_y | ə | sof_a_ |
| ʐ | d_r_y | ɝ | p_er_t |
| ʃ | _sh_y | ɚ | l_iver_ |
| ʒ | A_si_a | eĭ | m_a_te |
| h | _h_igh | oŭ | m_o_te |
| ɦ | a_h_oy | aĭ | m_igh_t |
| w | _w_ow | ɔĭ | H_oy_t |
| ʍ | _wh_y | m̩ | b_ottom_ |
| l | _l_ie | n̩ | butt_on_ |
| l̥ | p_l_y | l̩ | b_ottle_ |

Let us look at a sentence reduced to IPA symbols:

ʍɑt ɚ ju ˈkɛ̀:pɪŋ ɪn ðə bɑɾm əv ðæt ˈtʂ̧ɜŋk

("What are you keeping in the bottom of that trunk?")

Just to represent the sounds is considered rather traditional and old-fashioned. The school of scientific or structural linguists who follow the great American linguist Leonard Bloomfield, together with various European scholars, object to the limitations of phonetics and have gone one step further in developing what they term phonemics. They have endeavored to treat sounds by finding the minimum _distinctive_ unit of sound, which they call the phoneme, and to term the various forms of such a basic sound as its _allophones._ Thus in English _pin_ the _p_ represents the phoneme /p/. Now at the beginning of a word, a heavy puff of air is emitted as the lips open in pronouncing this sound (IPA p'). However, when this _p_ is final as in _top,_ there is little or no explosion (IPA p). Final _p_ then is an allophone of /p/. The slanted lines are the linguists's shorthand, indicating that letters between them stand for distinctive sound units in a given language.

Getting rid of the non-distinctive symbols, we can present our sample sentence in a frequently used type of phonemic transcription:

/ hwat ər yuw kiypiŋ in ðə batəm əv ðæt trʌŋk /

Something like this rather than the more fully detailed phonetic transcription we gave previously is what is usually meant when we speak of writing a language in a phonetic alphabet.

Charles A. Ferguson, Director of the Center for Applied Linguistics, has this to say about the phoneme: "The fundamental discovery of structural linguistics in the realm of speech sounds is that in any given language certain distinctions between sounds matter, and others do not, while the sound differences that matter for one language are not necessarily those that matter for another." He points out that the difference between the *s* sound in the word *seat* and the *s* sound in the word *salt* does not matter, and in fact it is hard to persuade the speaker of English that there is any difference at all between them. Yet the two *s* sounds are quite different and a speaker of Arabic notes right away that the *s* sound of *seat* is like his Arabic *sin* سِ while the *s* of English *salt* is like Arabic *ṣād* صْ. Contrariwise, in Arabic the sounds of English *e* in *bet* and *u* (/ʌ/) in *but* exist, but they do not *matter* in Arabic, that is they do not differentiate meaning. In linguistic terms, these differences are called non-distinctive, or non-contrastive. With such information on hand the language teacher knows on which features to concentrate.

There is much more to organized speech sounds, however, than the type or quality of sounds. For one thing there is also the quantity or length of sounds. This means, really, the duration taken to produce the sound or for how long the stream of air is emitted. Even in English, in places where there is no phonemic distinction, there are very real differences in length. Compare the duration of *rope* and *robe* and you will note that you hold the second word somewhat longer. In the IPA this would be indicated as follows: ɹoŭp ɹoˑŭb. In such languages as Czech, which have short and long vowels in which quantity is very important, length is marked by diacritics. Thus in the word *vidíte* (you see) the second *i* has the accent sign of length and is therefore longer than the first *i*. However, in Russian, a related Slavic language, length is not an important feature and most vowels are of medium length. Consonants, too, may be long; in effect, double consonants are really long consonants. In English these are not important, but in Italian they are frequent and of significance.

Then there is the matter of stress. Stress means the extra loudness or forcefulness with which a certain syllable of a word is pronounced. In English for example the stress usually falls on the first syllable, as it does in most Germanic tongues. Thus we say MAN-a-ger, and not man-A-ger or man-a-GER. In French, however, stress is light and tends to come on the last syllable, and that is one of the first things that comedians imitate when they are trying to take a French accent. Stress varies greatly between languages. In Russian, for example, there is what is called a "free accent" and it is difficult to predict although rules do exist for it. In Czech, however, the stress falls on the first syllable and in Polish usually on the next to the last.

There is still another type of accent, the pitch or tonal accent. While all languages have this in one form or another, in some languages it forms an integral part of the word. This is, in effect, a musical accent. Mandarin Chinese has four tones as follows:

| | | | |
|---|---|---|---|
| high level as in yī "1" | | low falling-rising | wǔ "5" |
| mid, rising to high in shí "10" | | falling | lyòu "6" |

Serbo-Croatian, the language of Yugoslavia, has the same number of tones but these tones occur only on the stressed syllable of a word, and length is also involved in these distinctions. Swedish and Norwegian also make tonal distinctions associated with a stress accent. In Swedish, for instance /bøner/, with loud stress and one tonal contour on the first syllable, means "peasants," while when it is pronounced with loud stress but a different tonal contour, it means "beans." Chinese, however, has a system both of the tonal and of the stress type. Mandarin /ian + zin/ with stress on the first syllable means "eye," while /ian ± zin/ with stress and falling tone on the second syllable means "glass."

All in all, a complete understanding of the sound system of even one language is a matter of enormous complexity. Fiction writers have speculated about systems on other planets and have conjectured as to whether the Martians may not use radar waves, odors, light beams, or some other kind of energy transmission. But as far as earth dwellers are concerned, no better system has yet been devised than that of signalling through organized speech sounds.

# Chapter 6

# The Structure of Language

*Analyzing Grammar*

Language not only has sound but also has form. We are used to referring to form merely as grammar, or even as grammar and syntax. Unfortunately, all too often in the past, grammar came to be regarded as the dullest of dull subjects, largely because of the unpalatable way in which it was served to school boys and girls.

To understand what makes language run, we must realize that since each language is a conventional set or code of symbols, it has ground rules that must be applied by anyone who uses it to communicate.

It is a curious fact that in our traditional courses in English grammar the bulk of attention was paid to the superficial rules while the really fundamental ones were taken for granted. Moreover, great concern was expressed with differences in social usage, with teachers doggedly attempting to discourage certain popular but disapproved usages in favor of patterns preferred by normative grammarians and writers of school texts.

Linguists, on the other hand, view grammar in quite a different light. They are more interested in seeing how languages work from the bottom up than in the don'ts and taboos of speech. In describing grammatical structures, just as in describing sounds, these linguists have settled upon a basic unit called the morpheme. Just as the phoneme is the minimum unit of sound, the morpheme (from *morph*, a Greek word for form) is defined as the minimum unit of structure. Words, sentences, and entire paragraphs, as it will be seen, can all be regarded as being built ultimately out of morphemes.

Roughly speaking, a morpheme is any one of the pieces that has a function in a word. For example, *distrustfulness* can be shown to have just four functional elements: *dis- trust -ful- -ness*.

The principle that requires us to look for morphemes as units of language is that whenever two different things are said which are associated in meaning and partly alike in sound, we are to assume that the sound similarity is what signals the meaning similarity. A linguistic investigator finds the morphemes in a strange language by comparing various items and looking for all such cases of two-fold similarity.

This procedure is not without its complications. Consider, for example, this set of English words:

| | | |
|---|---|---|
| rejection | reversion | reception |
| conjecture | conversion | conception |
| injection | inversion | inception |

Here, depending on how we feel today, it may or it may not seem that all the "ject's," the "vers's," and the "cept's," all the "re-'s," "con-'s," and "in-'s" show in each case a meaning similarity to go with the similarity in the sounds. The fact is that these (which were once Latin morphemes) lead a Zombie-like existence in English. This is true of many pieces of the Latin language. We can make up new Latin-pattern words that the Romans never heard of. Examples would be the anthropologist's terms "uxorilocal" and "virilocal" to distinguish whether a newly married couple set up housekeeping in the wife's former place of residence or in the husband's. So we can furnish ourselves with some evidence that most Latin morphemes have achieved some sort of a reincarnation as English morphemes today.

One of the main methods of operating in finding out about grammatical structure is called "immediate constituent analysis." Expressed in elementary terms, this means looking at chunks of language and finding out where they are most loosely put together. To take an obvious example, *ungentlemanly* is to be considered as made up of two parts, *un-* and *gentlemanly,* and not in any other imaginable way such as *ungentleman* and *-ly* or *ungentle* and *manly*. This, of course, is apparent from the meaning, but less clear-cut cases can be found even in English, and, when approaching a language not previously studied, very little may seem transparent. The linguistic analyst examines sets of words, or sets of sentences, or whatever size level of unit he is working on at the moment. Looking at lists of, say, words that seem to be able to function alike in the language, he tries to find others with pieces that can be considered replacements for parts in his specimens. Thus, if *ungentlemanly* were really a problem, it would be important when we discovered that there was a word *unfair,* which could serve as a model for *ungentlemanly* and which has no readily conceivable division except into *un-* and *fair.*

Immediate constituent analysis is pursued right on down to the point where we no longer can find smaller pieces which we can juggle and recombine in meaningful ways to make up other forms. At this point we have reached the ultimate morphemes. Just where this point is, is not always an easy question. Leonard Bloomfield felt that *fl-* as found in *flash, flicker, flare, flame,* or *gl-* as found in *gleam, glimmer, glitter, glow, glint* represented a morpheme. The modern theory of morphemics has not followed him in this. It is felt, rather, that at this point we are no longer dealing with really recombinable, or as they are technically called "commutable" units, and it is difficult to account for the pieces left over like "-eam," "-immer," "-itter," "-ow," "-int" as morphemes. Instead the tendency now is to call such things as the *gl- phonesthemes*—sound groups (*phon-*) that convey a certain feeling (*esth-* as in anesthetic) about the words in which they are found. The theory of phonesthemes is not yet well developed, but it is obviously going to play an important part in any reasonably complete understanding of human language that we look forward to achieving some day.

## Grammatical Functions

One emphasis of the linguistic approach to grammar, as can be seen from what we have said already, is on what goes together with what. Another focus of attention is on what function the various pieces play. One of the contributions of the structural linguists to clearing up our thinking along these lines has been to point out that languages operate with certain grammatical signposts, as we might call them. Viewed in this light, a good deal of any speech or text can be seen to be concerned with procedural rather than substantive matters. The linguistic scientists have been fond of pointing out the properties of sentences, such as the following:

"The vencular lobemities may have been molently perfluced." Here, in spite of the nonsense nature of the words, there is every appearance that *vencular* is an adjective, *lobemities* a noun in the plural, *molently* an adverb derived from an adjective, and *perfluced* the past participle of a verb; *vencular, molent, lobemity,* and *perfluce* could all perfectly well be technical terms in English that we just happen not to know. What gives the sentence its plausible cast is the signposts. The characteristic endings *-s, -ly,* and *-d* are some of the strongest indications; there are also *-ar* and *-ent,* which are common derivational endings of adjectives, the noun suffix *-ity* and the common verb prefix *per-*. The familiar, dependable short words like *the* and *may have been* are fully as important for their signpost functions as for any definite information they convey to us about the subject being discussed. Notice how we can be clear about the meaning of *the ship sails* or *ship the sails* where we might be confused by a headline or telegram SHIP SAILS. The term "function words" has been given to these small groups of words that serve as grammatical indicators, including prepositions, conjunctions, articles, auxiliary verbs, and the like. Note that it is only in the large classes of nouns, verbs, and adjectives that we can produce fake new words. Any adult who has learned more than one new preposition in the last seven years is somewhat phenomenal.

The word order also serves as a marker of what is going on in the sentence. The position of *vencular* before *lobemities* makes it seem like an adjective, or at least clearly a modifier of the following noun; we would have some of that effect even if we had only said that:

> "Temp wooch can be molently perfluced."

Lewis Carroll's *Looking-Glass* poem "Jabberwocky" begins with such a skeleton of procedural signposts in the right places accompanied by unfamiliar blobs where the main substantive content should be.

> 'Twas —————— and the —— -y —— -s
> Did —— and —— in the ——
> All —— -y were the —————— -s,
> And the —— —— s out- ——.

This creates part of the mood of the poem, especially in making us go along with Alice's reaction: "Somehow it seems to fill my head with ideas—only I don't exactly know what they are!"

The three marker devices we have mentioned—affixes to words, function words, and word order—seem to be pretty generally used by the languages of the world to convey the procedural workings of the grammatical machinery. The way they function and the extent of using the different types are subject to wide variation. Latin, for instance, relies heavily on word affixes while in Vietnamese it is almost stretching a point to find any.

The grouping of words furnished by speech melody in the intonation patterns of a language supplies another terribly important type of signpost, but we despair of illustrating that on the printed page.

By calling function words, affixes, word order, and intonation "signposts," we imply that they are pointing to some underlying structure. The descriptive linguist looks for the fundamental workings of the grammar of a language underneath these markers. What the structuralists see as really making grammar tick is the combining possibilities of morphemes, the ways in which two or more can be put together to form a larger unit, and how such units, in turn, can enter into larger combinations, and so on. Each language has its own basic recipes or types of patterns for building up words, word groups, clauses, sentences, and connected units of discourse. Sometimes the same constituent elements may be joined together according to more than one basic pattern. It is possible to say in Vietnamese

tên họ   (name, family)

and on one occasion mean name and surname and on another occasion mean the name of the family. It is the possibility of there being contrasting interpretations of this sort that shows us most clearly that there are in fact different blueprints for morpheme combinations.

Some types of modern linguistic theory, especially that which generally goes by the name of tagmemics, concentrate on the parts that enter into the combinations rather than on the combinations that the pieces go to make up. But this, not surprisingly, tends to amount to the same thing differently expressed.

The sorting of morphemes or words into groups according to the range of patterns they fit into determines the form classes of a language. This concept agrees fairly well with the traditional notion of parts of speech for the western European languages, but the form classes of Japanese, Marshalese (in the Marshall Islands of the Pacific), or many American Indian languages may be radically different in some ways from those to which we are accustomed. Also, there is the problem that ever since the Middle Ages there has been a tendency for all but the most careful writers on the subject to blur the distinction between grammatical function of words and their logical function. The obliteration of this essential difference was even considered a virtue in the 1660 *Grammaire de Port-Royal,* which probably represents some sort of opposite pole relative to modern descriptive linguistic practice.

Besides asking what patterns of combinations are possible, the other most interesting question for the linguistically minded investigator concerns what distinctions the speakers of a language are habitually called upon to make. These grammatical categories such as singular and plural, present and past tenses, and cases, modes, voices, and the like are among the most essential concerns of a learner of any language. Also, they provide some of the most interesting ways in which languages differ from one another. We obligatorily distinguish singular from plural, while in Chinese this is done only when there is some particular point to be made by doing so. Several types of such mandatory distinctions that are strange to English speakers were mentioned earlier, in Chapter 1.

The reader may hear in the future—or even have heard already—of new theories of the structure of language quite different from what we have presented here, called usually "generative grammar" or "transformational grammar." Such new developments, we feel safe to say, are a much more esoteric approach to language than we have dealt with here. At present the advocates of the structure and transform schools of thought are irreconcilable. They tend to use the same words in radically different meanings and often exhibit a propensity for demolishing straw dummies of the other approach. However, all serious study of language in the long run is likely to advance our real comprehension, and some more inclusive system may eventually emerge. In such a synthesis, before it in turn meets the onslaught of some still newer twist, an understanding of language structure along lines similar to the presentation in this chapter should be expected to play a part. We at least feel that it represents basic spade work which must be taken into account in working out the application of all more far-reaching general principles.

# Chapter 7

# How the Earth Dweller Writes

*The Place of Writing*

"Put it in writing" is a familiar request. So is "Drop me a line." However, about half of the earth's population could not accommodate you simply because it cannot read or write. Even in the United States there are many illiterates and semi-literates. The Armed Services found this out during World War II when they were obliged to set up courses in reading and writing for such persons. In today's world, nevertheless, the ability to read and write is no longer the special privilege that it was during the Middle Ages—in the Western world at least.

Writing is, as we can see, less universal than speaking; and in many speech communities of the world only one out of ten or even less is literate. An example of this is Nepal in south Asia. In such societies, of course, the ability to write is a status symbol, which is hardly the case in an advanced technological culture such as ours. In some areas of Africa and the Orient the public scrivener is a well paid and highly respected personage.

Furthermore, about half the languages of the world have

never had a writing system made up for them. True, these are mostly languages of little numerical significance, but in the aggregate their speakers add up to an appreciable body of compulsory illiterates.

How did the art of writing develop? Probably no one will ever know just when and where the first primitive man or woman made some sort of mark which carried meaning. Whenever this occurred, it was the first written symbolization. If it was used the way writing as we know it functions, we should really call it a written symbolization of a verbal symbolization. This is so because spoken words are symbols reflecting concepts which we wish to convey to others. Writing serves primarily to remind us of something we have said or might want to say sometime. For this very reason people are often reluctant to put statements in written form, especially when they represent negative criticism of others, although they do not hesitate to "sound off" verbally, when they know that no one is recording what they are saying. Consequently we will never know how Moses sounded at Mt. Sinai, how Mohammed sounded reciting *surahs* of his Koran, Jesus addressing His disciples, Alexander the Great as he harangued his troops, or how Abraham Lincoln sounded at Gettysburg. (Contemporaries of his report that, despite his eloquence, Lincoln's voice was somewhat shrill and not at all suave.)

At any rate, the earliest records of "writing" are inscriptions on caves, jugs, and artifacts found in archaeological expeditions. The inscriptions are sometimes actual drawings of objects, sometimes quite crude, but which leave no doubt as to what they are meant to convey. The earliest records of writing, according to some authorities, are to be found on clay, bone, shell, and stone; however, it is not always quite clear just *what* these early "writers" meant to say about those figures.

### Relations Among Alphabets

It should be mentioned that there are many theories among the world's peoples about the divine origin of writing. The ancient Egyptians, the Mayans of Mexico and Central America, and the

Japanese all have had theories that attributed their writing systems to divinities. Originally, the Egyptian system of hieroglyphics (meaning "sacred stone writing") was based on pictorial or facsimile representations. Thus to indicate "man," "woman," "sun," and the like, the Egyptians merely drew a picture of these objects. But since there is much that cannot be presented pictorially—for example, concepts like love, hate, honor, pity—attempts were made to expand the range of written expression.

How the Egyptians expanded their writing system is worth telling. For example, in ancient Egyptian the word for *sun* was *re*. The symbol for *sun* then came to be used occasionally in the written representation of any word in which the sound *re* occurred.

The Phoenicians went one step beyond the Egyptians in creating their special alphabet some 5,000 years ago. A graphic shape which had earlier represented an entire word came to be used for a single consonant which began the word.

The Hebrew alphabet still shows traces of its pictorial origin. The *a*, called *aleph*, for example, means "ox" and was originally

# יהדות ליטא

‏...המפליא בתולדותיהם היא העובדה שעל אף התמורות
המדיניות, החברתיות והרוחניות שעברו עליהם, הצליחו
לשמור על אופים המיוחד. הם לא נבלעו ולא נטמעו
בתוך קיבוצי יהודים אחרים... הם שמרו על הומו-
גניות. על מסורת רוחנית מיוחדת, תכונות מוסריות
משלהם וכל אלה נצטרפו יחד לכלל אורח חיים ספציפי.
יתר על כן, בתוקף סגולותיהם אלו זכו יהודי ליטא,

MODERN HEBREW

the head of an ox. The *b* is referred to in Hebrew as *beth,* which is the word for "house." The letter *g* is known as *gimel,* for "camel," the head of which is represented by this symbol.

The Semitic system of writing served as a partial basis for the earliest Greek alphabet. However, the Greeks made an important stride forward in that they were the first to arrive at the principle of treating the writing of vowels as just as important as the writing of consonants, and represented the former with special vowel letters.

The Roman or Latin alphabet developed mainly from capital letters of the Greek alphabet like today's B, C, V, O. From it a large number of variants developed, such as the Irish and the German Gothic, first used about the twelfth century and widely employed until the sixteenth century when the plainer Roman form took its place. The use of German Gothic, however, continued in Scandinavia until the nineteenth century; and in German today, it is used about half the time, alternating with the Roman form.

Another form of the Greek alphabet became the basis for the Coptic and Ethiopic systems of writing. The latter is in current use in Ethiopia and Eritrea today. Coptic survives, for religious purposes only, among the remnant of native Christians in Egypt.

Armenian legend credits the invention of the Armenian letters by Mesrop Mashtots in the fourth century to divine revelation. However, there was clearly also a human component in the origin of this alphabet, as Mesrop had studied the Greek

«Այգուն,այգուն իմ խցկի մոտ
Լուսամփոպ մինչ առաւոտ
Երգէ պլպուլն իմՄիսվանայ
Կիլիկիա,Կիլիկիա:«

Հայոց Բագրատունեաց Հաստատութեան անկումէն յետոյ, Կիլիկիոյ թարձունքներուն վրայ ապասման գտնող Հայ իշ-խաններ սկսան տակաւ զօրանալ։Ռուբինեան իշխաններէն Լեւոն Բ. իր քաջութեան եւ արիութեան շնորհիւ կարձա-նանայ թագաւորական գահին ու կ'ըլլայ հիմնադիրներէն Ռուբինեան Հարստութեան։

ARMENIAN

90

system of writing and many of the capital letters in Armenian show a clear resemblance to the small letters in Greek that represent similar sounds. The Georgian alphabet, used in the Soviet republic of Georgia in the Caucasus, was probably originally adapted from the Armenian system.

Природой здесь нам сужено,

В Европу прорубить окно.

CYRILLIC: RUSSIAN (PRESENT SPELLING)

Still another variant of the Greek alphabet is the Cyrillic or Slavic alphabet devised by the monks Cyril and Methodius who were sent out from Constantinople to convert the Slavs to Christianity. This is used by the Russians, Serbs, Bulgarians, Ukrainians, and Byelorussians and has been adapted to serve for many other languages spoken in the Soviet Union.

One of the most intriguing variations of the alphabet is the runes, used by the early Germanic scribes. These were scratched in armor, horns, obituary stones and the like, and were supposed to possess magical powers. Their origin is unknown, although Greek, Thracian, and Etruscan and Latin sources have been suggested. In Wagner's *Die Walküre*, Sigurd the Dragon Slayer climbed a mountain surrounded by fire and awakened a sleeping Valkyrie, Brynhild, with a kiss. Brynhild was a daughter of the gods and therefore skilled in all forms of magic, including the runes, and he asked her to teach him runes.

तास्सवितुर्वरेण्यं भर्गो देवस्य धीमहि।
धियो यो नः प्रचोदयात् ॥१०॥

DEVANAGARI: SANSKRIT

Another descendant of the Semitic alphabet is the ancient Devanagari of India in which Sanskrit is written. The Devanagari in turn was the ancestor of the present-day alphabets of

India and of various Southeast Asian languages such as Thai and Burmese. Some of these are indeed quite complex, with each symbol standing for a consonant or group of consonants followed by a certain vowel. One of these, the alphabet of Tamil, a tongue spoken in Ceylon, has over three hundred symbols and makes the Roman alphabet seem simple. Incidentally, this system is known as a "syllabic alphabet."

Even though syllabic alphabets are in many ways less efficient than the more familiar alphabetic system of writing— as used in most European languages—some newly devised writing systems have been of the syllabic type. The best established system of such a nature is used in northern Canada by the Cree and Eskimo, and to some extent for writing Ojibway and other Canadian Indian languages. In this system the basic shape of the letter represents some consonant sound, and the way it is turned indicates what vowel follows the consonant.

| ∨ Ċ ° | | | ∧ ] ∽ | | |
|---|---|---|---|---|---|
| pē | tā | w | pi | to | š |
| "he brings it" | | | "differently" | | |

The other region of the world where missionaries introduced syllabic alphabets was in southwestern China among the non-Chinese tribes. The Pollard script for Miao and others based on it are now being replaced by Roman alphabet systems under pressure from the Chinese Communist Government.

MIAO: HWA DIALECT, POLLARD SCRIPT

92

قسم دراسات الشرق الأوسط

جامعة تكساس أوستن

The ancient Semitic alphabet also came into great prominence in the form of the Arabic writing system, which spread with the spread of Islam. The Arabic letters do not show much of any obvious resemblance to the earlier Semitic ones from which they are historically derived. The most important reason for the discrepancy is probably that all Arabic script is based on a cursive, or handwriting, form of the alphabet. The Arabic alphabet spread even farther than the Arabic language. With some modifications and adaptations it serves today as the normal mode of writing Persian, Pushtu, Urdu, and Sindhi. It is the most common of three systems for Kurdish, which is also written in Roman and Cyrillic spellings. Formerly it was the standard for Turkish, Malay, Hausa, Swahili, and most of the languages of Muslim peoples in what is now the Soviet Union. Probably this script has had at least some use wherever the religion of Mohammed has taken root. Some historically interesting cases are its use for Somali in East Africa, Malagasy on Madagascar, and Sulu in the southern Philippines. Only the Roman and Cyrillic alphabets can claim that more languages have been written down in them.

## Signs for Words

But the descendants of picture-writing systems have by no means vanished from the face of the earth. Both China and Japan, and, to quite an extent, Korea, still make use of the Chinese characters. Like the ancient Egyptian system, the Chinese symbols originally were meant to represent certain objects. But this is only part of the story. The basic elements

93

子曰學而時習之不亦說乎有朋自遠方來不亦樂乎

人不知而不慍不亦君子乎

are used in a number of combinations to represent objects or ideas. At any rate, what makes the Chinese writing system particularly difficult is the number of combinations of elements that a learner must come to know. For instance, the character for "good" 好 consists of elements meaning "woman" and "son." The character for "love" 愛 *ai* consists of four elements meaning "claws," "a roof," "heart," and "move slowly." However, one finds Chinese even more complicated. For example, *nung* "nasal stoppage," written 齈 , consists of ten or eleven identifiable separate units, and a total of thirty-eight strokes. This is the most complex character listed in Matthews' Dictionary, the standard reference.

カゾクハ キョウ ハヤク オキテ、オスシヤ
サンドイッチヲ ツクリ、クルマニ ノッテ
ウエノ コウエン ヘ イキマシタ。

かぞくは きょう はやく おきて おすし
や、サンドイッチを つくり、くるまに のって
うえの こうえん へ いきました。

家族は 今日 早く 起きて おすしや サンド
イッチを 作り 車に 乗って 上野公園へ
行きました。

JAPANESE: CONVENTIONAL (KAISHO), GRASS (SOSHO), HIRAGANA, KATAKANA

95

Very early, the Japanese, adopting many features of Chinese culture, also adopted the characters. However, Japanese has up to three or more pronunciations of each of the Chinese characters. The first is a Nipponicized Chinese pronunciation of the character as of the date of the first borrowing (Go-on pronunciation), then another from the date of the second borrowing (Kun-on), and finally one or more purely Japanese pronunciations, often with hard and soft variations. For instance, the Chinese character 人 *jen* (which sounds to English speakers like our word "wren") is pronounced in various Japanese compounds as *nin* (Go-on), *jin* (Kun-on) and *hito* (soft from *bito*), the last and its alternate being the original Japanese word for "person." 門 *men* "door" or "gate" in Chinese is Japanese *mon* (Gon-on), *to,* in the meaning "door," or *kado,* in the meaning "gate," the latter two being Japanese pronunciations.

It is plain to see that to master a writing system such as the Chinese takes years and years, which has tended to create a really formidable Chinese wall for all those who wished to learn to read the literature written in this language. Attempts have been made in the past to simplify the Chinese writing system, but they have met with little success because the Chinese, and the Japanese as well, take great pride in the artistic and esthetic appearance of the characters used by them. At present under Mao Tse Tung, the Red regime is simplifying the characters, reducing the number of strokes which make them up. The regime is even sponsoring a system of Romanized writing to combat the widespread illiteracy. About twenty years ago, the Japanese also simplified the writing system, reducing the basic character inventory from 5,000 to approximately 1,850.

It should be mentioned that only Chinese makes use of characters exclusively. Japanese has developed two sets of symbols, called *hiragana* and *katakana,* which are syllabic alphabets representing the sounds of the language. They are used to indicate grammatical forms, such as verb ending. For example: *kaku* is "to write." "I wrote" is expressed as follows: *kakimashita.* Of this, the stem is *kaki* (書き) while *mashita* (ました) indicates the past.

Korean has gone further than Japanese and developed a complete alphabet—just as efficient as the Greek or Latin—with letters which look like extra Chinese characters. However, in writing Korean large numbers of Chinese characters are still used to represent Korean words with identical meanings. This is somewhat the way it would be in English if sentences were made up, to an appreciable extent, of symbols like @, $, &, %.

The Kanji or Chinese characters are written from top to bottom, most artistically with special brush and on rice paper. The Arabic and Hebrew alphabets go from right to left, while the Roman and Cyrillic alphabets are just the opposite, being written from left to right.

## Problems and Horizons

No system, no matter in what direction it is written, does a complete job of representing speech—which is, we have maintained, its primary function. In fact, writing is but a pale reflection of much that goes on in speaking. The intonation, which tells us so much about a speaker's attitude, receives only rudimentary representation by commas, periods, question marks and exclamation points. And tone of voice can be inferred only from parenthetical comments like "he said gruffly."

In any highly literate society, on the other hand, writing develops to a certain extent on its own, beyond its basic chore of reminding someone of possible speech. Often the writing has an influence on speech—most noticeably when "spelling pronunciations" develop, such as the sounding of the *t* in *often* or the *b* in *subtle*. Writing will at times convey some information that the spoken version of a message leaves out, as for example when English orthography distinguishes *pear* and *pair,* or when there are different Chinese characters for words with different meanings but the same pronunciation. Also, writing systems develop certain conventions of their own which are at best only deviously related to any of the devices used in speaking. Examples of this in our own culture would be most of the uses of capital letters, italics in printing, and much of our punctuation.

In our day and age of rapid communication the trend has been more and more to simplification of writing systems. Alphabet reform, like language reform, has been a real issue in world affairs. In his program of modernization Kemal Atatürk, in place of the Arabic alphabet previously used for Turkish, adopted the Roman alphabet and made this the official system.

With all due respect to the esthetic beauty of such writing systems as Chinese, it does seem that they take an inordinate time to master. Yet it must be admitted that, as many Chinese and foreign scholars point out, for a tongue like Chinese the pictographs are much more easily recognizable than are words which are written in the same manner but pronounced in different tones which change their meanings. There are, of course, various devices for indicating tonal distinctions in languages. Vietnamese, for example, has tried to solve the problem in using the Roman alphabet, by writing symbols over and under the vowels to indicate the proper one of the six standard tones, leaving tone number one unmarked. Thus one writes:

$$\text{ma} \quad \text{má} \quad \text{mà} \quad \text{mả} \quad \text{mã} \quad \text{mạ}$$

The above word has six different meanings according to the tone in which it is uttered. Nevertheless, this still does not solve the problem entirely for Vietnamese also has at least ten different vowels, for the writing of which the Latin letters were quite insufficient. The result is that a letter may have both a tone mark and another diacritic mark distinguishing the vowel. Examples:

$$\text{rằng} \qquad \text{giảm}$$

It has even been suggested that a completely new phonetically based alphabet for English would be a way out of the morass of our spelling conventions. George Bernard Shaw made provision in his will for an award to the inventor of the best new system. No public enthusiasm has been exhibited for the winning entry, and it seems unlikely that such a radical departure will leave any lasting mark.

One thing is sure: when people have adopted a certain writing system, they are reluctant to change. The distinguished

American linguist, Charles F. Hockett, notes: "The language changes as languages always change; but for some reason peoples are more conservative about writing systems than about any other human institution that can be named—even religion."

The conservatism of writing and the little it has changed over the centuries deserves comment in this day of split-second communication and automation. It should be emphasized that few really new advances were made in the writing process until the printing press was developed in the fifteenth century by the German Gutenberg. Then it became possible to make thousands of copies of any book without each volume being laboriously written by hand. Nineteenth- and twentieth-century technology revolutionized written communication. First came the telegraph, capable of sending the human word thousands of miles in a split second. The English sentence "What hath God wrought" was the first message thus to be transmitted, and it opened a new epoch. The typewriter was developed late in the nineteenth century and greatly speeded up the act of writing, which has again been accelerated by recent advances in designing electric typewriters.

However, here the written language barrier rears its head. Languages like Chinese, Japanese, Korean, and others that use ideographs are too complex to make any real use of typewriters. All the man-hours spent in merely committing a text to writing can be done in one tenth the time in an alphabet language.

Modern technology is bringing about tremendous advances in written communication, thanks to such processes as offset printing, multilithing, mimeographing, xeroxing, and photostating. IBM machines and input-output electric typewriters insure storage and retrieval of vast amounts of information in a fraction of the time formerly required. Thus, librarians and researchers are developing the new science of information dissemination and retrieval, which is becoming a vital part of library training.

Experimentation is going on constantly; all sorts of exciting developments are possible. A "speech typewriter" is being perfected that produces the written equivalent of what one speaks into it. Some machines seem to be advances beyond writing.

Information can be stored in special codes, or machine languages, designed for use in data processing operations.

New horizons are opening up in this whole area. The radio did not make people stop reading, as had been predicted in some quarters, but led to television, a fusion of the possibilities of the written and spoken word.

Daring advances are commonplace in the field of space communication. We have learned to use the moon as a rebroadcasting point from which signals can be ricocheted over vast distances. Telstar, an earth-controlled satellite, has put international television programs on the television screen in homes on opposite sides of the Atlantic. It goes without saying that these same facilities can be used to deliver newspapers and magazines. As a matter of fact, on April 24, 1962, the first transmission of television pictures by way of an orbiting satellite was announced by the U.S. Air Force. The transmitting waves went a thousand miles into the air from California to a two-year-old orbiting balloon, the Echo I, and bounced back to earth in Massachusetts. The signals traveled 3,000 to 4,000 miles to make their 2,700 mile cross-country jump. The first picture thus sent was really a bit of writing—merely the letters of M.I.T. (standing for Massachusetts Institute of Technology) flashed large across the screen. The possibilities are self-evident.

Writing has come a long way since primitive man scratched enigmatic messages on stones, bones, and the bark of trees.

# Chapter 8

# A Glance at Some Other Communication Systems

## Gestures

"Don't say anything—I understand," the television hero said to his heroine. Rephrased, this means that words are not always necessary to convey meanings. Perhaps our TV hero, in the story at least, could tell just what she meant by her beautiful eyes, her facial expression, and her gestures.

There are many ways of conveying meaning other than speaking, writing, or other verbal forms. For example, you are driving along the road; suddenly you see a sign; you drive along to a busy intersection and the traffic officer makes a signal for you to stop, then signals for you to drive on. You turn left, but before doing so you stretch out your left arm and point your finger in that direction. All this is communication and yet, not a single word has been spoken. But that is not all. Your wife strongly hints that she would like to go out, so you take her to a movie where you see still another example of non-verbal communication when the ushers make signs to one another to find two seats together.

But this by no means exhausts the repertoire of the ways in which messages can be sent. There appears to be no language whose speakers do not make use of gestures, or pasimology, as it is called. Athletic games like baseball, boxing, and football have a definite set of hand symbols understandable to participants from any part of our country. The American Indians often made use of a code of gestures for intertribal conferences. As recently as 1936 such a conference was called in Oklahoma and pictures and a record of the gestures used may be consulted in the Smithsonian Institution in Washington.

According to Mario Pei, a prolific writer on language subjects, it is possible that some seven hundred thousand distinct elementary gestures can be produced by facial expressions, postures, movement of arms, wrists, fingers, and their combinations. "It is quite conceivable, first, that a gestural system of communication could have arisen prior to and independently of spoken language; second, that such a system, had historical conditions been favorable, might have altogether supplanted the spoken tongue; third, that it could today supply the world's needs for an international common system."

I have heard people, particularly southern Europeans and Mediterraneans, criticized because "they talk with their hands." E. T. Hall, an eminent anthropologist, points out in his book *The Silent Language* that gestures are used by all peoples although they differ in form and meaning. The classic example of this is that a wave of the hand with palms down means "goodbye" or "go away" in America, but a wave of the hand with the palm up means "come here"—while just the opposite can be signified by these gestures in parts of Italy.

Although there is a myth that the Anglo-Saxon cultural pattern is undemonstrative this is not really so. We gesticulate far more than we imagine. Try talking without making any sort of movement of the hands, body, forehead, or face—you will find it almost impossible. Another revealing experiment is to turn on the television but turn off the sound. Notice that there is scarcely a moment that the actors do not make some kind of non-verbal symbol.

A number of attempts have been made to harness gestural symbols to the task of helping man solve his international communication problem. The most successful attempt so far has been in the International Sign Language for Tourists devised by Stephen Streeter, a Washington travel expert. This language consists of 72 symbols to express basic concepts such as "I'm hungry," "send a doctor," etc. A manual is available with explanations in some nine world languages.

In developing his International Sign Language the problem was that the whole thing was loaded with booby traps. For example, he learned that one of his symbols meant "go to the devil" in Brazil while he was obliged to give a wide berth to others which might have been offensive to certain religious and ethnic groups. E. T. Hall's *The Silent Language* gives many examples of how ignorance of the symbols of various cultures causes misunderstanding even when we have mastered the mechanics of the language involved.

In the Orient, there is the traditional dancing language of China, Korea, Japan, Vietnam, Indo-China, and Indonesia where hands rather than feet, as in Western dancing, carry the message. According to Pei there are in those conventionalized gestures 200 symbols to express various states of love.

The Trappist monks, whose rule includes a particularly rigorous discipline of silence, have developed an elaborate set of gesture symbols to enable them to carry on necessary communication without speaking. This is, of course, a higher level of organization in the use of gestures. Most gesture communication represents the largely unconscious accompaniment to speech. We also find isolated conventional signs like the hitch-hiker's thumbed request for a ride. The football referee's hand signals represent a small system of deliberately organized signs. Most gesture systems are limited to use for special purposes. Only in a few cases do we find basic communication carried out by gestural means, such as in the sign language of the deaf. Normal conversation can be carried on with only occasional recourse to spelling out English words by means of special alphabet-letter signals. A scientific investigation into the functioning of this system, using methods comparable to those employed by the investigation of language, has been inaugurated recently by the American linguist, William C. Stokoe, Jr., who says: "a symbol system by means of which persons carry on all the activities of their ordinary lives is, and ought to be treated as, a language."

People often ask why some sort of sign language did not originally develop instead of vocal speech. Darwin answered this by pointing out that it was a matter of efficiency, basically, since gestural language demands the use of hands while oral speech leaves the hands free for other tasks, plus the fact that gestural language requires light while oral speech can proceed in the dark. It becomes obvious when one examines the matter that, compared with oral speech, manual and other systems have many disadvantages which limit their range of expression.

## Codes

One of the most interesting forms of language is the whistle speech of the natives of Gomera in the Canary Islands by which the islanders communicate for miles. Meanings in it are, of course, carried by modulations in the whistling pattern. Similar systems have been reported as being in use in the French Pyrenees and Haiti.

Another intriguing "language" is that of the drums, a standard medium of communication in many parts of Africa south of the Sahara. So effective is this that natives are able to communicate from one village to another through the drumbeats. From all indications, however, the inroads of modern communication, including radio, loudspeakers, and television, are taking their toll of these primitive systems of communication.

Drum signal messages often follow the tonal patterns of words they represent. Mazateco, a language with an elaborately complicated tonal system, is also associated with a form of whistle speech, where ups and downs of pitch that ordinarily go with words are whistled.

Systems such as these are derivative from language; that is, they are ways of conveying a message consisting of a definite set of words. Some systems are in fact derivative from writing;

Morse code and semaphore signal codes are examples. In them the basic units stand for letters of the alphabet:

|   | a | b | c | d | e |
|---|---|---|---|---|---|
| International Morse Code: | $\cdot-$ | $-\cdot\cdot\cdot$ | $-\cdot-\cdot$ | $-\cdot\cdot$ | $\cdot$ |
| Semaphore flag: | ⌐ | ⌐ | ⌐ | ⌐ | ⌐ |

Just as writing is basically derivative from speech but develops in some ways independently (with small and capital letters), so to a lesser extent these systems have elements not directly dependent upon writing. Examples are:

| Morse Code: | $\cdot-\cdot-\cdot$ | End of transmission |
|---|---|---|
| | $-\cdot\cdot\cdot-$ | First of message begins here |
| Semaphore: | ↘ (or ↗ ) | |

After which signs A, B, . . . I, J represent, not letters but numerals, 1, 2, . . . 9, 0.

To this brief list may be added cable code, and international weather reporting code, recently elaborated by the Methodological Division of International Civilian Aviation and which operates according to five figure groups.

Then there is the language of flowers which, particularly in the days of chivalry, had definite meanings according to how the flowers were arranged. In past centuries, flicking a fan in a certain way had a definite meaning in the language of flirting. More modern is the language of teenage bobby-soxers. The bobby sox straight up means "open for a date," one fold means "going steady," rolled down means "taken"; beads knotted at the neck means "dated," and so on.

Engagement and wedding bands also exercise communicative functions. They have their "grammar rules" too, for if a woman in America wears a certain type of ring on the third finger of her left hand she is most likely engaged or married. In certain African tribes marriageable girls have definite styles of head-dress and married women another type. These are all systems in which only a small number of possible messages need to be kept straight. Perhaps as most typical of this sort we might cite the storm-warning flags hoisted at Coast Guard stations. Their meanings are: storm winds from the northeast; storm winds from the northwest; storm winds from the southeast; storm winds from the southwest; winds dangerous only to small craft; and HURRICANE! 🏴 🏴 🏴 🏴 ▶ 🏴

You can see that signaling systems are all around us. Some we don't even suspect. For example, beggars and vagabonds have a way in which they write on the walls of a house which warns their brethren either to avoid it or not, "hostile" or "soft touch."

Codes can be, and actually are, devised constantly for special purposes. For instance, the message of the fall of Troy was sent to Greece by lighting an immense fire on hill after hill. A bonfire is still a symbol of "help, come rescue us" on land and sea. In a recent movie, police planning a raid agreed on a series of symbols, the first of which was the Chief of Police lighting a cigarette. Translated, the message was, "Begin the raid." Of course, we all remember Paul Revere's famous lanterns: "One if by land and two if by sea."

### More Diffuse Systems

The pictorial form of communication is less tangible but very real. Everyone has heard that a picture is worth a thousand words. Actually, pictures are messages. People who know art can look at a picture, just as one listens to a speech or reads a letter, and interpret the message through the various clues given. Art interpreters refer to clues given by color, texture, shadings, tone, and arrangement. Modernistic art rebelled against the traditional pictorial realism and favors paintings and designs that are abstract. Instead of delivering an unmistakeable message, it merely suggests objects, moods, or concepts. However, pictorial representation may be the oldest written language known to man.

Music too has been called a language. Styles and patterns vary—as we quickly notice when listening to native Chinese music consisting of only a few chords—but the musical scale is a real alphabet, understood by musicians throughout the civilized world.

Music is even more symbolic than art and more subjective in interpretation, for the same musical selection that communi-

106

cates a message of joy to one person may bring a message of sorrow to his neighbor. The appeal of music is so universal that a nineteenth-century Frenchman devised an international world language based on the musical scales, and called it "Solresol." If this language had persisted, we might today walk into a restaurant and sing out in Solresol, "A hamburger with French fries and a double malt, please."

A language of fabrics is used by the *cognoscenti* in the textile field, and even today schools in Japan teach the language or art of *ikebana,* or flower arrangement. American lovers of Japanese things can attend classes in flower arranging, too.

Every time you stop for a traffic light you are responding to one of a vast complex of non-verbal systems used by earth dwellers to send messages to one another. We know that there are more than 2,800 different verbal languages. If it were possible to count the non-verbal systems of communication, we might find an even greater number.

What of space dwellers? Can we communicate with them? At this point, all we can say is, "No message yet!"

# Chapter 9

# *What Do You Mean —*
# *Semantics?*

*Different Ways of Meaning*

"What do you mean, 'snow'?" asks the Eskimo. "Falling snow, snow on the ground, snow in blocks for building igloos, or what? You can't use one word for all those different things."

"What do you mean, 'flier'?" we ask the Hopi who has just said *masa'ytaka*. "A dragonfly, an airplane, or a pilot? You can't use one word for all three." But the Hopi is perfectly happy to use his one word for anything that flies, so long as it is not a bird—for which he uses another word.

"What do you mean, 'democracy'?" asks the Communist. "Your people are all wage slaves who do not own the means of production."

"That's not true," we object, "and anyway it has nothing to do with democracy. 'Democracy' means just one thing: government by freely elected representatives and with the consent of the governed."

These are just a few examples of confusions that can arise over the meaning of what we say. Our negative reaction to the usages of the other speaker is not based on logic. The Eskimo's use of various words for "snow" seems unreasonable to us. But when English speakers live in the Arctic areas they start using different words too. One example is "sastrugi," borrowed from the Russian. We have to go to our dictionary to find that it means "wavelike ridges of hard snow formed on a level surface by the action of the wind . . . ," but this is an everyday word to Antarctic explorers.

Furthermore, we do practically the same thing with our word "water" that the Eskimo does with his "snow." We have a separate word for water while it is falling from the sky—rain. Any other time, it is just water. Whoever heard an English speaker say, "I stepped in some rain on the way here." He will always say "water," even though it was "rain" right up to the instant it hit the ground.

We have a similar reaction to Russian when it uses two words for "blue": *siniy* for dark blue and *goluboy* for light blue. "Blue is blue," we say. "What need is there for two different words?" But we do the same thing for the red part of the spectrum. When red gets pale enough we call it "pink." In English, "pink" is so different from "light red" that the latter term is used for a color that is also known as "burnt ocher," a bright, brownish-red color. But technically and logically the *siniy-goluboy* difference is just the same as the contrast between "red" and "pink." A color is *siniy* on the painter's palette until he mixes enough white with it. Then it becomes *goluboy*. It is the same with "red" in English. When the painter mixes enough white with the "red" on his palette, it becomes "pink."

So what of our complaints that Eskimos have "too many words for 'snow,' " or that Russians "have too many words for 'blue' "? We must finally admit that they are only prejudice, caused by our familiarity with English. After all, any divisions of color are arbitrary. A cylinder could be painted with a white ring around the top, a black ring around the bottom, and the rainbow colors in a ring around the middle. By careful blending, all of these could be spread into each other without any visible border between any color and the next, or between the lighter and darker shades of each color. In other words, all the hues of the rainbow and all their shades and tints merge into each other without any definite borders. Any division of this merging continuum into separate colors is arbitrary. It would be surprising to find that any two unrelated languages make exactly the same divisions. It should not be surprising when we find that some languages make as few as three major divisions while others make distinctions that are not found in English. A single name for colors in the cool part of the spectrum—indigo, blue, and blue-green—is common. Chinese has such a word which may also refer to gray or black and also carries an idea of the color being a characteristic of something. This word, *ch'ing,* would not be applied to colors like dyes. For paper and paint there are separate words. But *ch'ing* sky is blue, *ch'ing* grass is green, *ch'ing* mountains are purple, *ch'ing* cattle are black, and *ch'ing* horses are gray.

There is no end to vocabulary differences between languages, and when any language differs from our own, it seems strange to us. We cannot understand how some African languages have no common term for a male parent. Their words for "my father," or "his father," or "your father" are all different. But in everyday English we say "brother" or "sister" without any way to express "brother(s) and/or sister(s)" in a single word. Of course, there is "sibling," but this is almost a technical term of psychology and psychiatry. It was a good Old English word with its present meaning at the time of the Norman Conquest, but later on it disappeared from the language. It was revived at about the turn of the present century as a translation of the German *Geschwister.* This is an everyday German word in uses like *Hat er Geschwister?* "Does he have any brothers and sisters?" The German psychologists naturally used this word in concepts like "sibling rivalry," but to translate these terms into English, the obsolete word "sibling" had to be resurrected.

Or again, we find it strange that the Navajos use different words to describe the action of handing something to somebody.

These words all have the same first syllable, *san-,* but the rest of the word varies with the shape of the object passed:

> *sanleh*—long, flexible, like string.
> *sanlin*—long, rigid, like a stick.
> *sanilcos*—flat, flexible, like a piece of paper.

But is this really any stranger than the many English words to describe how we use a sharp-edged tool? Just a few of them: cut, chop, slash, carve, hew, slice, whittle, or hack.

## Definitions

The study of meaning is known as Semantics. This covers all the differences we have been talking about but it goes much further. It tries to explain what meaning is and how meanings really work. One of its conclusions was stated over 2,000 years ago by the Chinese philosopher, Hsün Tzu:

A name has no fixed standard. It is only by agreement that we apply a name. Once agreed, it becomes customary, and the standard is thus fixed. . . . A name has no fixed actuality; it is only a product of such agreement.

This idea has had hard sledding in the Western world ever since the time of Plato. He insisted that the idea of whiteness was more real than the actual whiteness of any object. But what is this idea of whiteness? The idea of whiteness, apart from any concrete thing that is white, is summed up only in the word "white." So Plato was really saying that the word "white" was more real than any white thing. This idea took firm hold in our civilization. In the Middle Ages the idea lost its vogue after the controversy between the Nominalists and the Realists. But the idea that "words are real" dies hard.

Any logical discussion makes it clear that the only useful definitions are those that both sides can agree on. Still, it is hard to convince ourselves that this is true. What happens if the two sides cannot agree on a definition? In the interest of clear understanding, they must agree to disagree. That is, we must admit that one definition is not really better than any other since any definition is only a way to help people agree that they are talking about the same thing.

This means that it is unscientific to accuse someone of "misusing" a word. This can be a shock. Is it wrong to say that the Communist in our example above is misusing the word "democracy"? When the linguist tells us it is certainly unscientific to make such a statement, we can hardly agree. He seems to be trying to tell us that the Communist form of government is as good as ours. This would indeed be shocking. But the linguist is saying nothing of the kind. He only asks us to accept the fact that we and they are using the same word with entirely different meanings. When we can't agree on a meaning we can only drop the word in question and use other ways of saying what we mean. This may be awkward, but note how it prevents useless arguments. If the Communist says, "You don't have universal worker ownership of the means of production," we are perfectly willing to agree. But this was what he meant by "democracy," or part of what he meant at least. Also when we say "You don't have a two-party system, or anything else to give you a choice between candidates by the voter," the Russian agrees willingly. But that was what we meant by "democracy," in part at least. So by dropping any word we cannot agree on, we eliminate misunderstanding and can have a more reasonable discussion. But as long as we argue about the correct meaning of "democracy" as a word, we are getting nowhere and preventing any possibility of understanding.

If there is no such thing as a "correct" definition, what are dictionaries for? A dictionary is a history, not a lawbook. If you do not know the meaning of a word, it can tell you how the word has been used in the past. *Time* magazine phrased it beautifully in reviewing a newly published dictionary:

When he set out in 1746 to write the first great English dictionary, Samuel Johnson intended his definitions to be laws that would firmly establish meanings. But usage thumbs its nose at laws; the dictionary nowadays is more a *Social Register* of words than a Supreme Court of language.

This really states the case. Choice of words is a matter of fashion and manners. "Correct" definitions are like "correct" clothes. They are the ones in favor with the people with whom we associate. Insisting on dictionary definitions is just snobbery, no better than insisting that all our friends must be people listed in the *Social Register*.

Even when we can agree on definitions many problems remain. In the sentence: "He sat in a chair," the meaning of "chair" is clear and matter-of-fact. But we say a murderer "got the chair" and the word suddenly has a very different meaning. If someone talks about "calling a chair" it probably means nothing to us. In some hill towns of the Orient, however, the sedan-chair is still a normal way to travel. There you can call a chair, just as we call a taxi, although usually not by telephone! So all of a sudden "calling a chair" makes sense.

This behavior of a perfectly simple word is not at all unusual. A bench is pretty much like a chair—something to sit on. But look what happens to the word in a court of law. There it means the place where the judge sits, or the judge himself, or the judge's job. Think of the simplest, plainest word you can and look it up in the big dictionary. The simpler and plainer it is, the more likely you are to find a long list of secondary, unusual meanings.

Words can be difficult in other ways. What a word refers to in the world of facts is called its "denotation." If we do not know the denotation of a word we simply fail to understand it. The word "chair" would denote nothing to an African Bushman or to any other tribesman who had never seen or used one. The connotation of a word adds to its denotation. The same individual in the world of facts may be called "American Indian," "noble savage," or "red varmint." Since all these terms are applied to the same individual they have the same denotation; they all point to the same person in the world of facts. This is sometimes difficult to realize because the three expressions do not mean the same thing at all. Such difference in meaning is known as "connotation." Although the three terms denote the same thing—the same person in this case—there are three entirely different connotations involved. Of course, only the term "American Indian" is an objective description. The American Indians were neither noble savages nor red varmints. They were, and are, good and bad, trustworthy and treacherous, or sometimes each in turn—just as we are, and everybody is, and people will probably always be.

Differences in connotation can lead to utter confusion, even international incidents. According to Edmund Glenn of the State Department's Language Services Division, in a conference a reference to the "expanding economy" of the United States produced a violent burst of Soviet opposition. The U.S. delegate was nonplussed, especially by the attitude of his European allies. The French delegation supported the United States publicly but privately criticized the mistake of backing the Soviets into a corner by such a "rigid and overbearing" attitude. The whole problem arose from the translation. The Russian translation, *rasshirayushchayasya ekonomiya* means "expanding economy" but it has a connotation of an economy that is expanding because of its own inherent characteristics. This runs counter to the Marxist insistence that capitalism carries the seed of its own destruction and will inevitably collapse of its own weight. The Soviet delegates were steeped in Marxist doctrine; to them the phrase was no less than rank heresy. Naturally, they could not sign a document that seemed to make a liar out of the men who wrote their gospel. The original phrase had no such intention. It simply referred to the American economy which is in fact expanding. The Russian phrase, moreover, was the best simple translation. Anything more accurate would involve some sort of an explanatory footnote or circumlocution. The whole trouble arose because the simple Russian phrase had a connotation entirely lacking in the original English.

The moral of this story is perfectly plain. To translate accurately, or even to work accurately in a single language, we must pay close attention to secondary meanings and connotations. As was noted with the word "chair," the simplest word does not have the same meaning to any two different people.

## Characteristic Flavors

An object borrowed from another culture often takes its name with it. Strange animals often bring their native names into another language. So can other things, moccasins or pemmican, for instance, or *teburu* (table) and *taipuraita* in Japanese, or *beisbol* and *jonron* (homerun) in Latin-American Spanish. Sometimes even borrowing of an abstract concept occurs. In such a case, the new word often seems specially typical of the culture that supplies it. The French word *éclat* seems somehow to mean much more than the English "sparkle." As a result, the word has been adopted, at least at the literary level, not only into English but also into most other European languages.

As another example, the Spanish guerrillas of the Peninsular Campaign against Napoleon were by no means the first partisan fighters. Many populations before and since have resisted aggression long after their organized armies have been defeated. But something special about the effectiveness of the Spaniards, or the interest of the English in the outcome of their struggle, carried their name solidly into the English language. So much is this true that the word is no longer written with italics like a more foreign word such as *éclat*. Even puns on guerrilla-gorilla seem rather strained since the word has won full acceptance.

A final example is the English concept of "fair play." This word has carried over into several foreign languages. Other people know perfectly well what is fair, of course, but just as *éclat* is peculiarly French, the idea of fair play seems peculiarly Anglo-Saxon. Pictures of German strikers show them carrying signs with the word "unfair." This word has carried over into German—the language of German labor anyway—just as *éclat* and "guerrilla" have carried over into English.

Anthropologists have long been conscious of this relationship between a language and a culture. The examples of borrowings given above have all been taken from Western European words where only a small facet of a foreign culture has stood out as having a special flavor among basically familiar patterns. When we are met by radically different cultures like those of the American Indians, we find ourselves in a whole new world of strange concepts. Appreciation of this led to the Whorfian Hypothesis which takes its name from Benjamin Lee Whorf. He suggested that the way a person talks dictates the way he thinks on any given subject. Our examples of the Eskimo and Hopi that opened this chapter were borrowed from one of Whorf's articles. There is a bit of a chicken-and-the-egg about the whole thing. Which came first, the way of thinking or the way of speech? This question may never be properly answered. It is difficult to say just how much is the effect of speech on thought and how much is the effect of thought on speech. But however it runs, the interaction between thought patterns and speech patterns is tremendous.

Examples are hard to explain or understand. New concepts, entirely different from anything we ever thought of before, are hard to grasp. The Hopi, for instance, thinks of time as separate units like beads on a string. Days obviously follow other days, and seasons come one after another, but the Hopi does not think of them as a continuous flow. Since the Hopi's time does not "move" from one unit to the next, he cannot see speed as we do. To him it is more a matter of intensity. Do not be discouraged if you have trouble grasping this concept. Time has been an ever-rolling stream to you since you first started to think in words. You cannot expect to cross over into the Hopi concept of units just by reading about it once. But if you ever have to work with Hopis you should expect to meet a great deal of difficulty in explaining to them why there should be a deadline for completing any given job.

Here is another thought: how would you like to translate a simple English text into Hopi? Even from English to Russian can give enough troubles and English and Russian are related languages—closely related compared to English and Hopi. The way of the translator is hard. Between any two languages denotations and connotations can vary tremendously. The translator must tread a narrow path between literal translation and free composition. Differing connotations between words that are literal equivalents force him one way, but if he goes all the way, he ends up with a new composition in the second language. Any translator will tell you that there is no simple answer. The translator just cannot satisfy everybody. The Italians put it well: *Traduttore—traditore,* "To translate is to betray."

A few examples again: a European visitor has trouble with our "Department of the Interior." To him this is the ministry that controls the police and security forces and little else. Only careful explanation will convince him that our Department takes care of mines, forests, Indian affairs, and fish and wildlife.

Bible translation offers many examples. A phrase like "from the heart" comes out "from the liver" or "from the throat" or "from the belly," depending on the language being used. To a Chinese the Apostles Creed makes good sense only if the ascended Christ sits "on the left hand of God, the Father Almighty." Similar examples could be cited without end.

The problem is compounded when translating literature as such. Boris Pasternak electrified the world with his *Doctor Zhivago* with its implied tone of criticism of the Soviet Union. A book of his earlier poems was reviewed by the *New York Times*. Admitting that the poems had been competently rendered into English, the reviewer still maintained that they were little more than an echo of the originals. He should hardly have expected more. A translation that carries even a clear echo of the original is a good translation. For further proof ask any Oriental what his country's poetry amounts to when translated into English.

*Approaches to Semantics*

A book of special importance to semantics was *The Meaning of Meaning* by Ogden and Richards. The book is heavy going even for the professional linguist but it opened new horizons in the analysis of verbal communication. To oversimplify, the authors state that the basic referents in the semantic system of any language are vastly less than the total vocabulary would suggest since simpler synonymous expressions are available. They claim that a study of these referents or basic irreducible designations would lead to a much clearer understanding of meanings.

One example of this study goes by the name of "content analysis." After World War II a large body of German propaganda was subjected to this process. In a nutshell the analysts tried to pierce through the fog of what was said to determine the actual meanings of the statements. It has been claimed that content analysis applied at the time that Hitler and his colleagues actually made their speeches could have prevented the Second World War. "If's" are cheap, of course, but it may be of some comfort to know that the same technique is being currently applied to the mass of Soviet declarations and propaganda.

Another important contribution to the study of meanings and human reactions to words and other symbols is a book, *Science and Sanity,* by the late Count Alfred Korzybski. This book is the source of a new discipline called "general semantics." Some adherents of the system claim that semantic reconditioning could solve almost all of the world's problems. Cautious linguists and social scientists feel this to be rather extreme. Most students of general semantics make no such claim, nor do such authorities in the field as Drs. Wendell Johnson, University of Iowa; S. I. Hayakawa, San Francisco State College; Harry Weinberg, Temple University; and the late Irving J. Lee, Northwestern University.

One of the "thinking habits" decried by general semantics is that of thinking in polar terms—good and evil, black and white, etc. There is a full scale of values between good and evil, just as there is a full range of grays between black and white. Dividing everything into the good and the evil is sloppy and dangerous thinking. Again, no two people, places, ideas, or grains of sand are identical. This isn't hard to accept if we talk about things concerning which we have little or no prejudice. For example, saying that no two cows are exactly the same (Cow$_1$ is not Cow$_2$) rouses little emotion. But when we talk about things that involve strong prejudices, our responses are different. For example, if someone says that no two Negroes are exactly alike or no two Jewish people are exactly alike, the response may be, "Don't give me that—they're all alike!" The trouble caused by this sort of thinking in today's world is all too apparent.

Korzybski's book is difficult to read. Books by his followers exist that are quite readable and enlightening. Dr. Lee was the leader in the field until his death. Some of the materials he developed have been adapted for a number of Chicago junior and senior high schools. The results of his course were studied at the Nettlehorst School. Here, 300 seventh- and eighth-graders with IQ's of 84 to 130 and from many different backgrounds were exposed to general semantics. The students listened and participated with great enthusiasm. Even more important, they seemed able to apply what they had learned to real life situations. The theories and techniques of general semantics cannot be dismissed lightly.

Linguists are just now returning to a study of meaning. Traditional studies of grammar were based primarily on meaning. When linguists sought to improve on these, they found structure, not meaning, to be the most reliable guide to the study of grammar. Impressed by this fact, the linguists at first rejected the field of meaning as too nebulous for serious study. This amounted to throwing the baby out with the bathwater. More recently things are seen in a better perspective and the study of meaning by linguists has been revived. Possibly, to avoid confusion with general semantics, the subject is now likely to be called "semology." By semantics or semology, it is still the study of meaning and a fascinating study it is.

# Chapter 10

# Languages and Riot Squads

*Linguistic Nationalism*

LANGUAGE RIOTS IN ASSAM! SCORES KILLED! FORTY PEOPLE DIE! 40,000 FLEE!

These are the type of headlines we saw in the international press in July, 1960. The violence lasted for more than two months, and the Indian Government transferred some officials in the state of Assam to less sensitive areas. Others were suspended, and frantic appeals for national unity echoed throughout the land.

The idea of bloodshed over linguistic problems startles Americans, yet from time immemorial men have been willing to spill their blood to defend ethnic and language rights. This is what happened when speakers of Assamese (comprising about half the 9,000,000 population of Assam) rebelled against what they considered domination by people of Bengali origin. When demands for adoption of Assamese as the official state tongue were not met by the Delhi government, the streets ran wild.

Language riots are, of course, the result of modern Babel and the competition among speech communities. Attachment to one's mother tongue is a universal phenomenon and emotionalism is liable to flare up when one group is convinced that its language and culture are being treated as inferior to that of

120

another, possibly a more powerful group. At the present, when so many peoples are flexing their collective muscles and demanding self-determination, language rights have become one of the hottest issues of the day.

There is probably no better example of the Pandora's box of linguistic troubles which can be released when nations emerge from colonialism than that of the Indian subcontinent. In 1946 Great Britain released its hold on India and this vast area split into Pakistan and India. The language problem immediately raised its head, as was to be expected, in view of the highly complex tangle of tongues which abound in that region.

Estimates of the number of major languages and dialects spoken on the Indian subcontinent go as high as 500. However, after years of British rule, English has become a convenient interlanguage, used to communicate with people from other regions and to conduct official business, although in reality only an elite minority of about 5 per cent speak much if any English. Independence gave the various groups, heady with the idea of liberation, an opportunity to put in their claims while plans were being made to abandon English entirely by 1960.

A glance at the diversified linguistic picture of the subcontinent is essential. Not less than five main linguistic families exist. For years they have eyed one another with hostility. These are the Aryan or Indic (Indo-European), the Dravidian, the Munda, Tibeto-Chinese, and the MonKhmer, represented by the Khasi. The largest and most important are the Aryan languages which have existed on the subcontinent for the last 3,000 years and to which ancient Sanskrit and modern Hindi both belong. The Dravidian languages are second in importance, covering roughly most of southern India and including the important Tamil, Telugu, Kanarese, and Malayalam tongues. The speakers of the Munda group are much more backward than the Aryans and Dravidians, although there is reason to believe that they may have been the first inhabitants of the subcontinent. The Tibeto-Chinese and the Khasi are fairly recent arrivals and are small in number and influence.

When India became independent, it declared Hindi to be

the over-all "union" language, but it also granted official status to twelve other important regional tongues of the country: Assamese, Bengali, Gujarati, Kannada (Kanarese), Kashmiri, Malayalam, Marathi, Oriya, Punjabi, Tamil, Telugu, and Urdu. In addition, Sanskrit enjoys official status and is used as a classical lingua franca among the Pandits or highly educated Hindus. English is, in effect, a co-partner with Hindi as an interlanguage.

However, the preferred position given to Hindi evoked linguistic jealousy among the proud Dravidians in the south. Even other Aryan speakers, such as the Bengalis who think of themselves as the cultural leaders of India, felt that they had been forced to take a back seat. In Pakistan, the choice of Urdu, although acceptable in West Pakistan, was questioned in East Pakistan (from which it is separated by almost 1,000 miles), where Bengali is the vernacular.

If there was, however, a single point which all agreed upon, it was that English had to go. India in its constitution had committed herself to displacing English by 1960 while Pakistan specified no date. But this was easier said than done and both countries find themselves today still leaning heavily on the tongue of their former British masters.

Amusingly enough, not so many years ago when Khrushchev and the now-disgraced Bulganin visited India, they repeated the slogan *Hindi Russi Bhai Bhai*—"Indians and Russians are brothers." Their listeners, particularly in the south, looked blank because few could understand what was meant. Even in India's north, a considerable part of the population is not able to understand Hindi. Professor W. Norman Brown of the University of Pennsylvania has noted that at a recent educational conference in Pakistan delegates from Bengal (East Pakistan) frequently complained that they could not understand speeches in Urdu.

There are tremendous problems to be faced whenever the use of a language is extended to new fields. All the terminology, all the reference books, all the precedents, cannot be translated overnight. It really should not surprise us at all that in India the courts, except on the lowest levels, could not be conducted even today in any tongue but English. Though terminology could be coined or borrowed from Sanskrit or Persian, it would be so new and unfamiliar that much of it would mean little to its listeners.

A leading Indian linguist recently pointed out to the authors what variation there is in the use of abstract terminology in his native land. An expression such as "salvation's true path" would be rendered by simple village people as *mukti-kī sacci saṛak,* by the Pandits or educated Hindus as *mukti-kī satya upay,* by cultured Moslems as *nájāt-kī haqq rāh* and by Indian students who read English as *salwēshan-kī trū pāth,"* in which the English phrase is borrowed but with sound and structure (e.g., the possessive *kī*) following Hindi patterns.

As regards modern scientific, technical, and sociological terminology, Indian and Pakistani dictionary makers have simply not been able to coin and popularize new vocabulary rapidly enough to keep up with the needs of the country and its growing industrialization and intellectual development. In the universities, according to reliable reports, university professors are required to fall back upon English constantly or to use it entirely in their courses.

Insight into the woes of multilingualism at the grass roots level is afforded in a field study by John Gumperz of the University of California. He studied at first hand the speech situation in a fairly typical Indian village whose inhabitants, mostly illiterate and semi-literate, spoke a Hindi dialect. Nevertheless, they had difficulty in understanding technical publications and lectures by outside speakers sent by Delhi. He found that few persons listened to the All India Radio news broadcasts because of problems in grasping their style and terminology. India's Community Development project is striving to remove this sort of barrier, but this example illustrates how literacy and other social factors complicate the task of "language engineering" involved in putting a backward language to use by all strata of the population.

Selig S. Harrison may be overstating the case, however, when he comments in his recent book *India: The Most Dangerous Decades,* "Unless central educational controls can assure sufficient learning in English or unless Hindi is taught on a scale which now seems unimaginable, it is entirely possible that India will be led in not too many years by a generation of bureaucrats and politicians literally unable to talk meaningfully to one another on a national stage."

Meanwhile, the linguistic cauldron continues to boil in India. A few years ago in Orissa, state police had to use tear gas to disperse mobs. Demonstrators stopped trains in Madras state. In Central India, knowing that language problems were being discussed, frenzied mobs broke into the legislature of Madhya Pradesh state, throwing stones, articles of clothing, paper files, and miscellaneous objects at the legislators.

Several years ago the Sikhs, a warlike, bearded sect numbering some five million in Punjab province, agitated for their language rights. Fearing that they would be swallowed up by Hindi speakers, they have continued to clamor for greater use of Punjabi, pressing their point with Nehru-like demonstrations. The leader of the Akali Dal (Soldiers of God), Master Tara Singh, in August, 1957, told members of the press that the Sikhs wished to consider themselves part of the Hindu society but not of the Hindu religion. He charged that the pro-Hindu Arya Samaj party was trying to "kill Sikhism" and that cigarettes, from which his people abstain, had been tossed into the sacred water tank of the Golden Temple of Amritsar and that several sleeping Sikhs had their beards shorn off.

The Sikhs finally settled for a two-way linguistic formula in which their mother tongue, Punjabi written in a special alphabet called Gurmukhi, would be used in the grade school, after which Hindi would be the language of instruction. But the right-wing Arya Samaj, preaching "Hindi for Indians," noisily protested this. Nobody as yet appears satisfied, and Tara Singh stated not long ago that, "Mr. Nehru and a few others are nationalist, but the government as a whole is a Hindi government." In early 1962, Master Tara again went on a forty-day hunger strike, trying to draw attention to Sikh claims.

Many students of India have expressed concern that this young democracy may dangerously weaken herself by granting too many small groups their linguistic and cultural autonomy—thus falling prey to the dread specter of "balkanization." For example, on July 30, 1960, India, in a move to end a fierce five-year war, granted the Naga tribesmen of northeast India a separate autonomous state. The new state was to be inhabited by a mere 350,000 Nagas, highly diverse in their ethnic make-up, comprising some fifteen tribes. Meanwhile in London, A. Z. Phizo, leader of the Naga-in-exile movement, has continued to protest this agreement, asserting that he and his followers were not fighting for a state within the Indian Union, but for an independent Naga nation. In August of 1962, Phizo issued a belligerent statement repeating his vow to continue the struggle for independence and threatened to appeal to the United Nations. Meanwhile, Delhi counters that the Nagas are a group of tribes rather than a single people.

The new states of the Indian subcontinent are finding it necessary to depend heavily on English in communicating both with one another and the remainder of the world. There has not been time enough to translate text and reference books for the new needs. It is being found also that too abrupt a change-over can lead to a Babel-like confusion of tongues. For this reason a special committee on higher education in India has warned against a tendency on the part of the universities to drop English as a medium of instruction before they are equipped sufficiently to communicate in the native tongues. The committee pointed out that it is in the national interest to retain English as the second language in all universities, that the change-over should proceed in stages, and that it ought to provide for a proper foundation in English for secondary school students planning to go on to the universities. It would be childish to deny that the shift to Hindi and the other twelve official tongues has not caused much difficulty and confusion. At any rate, English as a medium of instruction has virtually disappeared from the elementary and secondary schools, being retained only as a foreign language. India's universities vary, but in all cases there is a trend towards increased use of the regional languages.

Just south of India in Ceylon a chronic conflict exists

between speakers of Sinhalese, the official language, and Tamil. The Tamil Federal Party of Ceylon in April, 1963, launched still another campaign to bring about the exclusive use of Tamil in the Tamil areas of the country. According to B. Mendis, writing in the *Christian Science Monitor* of April 4, 1963, "The government has warned leaders of the party against the consequences of their activities, pointing to examples of arson, looting, and killing which followed in the past 'non-violent campaign' "; nevertheless, the Federal Party leaders have described their campaign as a non-violent movement to win a place for Tamil.

Of Ceylon's ten million or so population, about seven million speak Sinhalese, an Indic language which is the standard official one. English serves as an auxiliary for educational and technical purposes. Tamil (a Dravidian tongue) is spoken by about two and one-half million persons. It is mostly a language for informal situations, being much less used for formal and literary purposes than in India.

We probably have not heard the last of the difficulties in the subcontinent regarding language problems. On February 21, 1963, Socialist and right-wing (Jana-Sangh) deputies interrupted the annual address by President Sarvepalli Radhakrishnan because it was being delivered in English and demanded that he continue in Hindi. The Socialists finally walked out. It developed that the President is a native of the south India state of Andhra Pradesh and is not fluent in Hindi. Strong pressures are coming from the south where Radhakrishnan originates, and where Hindi is spreading only gradually, to extend the Hindi-English partnership beyond 1965, the new cut-off date provided by the constitution. Speaking on India in a TV presentation on February 2, 1963, titled "The World as Seen from New Delhi," Quincy Wright, Visiting Professor of Government at Columbia University, called the language snarl in India the number one problem.

Citizens of the almost monolingual United States and similar nations are often puzzled at countries like India and Pakistan and their unwillingness to adopt English, with its ready-made space age vocabularies and rich literature, as their

126

medium of expression. The answer is quite simple. It is primarily a case of national or ethnic pride. To the peoples of the Indian subcontinent, English, whether we like it or not, will always be the tongue of their former conquerors, the British Empire. At the same time, the Hindus, at least, have not forgotten that, while Europe was inhabited by barbarians, India had produced a highly advanced civilization and a philosophy and literature written in Sanskrit, the parent of modern Hindi-Urdu.

Perhaps even more striking in this connection is the case of modern Israel, with its immigrants from some seventy lands, but with English spoken by virtually all educated people. The reason that Hebrew, a language not spoken for millenia, was "revived" and made the official tongue is also because of the Israelis' consciousness of their ancient past, regard for the role of Hebrew in the development of the Judeo-Christian tradition, and desire to avoid any language reminiscent of former persecutors. Naturally, new terminology had to be supplied by coinage or borrowing, but the structure and basic vocabulary remain the same as in the Old Testament. Hebrew began to be "modernized" in the late nineteenth century and had gone far toward becoming "sociologically complete" by the time it was officially adopted in 1946. Now used in all phases of life, it is probably one of the most rapid cases in history of undisputed adoption of a language by a whole nation. The fact is that, if the Biblical Solomon or David were to come to life and return to Jerusalem, they would soon understand almost everything said except such terms as "radio" or "electric toaster."

In decided contrast, however, is the case of modern Ireland, or Eire, which, on achieving independence in the 1920's, declared Irish Gaelic, spoken by only a small group in a few counties, co-official with English and made it a compulsory school subject. Societies have been formed in Eire to further the use of the language. Literary competitions have been arranged and folk festivals organized by the government. Nevertheless, while feeling no less Irish, the citizens of Eire apparently do not feel a strong need of the ancestral tongue for other communication purposes. It is a question whether Gaelic will ever take the place of English which, although the tongue of Cromwell and other anti-Irish Britishers, has been the mother tongue since the sixteenth century and earlier. A report by Father C. L. O'Huallachain, a Dublin educator who recently spent a year studying applied linguistics in language instruction at Georgetown University, points out that, thanks in part to inadequate teaching measures, the achievement in Irish Gaelic-English bilingualism has to date been far below official expectations.

This brings us to a point which is not really receiving its just share of attention in political discussions today. It is that language—like religion—becomes the symbol of solidarity or even emancipation when a people feels insecure, threatened, and unprotected. Although it does not always lead to the sort of violence witnessed in India, it nevertheless does create tensions, or to use political science terminology, it acts as an irritant in the body politic.

Particularly in today's world the flame of nationalism burns brightly. Not only in Africa but elsewhere, the desire for self-determination brings group after group forward with claims for independence, or at least autonomous status with such privileges as the right to provide education in the native tongue.

If, however, the diversity of tongues on the Indian subcontinent appears to pose thorny problems, Africa south of the Sahara presents an even greater linguistic puzzle. A few years ago an African editor was beaten in Uganda for using the "wrong" forms of the Luganda tongue which had shortly before been standardized. This incident reflects the emotionalism surrounding language problems on that continent, where countries are desperately seeking a common language with which to communicate among their bewildering diversity of peoples and with the outside world. Unfortunately, political and social scientists slight this issue in favor of more "compelling" economic and political questions.

The enormity of Africa's language problem can only be grasped if one glances at a linguistic map of the continent. South of the Sahara alone, according to Joseph Greenberg, a prominent American anthropological linguist, there are 800 distinct tongues, not to mention countless dialects. Instead of the neat, mono-lithic blocks of language families found in such areas as western Europe or Latin America, the bewildering array of tongues reminds one of a crazy quilt. What makes matters even worse is that, unlike many if not most areas, there are no languages which are spoken by a majority of the population. Swahili and Hausa, the two leading tongues, are spoken by only about 8 per cent of the population. In large parts of Africa many tribes in neighboring villages can communicate only through French, English, or in some instances Portuguese or Arabic, the tongues of former or present colonial powers.

No one is more aware than the Africans themselves of the obstacles this places before the new nations in their striving for political solidarity and technological progress. According to UNESCO figures, approximately 70 per cent of all scientific writing is in French, German, and English, with English accounting for 62 per cent of the output. Sociologist Janet Roberts remarks of this that, "The scientific and technical material needed to convert basically agricultural states to industrial nations is largely restricted to three or four languages, including Russian, in which a growing bulk of research is being printed."

Technology is only one face of the coin. The other is the problem of political and social solidarity, which is obviously all the more difficult to achieve when, in addition to all other dif-ferences, mutual intelligibility is not present. On the eve of Ghana's independence, President Kwame Nkrumah had the following to say before that country's Parliament, "One of the most obvious difficulties which face Africa south of the Sahara is the multiplicity of languages and dialects. Everyone of us in this Assembly today has to conduct parliamentary business in a language which is not his own. I sometimes wonder how well the House of Commons in the United Kingdom, or the Senate of the United States, would manage if they suddenly found that they had to conduct their affairs in French or Spanish."

Let us glance a moment at Ghana's linguistic picture. Its six and a half million people speak close to a hundred languages. A half dozen or so of these are spoken by sizable groups. These are Twi, with almost three million, and Dagari, Ewe, Gą, Moshi-Dagbande, and Nzema, none of which is used by more than a quarter of a million while Hausa is understood in some areas as a lingua franca. Viewing this linguistic mosaic, the newly created state decided to adopt English as the official tongue. It is used in top-level governmental and commercial situations with native tongues for more informal exchange. Nevertheless, only a tiny minority, or an estimated 120,000, speak English more or less well, comprising an elite that has access to leadership and professional advancement.

If the new states are to become bilingual or trilingual, assuming that English or French will continue to be included, which native languages are to be chosen? Here it is almost impossible to make choices without treading on tribal and group sensitivities. Recent experiences reveal how these come into play. For example, the Nandis and Kipsigis of Kenya speak mutually intelligible tongues but have refused to accept literature in each other's tongue because they "could not understand it." A committee set up to solve the problem soon realized that the lack of comprehension stemmed from political rather than linguistic causes, and gave the two tongues equal status under the blanket term "Kalenjin."

In Uganda, a mission committee attempted to solve the language problem of a northern province in which tribes refused to communicate with one another despite very similar tongues. They created a composite language only to have one tribe whose tongue differed greatly reject it completely. Finally, the language did come into use and was known as the "church language." The Baganda of Uganda are extremely jealous of their tongue and refuse to allow any other language to be given preference over their native Luganda which at present shares official status with English. It is not strange, therefore, that even in Uganda, where political parties have had some ten years of experience under British tutelage, the Minister of Agriculture Joseph Mukasa not long ago termed tribalism the greatest threat to that relatively stable and prosperous land.

It would not be surprising if the new African governments,

themselves keenly sensitive to problems of self-determination, were eager to accord as much autonomy as possible to separate ethnic groups and their languages. There have been some steps in this direction. Nigeria, for example, has been allowing regional governments to establish advisory councils for the ethnic minorities which before independence were demanding the creation of autonomous states, as well as boundary revisions. But there exists in this the danger of "balkanization," or the splitting up of a country into a vast patchwork of ineffective rival groups, all vying for power. The diversity of language in Africa obviously aids and abets this threat.

There are two opposing forces at work in Africa today. One is tribalism and the other is nationalism, accompanied by varying degrees of internationalism. Leaders vary in this regard, which means that their view of self-determination for ethnic groups varies. For example, Nkrumah, Ghana's "Osafegyo," is generally favorable to pluralism, while Julius Nyerere, Prime Minister of Tanganyika, stands opposed to it and strives for unification. It is interesting that far more has been done with vernacular tongues in ex-English than in ex-French territories where the same sort of veneration of "pure" Parisian French exists among the elite as is the case in France itself.

Whatever may be the case, nevertheless, all of the new governments are striving for something termed "Africanization"— the replacing of Europeans by Africans in as many technical, social, and political positions as possible. But the accomplishment of this depends greatly upon two factors—ability to handle a European tongue, and education. The process is not an easy one and it does require time. In Senegal, for example, out of 253 secondary school teachers a few years ago, only seventeen were African and this is a situation still fairly typical.

It is for reasons like this that "neutral" tongues are of special interest. Professor Gilbert Ansre of the University of Ghana at Accra recently conducted a poll on language questions at that institution. Of the respondents, almost 100 per cent favored the continued use of English as the official tongue. Queries about other choices were inconclusive, with at least one student giving a reply typical of the thinking of many Africans, "I won't (*sic*) like my language not to be chosen." Other neutral possibilities in Africa are the pidgins and creoles. One of the American observers at the Second Meeting of the Inter-African Committee on Linguistics, held in the summer of 1962 in Brazzaville, recently declared that a positive accomplishment of that conclave, organized by Malcolm Guthrie of the University of London, was to recognize the great importance of these speech forms which grew up out of the need to communicate both with the white man and other Africans.

The best known such lingua franca is Swahili, which developed on a Bantu base as a medium between Arab slave traders and native Bantu peoples. It has nineteen different forms today, with the recognized standard that of Zanzibar, erstwhile center of the slave traffic. But since it is not a tribal tongue, it is accepted as a useful means of communication in East Africa (although its former association with the slave trade still makes it repugnant to a few).

A similar example of a lingua franca is Sango in the Central African Republic. Still others are Town Bemba in northern Rhodesia and Kitchen or Mine Kafir in South Africa, which developed to answer the needs of the diverse groups working in the diamond mines. The point here is that some of these mediums could be adopted, by agreement of a number of nations, to serve as a common tongue.

## Multi-lingual States

Implementation of any language policy, however, rests ultimately on the educational system. But as the experience of multi-language states reveals again and again, it imposes a heavy burden on a school system even to conduct instruction in two languages and brings up all sorts of questions regarding language usage in government offices and administrations. Witness to this are the recent language riots by Flemish-speaking citizens of Belgium, protesting alleged discrimination by French speakers. On the tenth of September, 1962, riot squads had to be called out in Antwerp to quiet demonstrators who had noisily interrupted a French language sermon in a church of that city. This was a reaction to a decision by the Bishop of Antwerp a week before that French language sermons should be given in five churches of that city. In Canada, similar agitation has taken place recently among French Canadians protesting the favored position of English. Although officially bilingual, only about 13 per cent of the population can actually speak both tongues, and of these 9 per cent are French Canadians. A French separatist movement has existed for some time, but it has not been a potent force in Canadian politics. In 1962, however, extremist elements carried out several acts of violence, one of these resulting in the death of a postman who had picked up a bomb wrapped in a package in a letter box. Angry slogans of separatism have since then occasionally appeared in French Canada, proclaiming *L'indépendance! Québec oui! Canada non!* Quite recently the Canadian Government, wishing to make French a working language in the civil service and bring French-Canadians to feel at home when they are dealing with or working for the federal service, set up a special bilingual school in Hull, Quebec. Selected officials will be sent to 10- to 12-week intensive courses in French or English, whichever is a second language. Half the students will be native French speakers, and half English. What can one say, then, about the problem of conducting primary education in eight languages as the East African state of Uganda does during the first three years?

Once more, of course, it becomes necessary to dispel the misconception endemic among laymen everywhere that some languages are "incapable" of expressing the concepts of modern civilization. Many Africans themselves look down their noses at the native languages, regarding them as inferior. English and French are considered tongues of prestige, despite whatever colonial "taint" they may have for ardent nationalists.

As we pointed out in the first chapter, any language can be used to express any thought through its structure and the coinage of new terms, but relatively little has been done to develop African tongues into "sociologically complete" idioms, able to cope with the verbal needs of a complex, industrial world.

Apparently the situation has not changed much since 1881 when Dr. Edward W. Blyden addressed Liberia College and complained about the lack of interest in African languages and cultures. President Nkrumah in 1960 pointed out that there were more students enrolled in Latin and Greek at the University of Ghana than in all the tongues of Africa and insisted that, "Emphasis must be laid on studying the living languages of Africa." Ironically enough, more African tongues were for many years taught at the University of London than in all the universities of their native continent combined.

In line with the growing desire to extend the use of these languages, various committees have been set up, such as Kenya's Swahili Committee. Using Rockefeller Foundation funds, the East Africa Committee has been offering prizes for original works in Swahili. Many of the states are setting up organizations to foster interest and research in the native tongues. For example, Ghana has created an Institute of African Studies and a Bureau of Ghana Languages.

While not all new states have to face linguistic problems as complex as those of India and the new African nations, it is instructive to observe how language policy has been handled in some other areas.

In Indonesia, another highly multi-lingual region, the problem was facilitated by general agreement upon the adoption of a lingua franca, formerly known as Bazaar Malay. Bahasa Indonesia, as it is now called, is being adapted to twentieth century needs by a language committee that periodically circulates lists of new social and technical terminology.

The Federation of Malaya, by contrast, is encountering more trouble in arriving at a solution. At least seventeen tongues are spoken in this country, part of the British Commonwealth. In the cities the predominant group is Chinese, while the Malayans populate the countryside. A few years ago it was decided to declare English and Malay both official tongues and so to develop Malay that it would become the sole official idiom after 1967. Despite this decision and vigorous efforts to promote Malay, there is an overwhelming trend toward English which, as in Africa, together with French, is the vehicle of economic advancement and higher education. R. P. LePage of the University of Malaya at Kuala Lumpur has noted that, if this trend continues, within ten or fifteen years, more than half of the population will be receiving their education in English, although studying Malay as a school subject at the same time.

A fascinating book could and ought to be written on the subject of language policies the world over, how they help or hinder a given nation's efficiency of communication, and the role they have played and are playing in socio-political development of the nation. Our discussion in the present chapter can only give a sampling of what such a work would include. In the remainder of this chapter a glance will be cast at linguistic policy in other areas.

One of the most important areas, as international politics go, is the Soviet Union. And, of course, much speculation is done by Kremlinologists or experts on Russia regarding the loyalty to the regime of the numerous people who make up that vast state. With at least 200 distinct tongues, the USSR has made Great Russian the language of intercommunication and just about everything of importance must appear in it. But there is no doubt that, among the Central Asian peoples, such as the Uzbeks and the Kazakhs, a free referendum would result in a decision to have an independent state, with their own tongue as the official medium. The population of the Ukrainian Soviet Socialist Republic is some forty million but, especially in the cities, many persons are exclusively Great Russian speakers. Ukrainian leaders abroad have done everything possible to encourage the setting up of an independent Ukrainian nation, and indeed one existed for a short time during the troubled days of the Bolshevik Revolution. The extent of separatist feeling in the Ukraine or elsewhere is, however, difficult to determine. One thing is sure, the separatist feelings still exist in the USSR. Soviet authorities and press thunder at them from time to time, with the charge of "bourgeois nationalism." This happens to authors who write about certain regional heroes and traditions. Obviously this would not encourage regional intellectuals to create in the other languages of the Soviet Union. At the same time, the native tongues are useful to the regime in carrying the message of Marxism to the grass roots.

It has been noted that when India first got its independence, it sent a commission to the Soviet Union to see how it had solved its multi-language problem. They, of course, saw how the regime had created alphabets (mostly an adaptation of the Cyrillic) for languages which had not been committed to writing and set up primary education in some sixty important tongues of the USSR, and how they had, with the limits described in the paragraph above, encouraged the development of the native cultures. This has profited them well, for it is used as evidence to the nations emerging from colonialism that the Soviet Union is the friend of small and oppressed peoples. For example, in Communist Rumania, a few years ago, the regime created an alphabet (Cyrillic, naturally) for the language of the Gagauzy, a semi-nomadic Turkic group numbering some 100,000, and also set up primary schools taught in this tongue. Such a tiny people would hardly pose a threat to the regime, and yet gestures like this are useful in winning over peoples of the East interested in self-determination. Incidentally, Rumania, of all the East European satellites, has the largest proportion and number of minorities, and it provides primary education and radio broadcasts in Hungarian, Slovak, Yiddish, German, and Ukrainian. Radio Bucharest also transmits programs in world languages like English, French, Russian, and even Spanish.

In a recent article Jaroslav Bilinsky of the University of Delaware furnished evidence that at present Soviet leaders in various regions are not entirely in agreement on the nature and application of the policies governing the status of Great Russian versus the local tongues. It is also interesting to note that from time to time complaints occur about the inadequate knowledge of Russian in non-Russian areas. In a statement in 1956 Mukhtidinov, an Uzbek who was later to become a member of the Central Presidium of the Communist Party, charged that lack of fluency in Russian was in such regions a hindrance to young men and women about to join the labor force. Still others complain about the heavy load of language learning (sometimes three languages in all) of youngsters in non-Russian areas.

## Linguistic Minorities

In the Middle East there are four million or more Kurds, a semi-nomadic Indo-Iranian people, related to the Persians, and living in Iraq, Iran, Turkey, and Lebanon. The Kurds, who have staged more than one rebellion in the past, and are excellent fighters, seem determined to claim more language and other privileges and are in fact clamoring for the creation of an independent Kurdistan. A large scale revolt mounted by Kurds against the government of Iraq in 1962 was suppressed only through the intervention of large military units equipped with heavy weapons. The quashing of this revolt (which received several full-page spreads in the *New York Times*) was rendered all the more delicate because the Kurds comprised influential segments of Iraq's army and police. Correspondent Dana Adams Schmidt, in a special article in the April 4, 1963, *New York Times,* noted from Beirut that a delegation representing Mullah Mustafa al Barzani and Kurdish rebels had been waiting in Baghdad for two weeks to negotiate with the Iraqi revolutionary government on "granting the Kurds national rights on the basis of centralization." Apparently the Baghdad government had been quite cool to these demands. Correspondent Schmidt remarked that, "It is a problem that, if left unsolved, could have repercussions in Turkey and Iran, which also have large Kurdish communities!" At the present writing, Iraqi government representatives are reported meeting with Kurdish leaders to attempt working out an accord.

As in the case with Kurdish, language acquires a special significance for peoples who have no political homeland. As has been pointed out time and again, agitation for language rights is often tantamount to a general appeal for improvement in status. One observer has stated that, when in the old Austro-Hungarian empire the ruling groups and the "Ukrainophiles" struggled furiously over the use of the Ukrainian tongue in the schools and courts, this was no mere squabble over language.

137

It was a bid by the Ukrainian peasantry to gain a greater voice in national economic life and in the main stream of affairs. In Poland, the Ukrainians again campaigned for a greater voice in national affairs, and complaints of discrimination reached considerable proportions. Every schoolboy knows that in Eastern Europe between World Wars I and II, although beautiful constitutions were written and adopted, promising full equality to minorities, many of the "rights" were hardly worth the paper they were printed on. In varying degrees the minorities were simply at a disadvantage economically, politically, and of course vocationally—where it hurt the most since many of them simply could not obtain employment or make a decent living.

While some language conflicts are acute and explosive, others are merely mild, more or less dormant, irritants which could be fanned into violence. Examples of this are some of the minority languages in Spain. The Basques are an intensely proud people and inhabit the Pyrenees around Bilbao (and across the border in France). While mostly bilingual, they hold tenaciously to their complex tongue which is known to almost no outsiders. Separatist tendencies have cropped up among them from time to time. Of much greater size is the Catalonian group, centered in Catalonia and Valencia with Barcelona as the main city. The Catalonians (whose Catalan language is closely related to Provençal across the France-Spain border) are also largely bilingual; they are hard-working, enterprising people who have more than once displayed strong separatist feelings and whose history includes periods of independence. If historical events had occurred otherwise, Catalonia might have become the central point of Spain rather than Castile. As for official policy, the late Spanish Republic had looked with some favor upon the claims of certain ethnic groups. There are signs that the present regime has in recent years been allowing somewhat more leeway to literary composition in minority tongues and dialects including Galician or "Gallego-Portuguese."

Again it cannot be overemphasized that language claims are often merely reflections of political, economic, social, and cultural conflicts within the body politic. Professor Gumperz of

138

California has warned that failure to specify the factors involved in detail, can result in a confusion between two quite different types of socio-political problems commonly referred to under the cover term "language policy." In one case, he notes, "a small elite using a literary language maintains a social control over a mass of illiterates, restraining access to power by artificially maintaining a language barrier." Medieval Europe with Latin, and the diglossia situation in Bengal with both Bengali and Urdu, and Greece with *Katharevousa* (classical) and *dhimotikos* (popular) forms vying with one another, are examples. In the other case, two already literate groups may be struggling for political control. Instances of this are the Hindi-Punjabi rivalry in Delhi and the conflict in Norway between *riksmål*, the traditional literary form heavily influenced by Danish, and *landsmål* based on peasant dialects of West Norway.

All this means that language claims can be dynamite almost everywhere in the world. There are those who say that had the ethnic picture of Eastern Europe been understood better by the forgers of the Versailles Treaty, particularly as regards such lands as Czechoslovakia, Poland, and Yugoslavia, World War II might have been averted. This does not change the facts of history, but may provide object lessons in avoiding future errors. Let's remember that Hitler's claims were at first claims of an ethnic and linguistic nature—demands for greater rights for German minorities or for their incorporation into the Third Reich. At the same time, he ranted against alleged discrimination against Germans in neighboring countries. These theories die hard, even in recent days. It is a fact that in the western territories of Poland, annexed from Germany after World War II, it was actually forbidden to speak German right after the end of the war.

Living proof that peoples can live side by side together despite ethnic, linguistic, and religious differences is furnished by the example of Switzerland, where four groups live together in harmony. These are the French speakers, the German speakers, the Italian speakers, and the Romansch group, barely 20,000 persons in the Upper and Lower Engadine. Although the German speakers are the most numerous and most influential, all nationalities feel that they are, above all, Swiss citizens, assured of equal rights and protection in a working democracy.

Students of nationality and language problems often throw up their hands in despair, feeling that animosity between people speaking different tongues is inevitable. This is no more so than the belief that peoples who speak similar or the same tongues will love one another. Wars between "brothers" are usually unparalleled in their ferocity, as witness our own Civil War, one of the bloodiest in all military history; or the Spanish Civil War; the Irish and the English; the Czechs and Slovaks; the Serbs and Croats; the Indian Hindus and the Pakistani. Moslems speak the same or similar tongues, and yet conflicts and tensions among them have been severe.

### Studying Socio-linguistic Problems

Enough has been said to suggest that the study of language policies and problems—a branch of the field of socio-linguistics—is one in which a vast number of elusive and sensitive political, economic, social, religious, and psychological factors are involved. Consequently, passions run high and there is always the danger of offending some group or party by appearing to favor the views of their opponents. Be that as it may, there is need for tackling some of the problems on a "team" basis, involving both linguists and political and social scientists, since the issues cut across so many disciplinary lines.

One of the specific bailiwicks of the linguist in all this is the study of bilingualism, or the use of more than one tongue in a given area. This phenomenon, of course, has not only political and social implications, but also important psychological effects on individuals. Ordinarily there is a linguistic "pecking order" in a polyglot community, as a result of which an individual may harbor an attitude of contempt for languages or dialects which enjoy low prestige, and refuse to learn or to employ them, preferring to concern himself with one of high prestige that he hopes will bring him access to better social groups and vocations. The offspring of recent immigrants in America have suffered from

140

this "low prestige syndrome" and the country has lost a valuable source of language power through their resistance to studying the ancestral tongues. All these factors, of course, must be studied and added to our corpus of information on second language learning in America and elsewhere.

Recently, researchers, aware of the dilemmas facing planners in bilingual areas, have begun to collect and classify information on "language situations" in the various countries of the world. A file of such data is being assembled at the Center for Applied Linguistics, an arm of the Modern Language Association, in Washington, D.C., and at the University of Indiana's Archive of the Languages of the World. The Center for Applied Linguistics has published a collection of articles about problems in this field called *Study of the Role of Second Language Learning in Asia, Africa, and Latin America.*

Increasing attention is being paid to the study of bilingualism in its many-sided manifestations. More and more, the subjective, intuitive approach of the past, with its vague terminology, is being replaced by more scientifically objective methods, sometimes employing statistical procedures. Einar Haugen of the University of Wisconsin has published a monumental study on Norwegian-English bilingualism in the United States. The book *Languages in Contact,* by Columbia University's Uriel Weinreich, affords a kaleidoscopic view of polyglot situations throughout the western world.

Joseph Greenberg of Columbia has devised a statistical scale running from 0 to 1 based on his formula $A = 1 - \sum (i)^2$, in which A is an index of linguistic diversity and $i$ is the proportion of speakers of each language to the total population. Let us say that in a certain country one-fourth of the people speak language A, one-fourth language B, and one-half language C, then the index figure of linguistic diversity is .6250. Using this scale, a country like Uruguay, where almost 100 per cent of the population speaks Spanish, would produce a figure of linguistic diversity equalling almost zero. For the Plateau Province of Northern Nigeria, where languages and dialects are particularly numerous, the figure would be close to one. One defect of this measure, however, is that it really does not take into consideration the bilingualism of an individual who might speak two, three or more tongues but is based on his one ascertainable mother tongue. One can say then that Greenberg's formula measures the language diversity of an area but not the multilingualism of its inhabitants.

A code for describing the languages of a country by their type and the role played by them in a communication network of a given country has been elaborated by William A. Stewart of the Center for Applied Linguistics. Here is his classification in brief:

| *Type of Language* | *Function* |
|---|---|
| S—Standard | o—official use |
| C—Classical | g—used primarily by single ethnic, cultural |
| V—Vernacular | group or sub-group |
| K—Creole | w—used for "wider communication" across |
| P—Pidgin | language boundaries (French and English as second languages, Esperanto) |
| A—Artificial | lish as second languages, Esperanto) |
| M—Marginal | e—educational use, as language of instruction (at various school levels) |
| | l—literary use, including scholarly writing |
| | r—religious use |
| | t—technical use, for access to international technical and scientific literature |

The value of this sort of system is that it permits the observer to put into perspective the relative role played by any language in a nation. Of course, many languages play multiple roles. Let us, for instance, analyze Afghanistan's communication by the Stewart method:

| Pashto | So | Standard, official language |
|---|---|---|
| Persian | So | Standard, official language (equal partner with Pashto) |
| Arabic | Clr | Classical language, used for literature and religion |
| English | Set | Standard language, used for education and technology |
| Russian | St | Standard language, used for technology |
| Uzbek | Vg | Vernacular, used by Uzbek group or minority |

As is true with all formulas, they are so elliptic that they require elaboration. The above picture would not be complete unless one added that, although Pashto and Persian are officially co-equal, Pashto is mostly used in informal, everyday communication while Persian is still employed for most official purposes. Also, the above does not include the smaller minorities which, of course, could be added and classified by the same symbols.

Charles A. Ferguson, Director of the Center for Applied Linguistics, has stressed the need for systematizing the information gathered on a land or region into profiles. Each profile, in his opinion, would include the following information:

1. The number of major languages spoken.
2. The pattern of dominance of one tongue vis-a-vis the others.
3. The national uses of each major language spoken in the country.
4. The extent of written uses of the major languages.
5. The degree of standardization and variations from the established norm.

In his article "The Language Factor in National Development," from the *Study of the Role of Second Languages in Asia, Africa and Latin America,* Ferguson describes certain of his scales which we will discuss briefly. *W0* refers to tongues not used for normal written purposes. Most of the world's idioms fall into this category, even though a few translations of religious or other material exist in them. Going up the scale, we come to *W1* which takes in languages used for normal written purposes, such as Thai, Amharic, or Slovenian. *W2* embraces tongues in which original research in physical sciences is regularly published. This is a limited category, covering tongues such as Czech, Italian, and Dutch. Finally, *W3* includes the small number of tongues such as Russian, English, French, German, in which translations and resumes of scientific work in other tongues are regularly published.

All these evaluative procedures are merely a series of approximations in the effort to arrive at more precise instruments or, as Ferguson terms them, "national language profiles" which are of help to the linguist, language teacher, social scientist, and language planners, to say nothing of commissions entrusted with deciding the merits of conflicting linguistic claims. With such profiles available, observers of world events will be better equipped to understand what the fuss is about when rival groups in newly emergent lands charge that their language rights have been violated.

Trained people might also be thus enabled to detect the brief items in the daily press that will become tomorrow's headlines. More attention to what is behind language conflicts might provide the stitch in time to enable political leaders to alleviate these frictions before they erupt into major crises.

# Chapter 11

# The Dream of a World Language

*The Language Barrier*

The Old Testament described the multiplicity of languages as an affliction visited on mankind, and history is replete with confusions resulting from language barriers. Modern examples are at hand:

A Venezuelan shipper sends an order for automobile spare parts to Italy—and is shipped tractor parts instead. The British Foreign Office uses the word *requérir* ("to demand") incorrectly —and an incensed French general demands an apology. American tourists in a Far Eastern metropolis attempt to communicate in sign language—and are severely mauled because their signs are interpreted as insults. People drown unnecessarily in a sea disaster (the *Andrea Doria*) because they cannot understand rescue directions given in a tongue other than their own.

Surely we were better off during the Middle Ages, when everything of international importance was expressed in Latin. Can't we appreciate the advantages of a universal language and devise one? A world language has been one of the most persistent dreams of man from ages immemorial. No less than six hundred schemes for a universal language have been proposed by men and women seeking a solution to this knottiest of communication problems. The parade of language planners has been a colorful and varied one and has included learned scholars and dilettantes, scientists and crackpots.

Descartes, for example, speculated about a language so perfect in its symbolism that it would be impossible for human beings to err in it. In the nineteenth century a man named Sodre invented Solresol, a universal language based on the musical scale. More recently some scholars have devised Translingua Script, which makes use of numerical codes. For example, a tree would be known in every country by the number 31 and a man by 10 and so on.

Several billion earth dwellers have, however, remained blissfully unaffected by the hundreds of schemes which have been dreamed up to pull them out of their linguistic imbroglio. Most of the languages which have been offered have never gone much farther than the walls of the inventor's own study or beyond a handful of devotees. Only three languages have made some sort of dent in the field.

## Volapük

The first artificial medium to enjoy mass appeal was Volapük, devised in 1879 by a German Monsignor named Johann Martin Schleyer, a man whose linguistic prowess became legendary—he was reputed to speak over seventy languages. Schleyer—arbitrarily it would seem by modern scientific linguistic standards—created his Volapük (meaning "world speech") out of English, French, German, and the Romance languages, with heaviest emphasis on Germanic as a source of roots. The Lord's Prayer in Volapük appeared as follows:

"O Fat obas, kel binol in süls, paisaludomöz nem ola! Kömomöd monargän ola! Jenomöz vil olik, as in sül i su tal! Bodi obsik vädeliki givolös obes adelo! E pardolos obes debis obsik, äs id obs aipardobs debeles obas. E no obis nindukoläs in tentadi; sed aidalivolös obis de bad. Jenosöd!

146

Volapük came along at a time when the atmosphere was particularly receptive to an idea of this sort. It became the rage of Europe, from 1879 to 1889, and societies were formed in which pastry cooks hobnobbed with archdukes in a fraternal effort to master the new "world" language. In the United States, the American Philosophical Society (founded by Benjamin Franklin) considered supporting the language, but finally decided that it was too difficult. Some Parisian department stores even gave their sales personnel lessons in the new idiom.

The success of Volapük was, however, shortlived, largely because of the unnecessary difficulty of its grammar with complicated case-endings and a sound system which included umlauts such as the German *ü* and *ö*. Amusingly enough, it collapsed entirely in 1889 at an international conference of Volapük speakers when enthusiasts, trying to deliver speeches in the language, found it too cumbersome to use.

## Esperanto

Before Volapük was decently buried, a new contender appeared. This was Esperanto, brain-child of Dr. Ludwik Zamenhof, a Polish doctor reared in the city of Bialystok where Poles, Lithuanians, Ukrainians, Germans, Russians, and Jews lived together in uneasy hostility. The idealistic doctor came to feel that at the base of tension among peoples was the language problem, and believed that a universal language would bring peace and understanding.

The Polish doctor fashioned his international language out of English, German, and the Romance tongues, with the heaviest representation from the latter group. Profiting from the experience of Volapük, Zamenhof aimed—quite successfully—at utmost simplicity in designing his Esperanto.

The basic grammar, consisting of only sixteen rules, is simplicity itself and can actually be learned in a few hours. However, to learn to write and speak the language is quite another matter. The sound system is simple for most Europeans although it might not necessarily be so for persons speaking certain Oriental tongues.

Here is a sample of Esperanto:

| Esperanto | English |
|---|---|
| La astronomo, per speciala teleskopo fotografas la sunon, la lunon, kaj la planedojn. | The astronomer, by means of a special telescope, photographs the sun, the moon, and the planets. |
| Modernaj delikataj instrumentoj permesas la detalan ekzamenon de la strukturo de la atomo. | Modern, delicate instruments permit the detailed examination of the structure of the atom. |
| La teorio de Einstein, la nova principo de relativeco, presentas komplikan problemon. | The Einstein theory, the new principle of relativity, presents a complex problem. |

Today, almost seventy-five years since its origination and fifty-seven years after the first Esperanto World Congress, which ushered in the period of its practical use, the artificial tongue is still quite alive. But many students consider that Esperanto is more of an idealistic movement than it is a language. Each year, Esperantists hold a Universal Congress. A wide range of programs in cultural and social activities is offered, as well as several score specialized conferences, all in the *internacia lingvo*. At many places in the world, the wearer of the Esperantists' green badge (green for hope) can rely upon fellow members for assistance in getting around. At the World's Fair in Brussels, for instance, Esperanto interpreters were available along with those in principal languages.

According to Dr. William Solzbacher, one of the leading Esperantists in the United States, more than fifty scholarly publications in fifteen countries publish articles or summaries in Esperanto, and about 145 periodicals are printed entirely in the tongue. Fifteen radio stations in Rome, Paris, Vienna, Warsaw, Sofia, Valencia, Caracas, Pyongyang, and other cities broadcast programs in Esperanto. The Voice of America has used the language in four series of shortwave programs in the past two years and has received almost two thousand letters in Esperanto from ninety-one countries, including every Iron Curtain country except Albania. Esperanto is taught by about seven hundred schools in forty countries. When the University of Leningrad, breaking a long-standing ban, announced after-hours classes in Esperanto, there was a rush by applicants. Although the Esperanto organizations number only about 110,000 actual members, roughly one million persons make some use of the language. There now are even some native speakers, raised in homes where Esperanto was used as the household language. It is the only interlanguage that can claim a considerable literature, with some 8,400 titles that include original works as well as translations of the Bible, *The Divine Comedy,* and other classics.

## Interlingua

As inevitably occurs, one splinter group after another has broken away from Esperanto to form rival offshoots, such as Ido, Novial, and Occidental. Neverthless none of these has ever made much headway.

The only language which has seriously challenged Esperanto's pre-eminence is Interlingua, presented to the world by the American linguist Dr. Alexander Gode, whose work over a period of twenty years was supported by a wealthy "angel," Mrs. Alice Vanderbuilt Morris, who was converted to the idea of a world language.

Interlingua is what its founders call an extracted rather than a derived language. This means that a given word is generally taken in toto and subjected to little or no modification. Other artificial languages have generally altered considerably to conform to prescribed patterns. The Interlingua vocabulary is taken from French, Italian, Spanish, English and, to a much lesser extent, German and Russian. Only words that appear in at least three of these tongues are adopted. When no term meets these requirements, a word is usually taken from Latin. The developers made attempts to construct the language as scientifically as possible in an effort to arrive at what the architects of Interlingua term "standard average European." The Interlinguists claim that it can be read with little or no previous study by persons familiar with higher education. Its grammatical structure is of the same order as Esperanto and can be learned in a few hours. A book recently appeared comparing the difficulties of these two languages. It was done by an Esperantist, and the findings were favorable to Esperanto.

Here is an example of Interlingua:

| INTERLINGUA | ENGLISH |
|---|---|
| Professor H. Oberth, un del pioneros in le campo del rochetteria scientific in Germania e plus recentemente un associato de Dr. W. von Braun in su recercas de roccheteria al arsenal Redstone in Alabama, ha elaborate un vehiculo adoptate al exploration del luna. Un tal vehiculo debe esser capace a superar le difficultates extraordinari del terreno e del ambiente del luna que es characterisate per le absentia de omne atmosphere, per un gravitate reducite, per extrememente acute alterationes de temperatura, e per un superficie plus pulverose que ullo cognoscite in terra. | Professor H. Oberth, one of the pioneers in the field of scientific rocketry in Germany and more recently an associate of Dr. W. von Braun in his research on rocketry at the Redstone Arsenal in Alabama, has elaborated plans for a vehicle adapted for lunar exploration. Such a vehicle must be capable of overcoming the extraordinary difficulties of the terrain and surroundings of the moon, characterized by the absence of any atmosphere, by reduced gravity, by extremely sharp changes of temperature, and by a more dusty surface than any known on earth. |

For the present at least, the aims of Interlingua are more modest than those of Esperanto. No real attempt has been made to promote it as a spoken language, although one of the writers heard and understood a talk given in it at a meeting of the Modern Language Association of America. Its first objective is to secure acceptance as a medium of scientific and scholarly communication. It has done quite well in the dozen years of its existence, and by now, some twenty journals make use of Interlingua, mostly for summaries. The Interlingua Division of Science Service, Inc., in Washington, D.C., attempts to promote Interlingua by offering to provide summaries and abstracts in that language for specialized journals and resumés for conferences of international research significance. (This organization also publishes an Interlingua version of *Science News Letter*.) By now there are in Interlingua several newsletters for sub-disciplines in which no specific periodicals are available. According to Dr. Alexander Gode, "The community of those who can be reached through Interlingua includes anyone with fair or full qualifications to grasp the technical import of the same message if presented in either French, Italian, Spanish, English, Greek, or Latin. In many scientific disciplines this makes for the possibility of complete and world-wide coverage through Interlingua . . . on the basis of what the reader knows and has known all along by virtue of his professional training."

## Other Approaches

The trouble with artificial languages is that, although arousing tremendous enthusiasm among their devotees, they do not attract enough mass support to achieve their objectives. And yet they have proved that they are fully capable of performing the written and spoken communication tasks of modern technological societies.

One more method of arriving at an artificial international auxiliary language has been suggested. The Russian linguist N. D. Andreyev believes that intermediary languages containing most of the features shared by the major natural languages will necessarily be developed in work on machine translation done by electronic computers. When the ideal intermediate language has been hammered out, Andreyev feels, it will be usable for human international communication. This amounts to saying that since people have botched the job, machines will do it for them.

Another school of thought recommends the simplification of existing languages. The best known of these attempts has been Basic English, devised by the British philosopher, C. K. Ogden, and promoted in America by Harvard Professor I. A. Richards. With its vocabulary of some eight hundred words and about sixteen general-purpose verbs, "Basic" sounds terribly easy. In reality, however, it requires skill to manipulate this small stock of words so that complex concepts can be expressed in it. An Esperantist has pointed out that to render "The watermelon tastes good," one must say something like, "The large round, sweet vegetable has a good taste." Basic English reached its peak during World War II when it received a strong endorsement from Sir Winston Churchill and the British Government. This, of course, caused the charge of "imperialism" to be leveled against it.

Here is a sample of Basic English:

| BASIC ENGLISH (NEW TESTAMENT) | KING JAMES BIBLE (ACTS 4:32) |
|---|---|
| And all those who were of the faith were one in heart and soul: and not one of them said that any of the things which he had was his property only; but they had all things in common. . . . And no one among them was in need; for everyone who had land or houses, exchanging them for money, took the price of them, and put it at the feet of the Apostles for distribution to everyone as he had need. | And the multitude of them that believed were of one heart and one soul: neither said any of them that ought of the things which he possessed was his own; but they had all things common. . . . Neither was there any among them that lacked: for as many as were possessors of lands or houses sold them, and brought the prices of the things that were sold, and laid them down at the apostles' feet: and distribution was made unto every man according as he had need. |

Another school of thought vigorously opposes "made" or "simplified" languages, preferring to take their languages "straight." A large number of natural languages have been advocated as world auxiliaries, including French, English, German, Russian, Spanish, Italian, Greek, Chinese, Latin, Hebrew, and even Yiddish. Only French and English have any real chance of acceptance in the Western world, because these two languages are actually functioning as auxiliaries in almost every continent of the globe.

India and Pakistan, which had hoped to establish Hindi and Urdu respectively as their number one tongues by 1960, have realized that they cannot do so and will have to rely on English for some time to come. Ironically enough, at the bitterly anti-Western Bandung conference—to which Britain and the United States were not invited—English, which was familiar to the largest number of delegates, had to be used as the working language. Today, in fact, the use of English as a language of wider communication is expanding rapidly all over the world.

In almost any country of Africa, Latin America, or Asia outside Communist China, there is a tremendous demand for teachers of English as a second language.

Some observers even advise adoption of a multiple system of languages, according to which the world would be divided into a number of zones and a different combination of natural languages used in each. This would mean, for instance, that each country in the "zone of the Far East" would use the native language plus English and Chinese. The trouble with this sort of plan is that it would perpetuate the very thing which it tries to combat, at the same time placing an enormous burden of language learning on children in areas speaking little-known tongues.

With such conflict and partisan feelings about one or another proposed "interlanguage," it is more encouraging to turn to the growing trend toward adopting limited international codes in a variety of fields. One might well call these "sub-languages."

A language of written symbols has been one of the most persistent schemes for improving international communication. Recently, Rudolf Modley, Ford Foundation consultant, speaking at the New York Conference of Communication Arts, pleaded for the development of an international science of "symbology." He provided strong evidence of how this symbology can be helpful in such specialized areas as machine tool design. For example, control panels would be lettered in internationally recognizable symbols.

Another triumph for touring motorists was achieved not long ago when some forty road symbols were adopted by most Western nations as official traffic and driving directions.

The universality of numbers has persistently suggested their use as an international code. Most recently, Professor Erich Funke of the University of Iowa devised his Translingua Script, based on arabic numerals. Dictionaries in all the important languages would carry Translingua Script word equivalents.

Progress has been made by the Federal Aviation Agency with Basic English for international aviation communication, since its short vocabulary is useful for limited conversations such as occur between air and ground. Unfortunately, the use of English in any form presents problems. Certain sounds, such as those for *f* and *s*, do not transmit well and can be confused. Monosyllables, as in the case of *five* and *nine*, can be confused also. Moreover, there is scarcely an English sound that is not difficult to pronounce for one nationality or another. Scandinavians have trouble with *j*'s and the Japanese with *l* and *r*.

Additional codes are being devised in other fields. Specialists in documentation, here concerned with the world-wide collection and retrieval of information, have made increasing use of data processing machines and have developed international codes and symbols to control greater amounts of information than ever before.

One of the challenging by-products of "intelligent machine" research is the development of an international computer language. According to Bell Telephone Research scientist John R. Pierce, this would really consist of various forms of an "artificial, unambiguous, logical mathematical language" understandable to all computer experts.

And so the controversy rages on. Esperanto and Interlingua enthusiasts argue that these languages, which are perfectly regular, take about one twentieth the time to learn that is required for, say, a West European language. They point out that since these are not identified with any specific nation, they are free of any political taint, or the charge of imperialism, which makes such languages as English and French unacceptable to some countries, particularly the small, emergent nations. Their opponents retort by alleging that for most people the artificiality of these tongues gives them the feeling that they are not learning real languages. The fact that languages like Esperanto are not rooted in a specific nation deprives their learners of access to the rich cultural heritage which the major languages afford. They argue that the extra effort to learn a natural language is well worth while when one considers the millions who can be reached in the Romance languages, German, or for that matter Arabic, Russian, or Chinese.

In the Communist world, of course, it is Russian which is being promoted as the "world language of communism." Its teaching is compulsory in the schools of most of the satellites, and "friendship societies" attempt to interest adults in this Slavic tongue. Although Russian is definitely making inroads, its grammatical complexity and longer learning time put it at a disadvantage except among fellow Slavs. The curtain on artificial languages has lifted a bit, and announcements of after-hours teaching of Esperanto brought long lines of applicants in Leningrad. Eastern Europe's greatest activity is in Poland, home of the Esperanto movement. An Esperanto exhibition in the summer of 1959 brought visitors from many parts of the globe to Warsaw.

What are the prospects for a universally acceptable auxiliary language? Mario Pei's *One Language for the World*, published in 1958, said the answer would not come through creating new, artificial languages, since some that exist are adequate already. The only real solution must be reached by joint agreement of all nations. Pei proposed that an international conference be called to discuss the merits of a number of languages and that one be adopted by majority vote. Following this, each nation would pledge itself to teach that language from kindergarten up. Dr. Pei believes that the world could become bilingual within a generation, sweeping away many of the barriers that beset international communication today.

Since such an international language would be taught mainly to children, the difficulties that adults might experience in learning it should not be a consideration in selecting it. Under Professor Pei's rules, Mandarin Chinese—written in a Latin alphabet—would be the logical choice, however unlikely it might seem in today's political situation.

Dr. Pei sent copies of his book to the heads of sovereign states. From all indications there has been no wholesale movement to take concerted action on this matter.

# Chapter 12

# Language-Handicapped Americans

*Language Unpreparedness*

During the Korean War, an American Army battalion was moving along the rugged terrain when an excited native darted out in front, trying desperately to make himself understood. According to Associated Press correspondent Harold Martin, the unit was badly bloodied because no one was able to understand the friendly Korean's warning that they were marching right into a Communist ambush.

This was scarcely the first time that our language lack had taken its grisly toll. We will probably never know how many World War II GI's might still be alive today if more of them had been able to understand and speak everyday Italian during the campaign in "Europe's soft underbelly"; Arabic or French in the North African action; or Chinese, Japanese, Burmese, Karen, or Kachin in the China-Burma-India theater. Just after the Normandy landing a screening of some 20,000 troops turned up a meager twenty officers and men with sufficient French to read a French intelligence report, conduct thorough interrogations of war prisoners or refugees, talk with French military and port authorities, or read a simple newspaper editorial.

These men were, of course, members of that "lost generation" which had been "educated for living" after the First World War. Educational planners and administrators, particularly those of the ultra-progressive persuasion, had assured the nation that Americans would be born, live, and die without ever having use for anything but English. Although coals have been heaped upon the head of John Dewey for inspiring this hostility to foreign languages and other "hard" subjects, such sentiments were pretty much read into that philosopher's rather abstruse prose.

Just what is it, then, that has made Americans so allergic to foreign tongues? One of the underlying reasons has been our particular development as a pioneer people with little time for such "frills" as foreign languages. Another important factor has been geography. There are indeed few areas in the world where one can travel, say, as far as the distance between Portland, Maine, and Portland, Oregon—some 4,000 miles—without switching idioms. Moreover, our social development followed the melting pot principle, which meant that whatever were the ethnic origins of individuals, they were Americans all. Few Americans travelled extensively at that time, and knowledge of additional languages was superfluous.

Then came World War I with its strong wave of hysteria against everything German—and, by extension, anything at all "foreign." Sauerkraut was re-baptized "liberty cabbage." Some twenty states passed legislation banning any language but English as a medium of instruction. (Such legislation was annulled by the Supreme Court in 1923.)

The isolationism of the years following the First World War extended well into the 1930's, and was reinforced by a view of the oceans as permanent, impregnable defenses. Then World War II broke out. Eleven million American men and women were deployed over a global battlefront—and found themselves handicapped by ignorance of the languages of their allies as well as those of the enemy. "Snafus," misunderstandings and spilled blood were the price paid. Intensive programs to give our GI's basic know-how in some forty tongues were launched. It was a heroic effort, highly successful in many cases, but it could not conceal our language handicaps.

Emerging from the conflict as the leader of the Free World, the United States needed even more tongues to conduct the purely official tasks of diplomacy, and to counteract the insidious image of America projected by hostile forces abroad. According to this image we are interested only in Coca-Cola, the acquisition of dollars, and the exploitation of the "little fellow." The "Let 'em learn English" attitude of monoglot Americans did nothing to help matters.

Perhaps no single group in America's history had ever been made more dramatically aware of the pitfalls of language ignorance than were our veterans who had been its greatest victims. As ardent goodwill ambassadors for the cause of foreign tongues, they made beelines to the registrar's office to sign up for whatever idioms were available. Their strong motivation, maturity, and enthusiasm made them the most avid and successful language buffs in our history.

Second language learning was at long last given a new lease on life. Educational administrators—many of whom had been violently opposed to the subject as impractical—espoused the cause. Among the converts was Dr. Earl J. McGrath, former U.S. Commissioner of Education and presently at Columbia University's Teacher's College. His talk in 1952 in St. Louis helped trigger the trend toward foreign languages in the elementary schools (FLES). He had the courage to say, "For some years I unwisely took the position that a foreign language did not constitute an indispensable element in a general education program. This position, I am happy to say, I have reversed . . . . "

In the brave new postwar world, schools vied to do something about our pathetic lack of linguistic facilities. New courses were set up, both in language and area subjects. The number of non-Western courses increased. Language laboratories were established. Enrollments went upward. The foundations, particularly Ford, Carnegie, and Rockefeller, eager to do something about our faulty resources in this field, made millions available for improving the status of language teaching. An example of this was the Program in Oriental Languages, underwritten by the Ford Foundation and administered by the American Council of Learned Societies. This program supplied monies for new language and area courses in Eastern tongues, as well as for the production of much-needed texts. In 1952 the Rockefeller Foundation awarded a $235,000 grant to the Modern Language Association of America for a six-year study of foreign language teachers' recommendations to strengthen and improve instruction at all levels of American education. By 1958 a consensus of the profession had been pretty well reached. On the groundwork of the information thus gathered the National Defense Education Act was passed by the 85th Congress, in 1958. Its target was the development of language study, together with science and mathematics.

An upward swing in the language field began in 1945 and continued for the next dozen years. Most popular were Russian and other Slavic tongues, Chinese, Japanese, Arabic and a few Eastern idioms. Yet the rate of growth was still too slow and the filling of the gaps haphazard. The late Secretary of State John Foster Dulles had occasion to observe, "The United States carries new responsibilities in many quarters of the globe, and we are at a serious disadvantage because of the difficulty of finding persons who can deal with the foreign language problem. Interpreters are no substitute." Testifying before the 85th Congress in 1957, he pointed out that fully one-half of our career foreign service officers did not at that time have a "useful" knowledge of any second tongue, while of the incoming recruits otherwise well qualified, only a quarter could handle any tongue but English with moderate fluency. It ought to be pointed out here that by "useful" the State Department means a knowledge adequate to handle routine matters at a foreign service post.

## The Language Gap

Our cavalier attitude toward foreign tongues contrasts sharply with that of the Soviets, who are leaving no stone unturned to see to it that the message of the Kremlin can be carried to the peoples of the world in their own tongues. Russian youngsters begin French, German, or English in the fifth grade at the age of eleven or twelve and continue it for six or seven years. At the *vuz* or college level, from two to five years more of this study awaits them. A spotting system keeps a constant lookout for linguistically gifted youngsters, who receive scholarships to attend institutes where they receive five or six years of all-out training in an important world tongue, plus a secondary language.

Nicholas De Witt, a leading authority on Soviet education, points out that in science and engineering curricula, the study of languages like English or German is on a par with that of scientific subjects. Daring experimentation is being carried on by introducing young tots to other idioms. A vast network of special schools is being set up, where youngsters of eight or nine begin to study Chinese, Arabic, Persian, Hindi, Urdu, English, French, or German. Beginning in the seventh grade, they study subjects such as geography and history in the foreign tongue itself. Although a mere 40,000 or so college students are studying Russian here, the number of Soviet citizens of all ages burning the midnight oil to master English easily exceeds ten million.

It is small wonder, then, that the linguistic prowess of the Russians—though sometimes grossly exaggerated—has attracted international attention. When Libya was set up as an independent state after World War II, Moscow sent fourteen Arabic speakers to their mission while our own contained only one person familiar with this Middle Eastern tongue, who was shortly afterward transferred to a post in the non-Arabic world. An American congressman returning from Africa several years ago claimed that at the Soviet embassy in Khartoum, capital of Sudan, even the chauffeurs were able to speak Arabic!

Persons who have not yet adjusted their thinking to the needs of the jet and space age still raise the oft-asked question, "What difference does it make whether we know languages or not?" Perhaps the best rejoinder to this is a true story which made the rounds in Washington. When we established a diplomatic mission in a newly formed Far Eastern state about fifteen years ago, we had no one who could handle its official tongue. It was necessary to rely on native translators to peruse the press. The latter, out of an Oriental sense of deference to their employers, chose only those items which were favorable to the United States. When we sent out officers trained in the language, able to read periodicals and attend sessions of the legislature, they found that the entire land was in the grip of a virulent wave of anti-Americanism. The remarkable thing about this was that, thanks to the knowledge of several persons armed with a linguistic skill, we were able to read a danger signal and re-orient our entire information program in a strategic section of the Far East.

The dependence upon foreign nationals for language work overseas scarcely needs further comment, especially if sensitive materials are involved. And one does not need to be a graduate of The Harvard School of Business to realize the dangers of not being able to determine the accuracy of translations or interpretations made by employees. It is for this reason that the Italians have a saying, "Traduttore, Traditore," which means "To translate is to deceive." But common sense tells us that the burden lies not on the interpreter or translator but on the employer who must seek means of checking the quality and reliability of work done for him.

Apparently our language gap in the field of overseasmanship is as old as the republic. During the Revolutionary War when Benjamin Franklin represented us in Paris, he complained that his French was so poor that he had difficulty in understanding the tongue. Things were not much better a hundred years later when John A. Kasson, our Minister to Austria, filed a dispatch in 1881 with the following sentiments on our use of interpreters:

"... We have few native-born Consuls who are really masters of any other language than English. ... As a rule such agents content themselves with mere routine, and for ordinary intercourse depend upon some poorly paid interpreter of foreign origin, of whom the English language becomes in turn the victim. The same is true of some of our legations. The real interpreter of our interests becomes at last an irresponsible and partially educated foreigner." He added:

"It is to be greatly desired that the United States should escape from this condition of inferiority. . . ."

When it comes to language knowledge, however, the number of speakers we have available in a given tongue may not be as important as the fact that we do have someone at our disposal. Speaking at the University of Kentucky Modern Language Conference at Lexington in 1952, U.S. Air Force Lieutenant Colonel Middleton declared that it is quite possible that one officer with the knowledge of a remote but strategic language and area might be more important in future conflict than an entire nuclear bombing crew. It is interesting to note that Radio Moscow broadcasts more hours in non-official vernaculars such as Kurdish than does the radio system of any other nation. Apparently the Russians believe that minor languages may assume major importance in the future.

Months before Sputnik I was shot into space the proposed launching was described in its broad outlines in a Soviet popular science journal readily available in this country. Yet no particular attention was paid to it. Why? Perhaps partly because only one-tenth of one per cent of American scientists and engineers are able to read Russian in which, together with English and German, the bulk of the world's technical publications appear.

The price of linguistic ignorance is being paid day after day at a high rate of compound interest. Not many years ago an article appeared in a Soviet scientific journal on contact relay networks. This went unnoticed here while a project was set up duplicating the identical experiment. Writing in the *Scientific American,* William Locke of the Massachusetts Institute of Technology estimated that the cost to us in duplicated research was at least $200,000 on this project. The Soviets not only place great emphasis on language study by their scientists, but have set up facilities for rapid abstracting and translation of practically everything of technical importance appearing in foreign tongues. Recently, staff members of the Stanford Research Institute at

Menlo Park, California, went so far as to say that one of the best ways for an American scientist to keep abreast of developments in his own field in the United States is to follow Russian summaries and abstracts! It is, of course, encouraging that serious attention has been paid of late to the translation problem and that the National Science Foundation has taken important measures to assure rapid perusal of important research in Russian and other tongues and to make abstracts and translations available. But it must be emphasized that if a researcher cannot scan and read materials in the original, a time lag results.

Busy scientists, and others who have been pinning fond hopes on an early break-through in machine translation—perhaps out of an understandable concern over the toil and strain of language study—should be less sanguine. Mechanical translation is still at a crude stage, although at least fifteen centers in several countries are studying methods and techniques (largely through the use of digital computers) of perfecting this art. Translations of limited types of scientific texts have been done by machine, but human translators are still less expensive—and much more resourceful. The so-called "intelligent" machines can do only what humans program into them. Up till now mechanical translation has probably done more to inform us about the structure of language then to reduce our backlog of untranslated writings. A prominent linguist has even gone so far as to say of translation by machine that it has drawn many capable people into activities of dubious value. And even more than the waste of money, there is reason to regret the loss of talent to this economically dubious enterprise. He believes that a great deal more and better research could have been performed if even a fraction of the funds spent on "MT" had been allotted directly to fundamental research on linguistics.

## Our Government's Needs

Nor is machine translation easing the job of our foreign representatives, who number about a million and a half, or one per cent of our population. These people are deployed over more than a hundred countries and play a major role in shaping the American image beyond our borders.

Passports issued to Americans are accompanied by a letter from the President of the United States reminding them that, on their sojourns abroad, their actions reflect upon their homeland. Sadly enough, only about one out of twenty American tourists can go beyond the "Où est la plume de ma tante?" stage in a foreign language. This makes it practically impossible to give curious foreigners a coherent account of how normal, workaday Americans live, work and play—much less to discuss abstract ideas and philosophies.

The acute need for lingual skills motivated the Government and the Armed Services to set up facilities on a scale never witnessed before. Immediately following the Second World War the Army set up its Army Language School in Monterey, California, teaching twenty-nine Eastern and Western tongues. The Navy established its Naval Intelligence School, and the Department of State its Foreign Service Institute in the nation's capital. The Naval Intelligence School has offered, usually, eight languages, while the Foreign Service Institute has provided instruction in well over forty tongues. The Army Language School, with some 1,500 students and 500 instructors, is perhaps the largest full-time language school in the Free World. Members of the language profession generally consider that the scope and quality of the work being done at these schools is of extremely high quality, often surpassing instruction at academic centers where old-fashioned standards, texts, and techniques often still account for pitiful results.

The role of the Foreign Service Institute has been of special significance, particularly since it has accepted a large number of employees of the United States Information Agency, the Agency for International Development (formerly the ECA and ICA), the Department of Agriculture, and even the Air Force and the other services. Yet, despite its genuine successes, the demands made upon it because of our tremendous need for languages caused the then Under Secretary of State Walter Bedell Smith, in 1954, to charge the Wriston Committee with presenting a plan whereby the Institute's work could be made even more effective.

The results of the Wriston report were of the utmost significance for overseasmanship. It expressed dissatisfaction with the relatively low language competence of our diplomats and recommended that drastic measures be taken. On November 2, 1956, the Secretary of State approved a new language policy which read, "Each officer will be encouraged to acquire a 'useful' knowledge of two foreign languages, as well as sufficient command of the language of each post of assignment to be able to use greetings, ordinary social expressions, and numbers; ask simple questions and give simple directions; and to recognize proper names, street signs, and office and shop designations. The acquisition of a 'useful' knowledge of one of the widely-used languages within the next five years or within five years of the date of appointment to the Foreign Service." Teeth were put into this by denying promotions to newly appointed Foreign Service Officers until they had taken tests demonstrating proficiency in at least one foreign tongue.

These measures by the State Department were followed by new policy statements by the then International Cooperation Administration (ICA), our technical assistance arm, and the United States Information Agency (USIA), charged with informing the rest of the world about America. Nor did it stop there. In 1960 Congress made the following statement for the first time in the country's history: "It is the policy of the Congress that Chiefs of Mission and Foreign Service officers appointed or assigned to serve in foreign countries shall have, to the maximum practicable extent, among their qualifications, a useful knowledge of the principal language or dialect of the country in which they serve."

The sharp increase in military and governmental language teaching, from an extremely low point before World War II, has been noted in previous chapters. In many ways the armed services and government are far ahead of the academic sector and the public school in building the sort of language facilities that are needed in today's world. The Defense Department has consolidated language efforts under a single Defense Language Institute, with a West Coast Branch at the former Army Language School in Monterey, California, and one representing an extension of the Navy Language School on the East Coast at Anacostia, Washington, D.C. The Foreign Service Institute continues to expand, adding needed courses in more languages and areas. An African department has been added in the last few years. In 1962 it offered courses in Swahili, Hausa, and about half a dozen other African languages to foreign service officers. With the help of National Defense Education Act (NDEA) funds the Institute has also undertaken a broad program of publication of its texts, mostly under the U.S. Government Printing Office imprint. Thus far, texts based on scientific linguistic principles have been published in French, Spanish, Bulgarian, Japanese, Chinese and in Igbo, Yoruba, and Twi, three African tongues. Other manuals such as "Basic Hungarian" are in various stages of preparation.

"Language is ordnance" might well be considered one of the new mottos in Government service today. Even the Marine Corps guards bound for overseas duty must now take a minimum of a hundred hours or so of the language of the country. Between 1954 and 1962 there was a 1,200 per cent increase in the number of persons voluntarily studying tongues in our State Department outposts throughout the globe. There were some 9,000 in all, including wives of our civilian and military representatives learning some sixty languages in over two hundred sites. The Peace Corps has perhaps offered the most glowing example, since up to 450 intensive hours in the language of the country of destination is required of all trainees. Thus far, training has been conducted in thirty-three languages, including Nepali, Nyanja (an African tongue), Persian, Tagalog, spoken in the Philippines, and Quechua, an important Indian idiom of the South American Andes region. More than one Peace Corps hopeful has been "washed out" because of inability to perform at a prescribed minimum in another tongue.

Despite these encouraging advances, the needs remain so gigantic that we still have far to go. This was spelled out, as

166

far as our diplomatic corps is concerned, by Dr. James B. Frith, Assistant Dean of the School of Languages of the Foreign Service Institute at the 14th Georgetown University Roundtable Conference on Languages and Linguistics on April 5, 1963. In his talk titled "Language Learning in the Foreign Affairs Community" he pointed out that up to the outbreak of the Second World War there were only fifty-eight countries in which we had embassies or legations, as contrasted with 109 in January 1963. Although twelve languages might have been useful then, it was actually quite possible to conduct all official business, most of it connected with routine matters related to the welfare of Americans abroad, in French or English. Today, Dr. Frith emphasized, that our diplomats find themselves "eyeball to eyeball" with a bewildering number of peoples and lands. Based on a systematic study of the language situation in the various countries to which we send representatives, the Department of State came to the conclusion that foreign service officers have a genuine need for between 97 and 154 languages! Here is the list:

### LANGUAGES MOST USEFUL IN DEPARTMENT OF STATE FOREIGN SERVICE POSTS

*Akan (*Twi)
*Amharic
Arabic (*Eastern, *Western)
Armenian
Assamese
Aymará
*Azerbaijani
*Bambara-Malinke [Mandingo]
Basque
Bassa [Kru-Bassa]

*Baule [Anyi-Baule]
Beja [not included]
*Bemba
*Bengali
Berber [Shilha, Rif]
*Bulgarian
Bulu [Fang-Bulu]
*Burmese
*Cambodian
Catalan

* In this list, an asterisk marks languages which are primary—that is the principal local language of one or more points. Parenthetic enclosures distinguish regional variants which may not be mutually intelligible. Hyphen indicates mutually intelligible variants. Brackets enclose the name under which these languages appear in the list given on pp. 40–55 when this is different from the way these appear here (except that absence of prefixes on the Bantu languages is disregarded).

*Chinese (*Amoy, *Cantonese,
    *Fukienese, *Mandarin,
    Swatow)
Chokwe [ci Cokwe]
*Czech
*Danish
*Duala
*Dutch [Dutch-Flemish]
Estonian
*Ewe [Ewe-Fon]
*Ewondo [Fang-Bulu]
Fanagalo [(a Bantu Pidgin)]
*Fijian
*Finnish
*Flemish [Dutch-Flemish]
*Fon [Ewe-Fon]
*French
*Fula [Fulani]
*Ga [Gą]
*Gaelic
Galla
Georgian
*German
*Greek
Guaraní
*Gujarati
*Haitian Creole [Caribbean
    French Creole]
*Hausa
*Hebrew
*Hindi [Hindi-Urdu]
*Hungarian
*Icelandic
*Igbo
Ilocano
*Indonesian [Indonesian-Malay]
*Italian
*Japanese
Javanese
Kannada

Kazakh
*Kikongo [ki Kongo]
Kikuyu [ki Kuyu]
*Kimbundu [ki Mbundu]
*Kinyarwanda [kinya Rwanda]
Kirghiz
*Kituba-Monokutuba [(a lingua
    franca based on Kikongo)]
*Korean
*Krio
Kurdish
*Lamba
*Lao [Thai-Lao]
Latvian
*Lingala [li Ngala]
Lithuanian
Luba
*Luganda [lu Ganda]
Lunda [not included]
Luo [Achooli-Luo]
Macedonian
*Malagasy
*Malay [Indonesian-Malay]
Malayalam
*Maltese [Arabic]
*Marathi
*Martinique Creole
Masai
Maya [Yucatec]
Mende
*More [Mossi]
*Nepali
*Norwegian
Nubian
Nyamwezi-Sukuma [kinya
    Mwezi-ki Sukuma]
*Nyanja
*Okinawan [Ryukyu]
Oriya
*Panjabi [Punjabi]

* See footnote on preceding page.

*Papiamento
*Pashtu
*Persian [Persian-Tajik]
*Persian (Afghan)
 [Persian-Tajik]
*Polish
*Portuguese
*Quechua
*Rumanian
*Rundi
*Russian
*Sango [Sango-Ngbandi]
*Sara
*Serbo-Croatian
 Serer
*Shona
 Sindebele [isi Zulu-isi Xhosa]
 Sindhi
*Singhalese [Sinhalese]
 Slovak
 Slovenian
*Somali
 Soninke [not included]
 Sotho
*Spanish
*Susu
*Swahili

*Swedish
*Tagalog
*Tamil
 Telugu
 Temne
*Thai [Thai-Lao]
 Tigre
*Tigrinya
 Tshwa [shi Tswa]
*Tsonga [Thonga]
 Tswana
*Turkish
 Ukrainian
 Umbundu [uMbandu]
*Urdu [Hindi-Urdu]
 Uzbek
 Vai
*Vietnamese
*Visayan
 Welsh
 White Russian [Byelorussian]
*Wolof
 Yakut
*Yoruba
*Zarma-Songhai [Songhai]
 Zulu [isi Zulu-isi Xhosa]
 Zulu-Xhosa

* See footnote on page 167.

The following tabulation lists the languages which are primary at one or more Foreign Service posts and useful in some degree for foreign affairs personnel at five or more points.

| | | |
|---|---|---|
| Afrikaans | Fula | Portuguese |
| Arabic (Eastern) | German | Russian |
| Arabic (Western) | Hausa | Spanish |
| Chinese (Cantonese) | Hindi | Swahili |
| Chinese (Mandarin) | Italian | Tamil |
| Dutch | Japanese | Turkish |
| English | Persian | Urdu |
| French | | |

It would be naive for some time to come to expect our academic institutions to cover the nation's needs in non-Western languages. According to an MLA survey, of the almost three million students enrolled in modern college language courses in 1960 only 2.4 per cent were studying tongues other than French, Spanish, German, Russian, or Italian.

In 1959 the U.S. Commissioner of Education pointed out that 80 per cent of the world's population speaks languages taught little or not at all in our schools. The Modern Language Association survey reported that in 1960 somewhat over 12,000 students were enrolled in the "critical" non-western tongues. Bengali, spoken by over 70 million in South Asia, claimed a total of nine students. Indonesian, the official medium of some 90 million, was being studied by only thirteen. The tongue of Vietnam, a prime trouble spot in southeast Asia, was being learned by thirty-eight, while Burmese, spoken by some 12 million in a vitally strategic area, claimed twenty-five. Czech, the mother tongue of 12 million in Russia's chief satellite, attracted ninety learners that year. Finally, although sub-Saharan Africa has some 800 distinct tongues, with over 200 million speakers, we had only sixty persons enrolled in a half dozen of these idioms. More encouraging, between 1958 and 1960 enrollment in Chinese tripled, going from 651 to 1771; Arabic from 364 to 533; and Hindi from 28 to 106.

A word of warning and explanation must be interjected here. The number of students enrolled in a given language does not equal the number of persons who gain any real facility in reading, writing, or speaking it. The simple reason for this is that all too small a percentage ever get to the intermediate or advanced stages. In both high school and college the overwhelming majority take only two years of non-intensive work. Dr. Conant has remarked in his book, *The American High School Today,* that fewer than four years is almost a waste of time, comparable with drilling for oil without waiting to strike a deposit. Moreover, all too many of the 12,000 students pursuing a "critical language" (with or without an NDEA fellowship), although graduate students, are obliged to work on the elementary phases of their languages since they have had little or no opportunity to begin their study previously.

Granting freely that we are short of language power, and that additional languages ought to be taught, which of the earth's 3,000 or so tongues should be added to the curriculum? To answer this question one would need the combined powers of a soothsayer able to predict all the geopolitical changes due to occur on earth and perhaps other planets in the years to come. Obviously, the best we can do is to make "educated guesses" or —to use a term much in favor among social scientists—"extrapolations" of future developments based on present knowledge and trends.

On March 27-28, 1961, linguistic experts met to grapple with just this problem at the Brookings Institution in Washington. Chaired by Austin E. Fife of Utah State University and organized under the joint auspices of the Modern Language Association and the U.S. Office of Education, the Neglected Languages Conference attempted to decide which languages ought to be stressed and what measures taken to improve their teaching.

The authors, attending the above conference, were definitely impressed by the elusiveness of its objectives. At any rate, a list of target languages was drawn up according to seeming importance. The official or "national languages" of other nations, such as Modern Greek and Pashto, were automatically assigned to Priority 1. Priority 2 included "languages of regional or cultural significance," such as Slovenian, a tongue of Yugoslavia, and Sierra Leone Krio, an important medium of communication in the new African state of Sierra Leone and surrounding territory. Priority 3 was a sort of "catch-all" of tongues of some special importance, such as Basque, spoken by a group with marked ethnic consciousness in the Spanish and French Pyrenees; Galla, a leading minority tongue of Ethiopia; Nahuatl, an important Indian idiom of northern Mexico; Tswana, Fang-Bulu, Kpelle, and a number of other African languages. Recognizing the difficulty of predicting which will be the "languages of tomorrow," Professor Fife said, "Global linguistic geography itself is in upheaval. Not having resources or manpower to develop materials and programs for the hundreds of mother tongues that pack the earth, we need a crystal ball in which we can perceive regional lingua francas that will emerge as vehicles of cultural and political action. Should we bet heavily on Hindi because it looms a sure winner, or should we play Bengali, Marathi, Telugu, etc.?"

Just how well equipped are we today with personnel able to handle the important world tongues? About fifteen years ago the American Council of Learned Societies in its survey of personnel in the humanities made an attempt through questionnaire to identify the individuals with a knowledge of non-western tongues and areas. Two years ago the Center for Applied Linguistics began its Roster of Linguists, intended to locate persons trained in linguistic science, those with experience in teaching English as a second language, and persons with knowledge of tongues other than French, German, Spanish, and Italian (which are now being surveyed by a special study of the Modern Language Association). The Center recently issued a statistical report of the first 1,875 questionnaires received.

While the findings of the Center's Roster are only partial for some tongues, they are fairly inclusive for others. As is the case with most statistical reports of this sort, the findings are depressing. Albanian was claimed by only ten persons. Only six persons indicated familiarity with Tibetan, an equal number with Vietnamese, five with Cambodian, four with Laotian. Chinese, spoken in five forms by some 600 million, was reported by 352 individuals, of whom only forty-seven indicated advanced or native mastery. Arabic, key idiom of the Middle East, was reported by 144 with only one-third noting high fluency. A total of thirty-nine Americans were located who had some acquaintance with as many sub-Saharan African tongues, with only five rating themselves fluent.

Figures, however, are cold bits of information in comparison with the "real life" situations arising in our encounters with the peoples of the world. Significantly enough, however, in such cases the needed tongue is not always a language like Tigrinya, Malagasy, or Burmese. The Department of State's Language Services Division, charged with supplying interpreters (as well as translators) for most official purposes, is at times hard put to furnish personnel in the less exotic tongues. A good case in point is Portuguese. The Division will probably have to go directly to Brazil to recruit enough speakers well enough versed in both English and Portuguese and able to perform interpretation of a conference or escort-group type. Language Services Division representatives have been obliged to travel all the way to Japan to help fill our needs for Japanese-English interpreters.

We will eventually have to face the fact that for many languages we cannot indefinitely rely upon *émigrés* and refugees. A case in point is Russian, since White Russian immigrants are well advanced in age and World War II DP's are only a limited source. At the same time, few college graduates can pass the demanding interpreter exams merely on the basis of academic studies. It is interesting to note that although the regular staff of the Language Services Division is mostly American, they require additional help in the form of part-time contract personnel of foreign birth. The Division ordinarily will not consider anyone who has not lived in the country where a language is spoken for at least two years, since first-class translation depends on a knowledge both of the mechanics of a tongue and the socio-cultural background of the speakers. Interpreting, the oral side of this art, is one of the most complex skills, as visitors to the United Nations have been able to appreciate. Only about one bilingual person in ten can pass the State Department's test for conference interpreting, be it simultaneous in which he is required to interpret in unison with the speaker, or consecutive in which he translates afterwards. Less demanding is escort work in which the interpreter accompanies official delegations (trade unionists, civilian and military officials, educators, etc.) on their escorted tours throughout the country. There is by now almost no city of a hundred thousand population which has not received visits from these foreign guests who represent scores of lands and whose impression of America will influence their country's policy. The effectiveness of the escort interpreter at this "grass roots" level can help create goodwill—or the opposite.

All this means that we simply have not come far enough in our task of training language specialists since World War II. Not long ago George Winchester Stone, Jr., Executive Secretary of the Modern Language Association, in a statement prepared for Senate hearings, commented, "But with all the improvement demonstrable statistically in terms of increased enrollments, early beginnings, longer sequences, and the study of an increasing variety of languages, we in the United States are still one of the least developed countries of the world linguistically. And this at a time when our position as an economic world leader demands more than ever that we be able to communicate with other peoples."

Little more need be said about our national syndrome of linguistic ignorance and our allergy to doing something about it. At a time when serious plans are being made for landings on Venus, Mars, and even other planets, it is ironic that we have not yet solved the problem of communication with our fellowman on terra firma. And although Telstar is capable of bringing us television shows from the remotest points, not excluding Timbuctoo and Kuala Lumpur, too many of us can understand only the picture and not the sounds.

# Chapter 13

# Bright Spots on the Language Horizon

*Commendable Efforts*

The preceding chapter was largely negative in tone, pointing out the gaps in our language training picture. In the present one, by contrast, we will try to show how, both in the United States and other parts of the globe, attempts are being made to modernize and improve foreign language instruction. And, finally, in the concluding chapter a blueprint will be drawn of the type of language facilities the authors feel America ought to have.

In general, the trend for foreign language study has been an upward one since World War II. It was, however, not until the Soviet launching of the first Sputnik that the nation was electrified into realizing how backward we were, not only in science and math teaching, but in the language field as well. In record time the 85th Congress passed the National Defense Education Act authorizing the expenditure of over $700 million for the improvement of instruction in these three areas. The Office of Education in the Department of Health, Education and Welfare was entrusted with the task of administering the Act.

While the NDEA has made some real contributions to building up our language facilities, it should not be thought that little more remains to be done. Among its positive accomplishments is the encouragement of the study of the neglected strategic tongues. In the past five years more than a thousand fellowships have been granted to graduate students for study of over fifty of the eighty-three tongues on the "critical list" compiled for the Office of Education, and ranging from Swedish to Yoruba, an important African idiom. The NDEA has also supplied matching funds to fifty-six universities for setting up language-area centers, for Slavic, Latin-American, Oriental, and African tongues. In 1960, according to the Modern Language Association, there were 12,000 students in all our higher institutions learning critical tongues, many of them at NDEA-supported language and area centers. Support has also been made available in the form of matching funds for the building of over 4,000 language laboratories in public schools, and to finance the costs of state foreign language supervisors, who now number over thirty. Summer institutes held at colleges throughout the nation have given over 10,000 public school teachers the opportunity to study applied linguistics and improve their fluency in the language taught by them. Finally, NDEA funds have been granted for research projects in linguistics and language teaching methodology. One of these, for example, studied the accomplishments of two groups of students of German, one taught by the conventional grammar method, the other by the spoken approach.

It is significant to note that Dean Howard Sollenberger of the Foreign Service Institute Language School of the State Department has estimated that ten years will be required before appreciable gains in qualified language manpower are felt as a result of the NDEA.

## Rising Enrollments

While the quality of language instruction may not always have improved, it is a fact that the quantity of students enrolled in foreign tongues has been increasing steadily since 1945, with the most dramatic upsurge since 1957. Ten years ago over half of our high schools offered no modern language, and only about 15 per cent of the total high school population studied this subject. At present about 20 per cent are taking French, Spanish, German, and a few other tongues, while the number of schools offering at least one modern language has increased to about 70 per cent. But lest we gloat over this, it should be pointed out that in 1914 over 40 per cent of our secondary school youngsters were learning a modern idiom, twice the proportion doing so today!

In some states, according to Modern Language Association statistics, enrollments have made very striking gains. In Delaware, for example, the percentage of secondary school students enrolled in a modern tongue climbed from 1.6 in 1954 to 34 in 1959; in Kansas, from 2.3 per cent to 13.2 per cent; and in the state of Washington, from 11.5 to 22.2 per cent during the same period. Private schools, of course, have traditionally insisted on language study and about 82 per cent of the pupils in grades nine through twelve of 1,278 independent schools canvassed in 1959 were enrolled in a modern tongue.

As for FLES—the movement to introduce foreign languages in the elementary schools—there is both progress and failure to report. On the surface it is impressive to hear that over a million youngsters are now studying a modern tongue in grade school. While there are some excellent FLES programs, well over half of them are conducted after-hours and outside the regular school curriculum. Many of them meet for only fifteen or twenty minutes, twice a week, learning a few phrases and a few songs. And yet Drs. Arnold Gesell and Frances L. Ilg of the Gesell Institute of Child Development have declared that, "The present trend toward providing opportunities for second-language learning in the early grades indicates a clearer recognition of the patterns and sequences of child development. The young child enjoys language experience. . . . With favorable motivation he is emotionally amenable to a second and even a third language. This holds true for nursery school and kindergarten age levels." It would seem a pity that so little is done to introduce American youngsters to a second tongue at an earlier age.

Another authority, Dr. Wilder Penfield, of the Montreal Neurological Institute, whose own children since kindergarten have been studying French and German along with English, has endorsed FLES on purely scientific grounds. The physiological development of the "organ of the mind," he stated in 1953, "causes it to specialize in the learning of language before the ages of 10 and 14. After that, gradually, inevitably, it seems to become rigid, slow, less receptive." He also added, "One who is mindful of the changing physiology of the human brain might marvel at educational curricula. Why should foreign languages . . . make their first appearance long after a boy or girl has lost full capacity for language learning?" The full impact of a statement like this is only felt, however, if one observes youngsters learning other tongues and hearing them cope equally well with Chinese, Swahili, Bulgarian, German, or Arabic sounds.

That the idea of the early introduction of language is not really new is evidenced by a bit of Americana. In 1774 John Adams wrote to his wife Abigail, "Above all . . . let your ardent Anxiety be to mould the Minds and Manners of our Children. . . . Fix their Ambition upon great and solid objects, and their Contempt upon little frivolous and useless ones. It is Time, my dear, for you to begin to teach them French."

At any rate, it would seem a pity that not more is being done to introduce American youngsters to a second tongue at an earlier age—at present barely one youngster out of ten goes to a school offering this subject. On the plus side, however, the fact that the general public is so receptive to FLES is an encouraging sign that language planners ought to utilize to the utmost.

College enrollments have also taken an upward turn. Of the 2,720,055 students in 1,206 higher institutions in 1960, approximately 20 per cent were enrolled in modern language classes, representing a 12.4 per cent rise over 1959. The breakdown in percentages of languages studied by college students in that year was as follows: French 37.7; Spanish 28.4; German 24.4; Russian 5.2; Italian 1.9; and other modern tongues 2.4. On the credit side, also, a growing number of colleges are bringing back or introducing the language requirement both for admission and for graduation

At the college level there has been a heartening tendency toward teaching about heretofore neglected areas. With matching NDEA funds fifty-six universities have set up "language and area centers" devoted not only to the languages but also to the economics, geography, history, literature, and arts of important world regions. Students of these programs work toward graduate degrees as area specialists on Russia and East Europe, South Asia and Southeast Asia, Africa or Latin America. A number of smaller colleges are also beginning to follow the practice of cooperative sharing of instructors in hard-to-get language and area subjects and to defray their costs jointly. Thus, several colleges within a limited geographical area can now afford to offer, let's say, Russian, Chinese, or African languages and history without employing a full-time specialist.

Courses on the non-Western world are beginning to appear for the generalist as well as for the language-area specialist. For example, the University of Wisconsin has introduced an undergraduate course in the civilization of India, modeled after a course given at the University of Chicago's South Asia Center. When the Center for Middle Eastern Studies was set up at Harvard a few years after World War II, there was no general course on the Middle East. A survey course was promptly added to the curriculum. A similar offering for the Far East, known by its students as "Rice Paddies," now also graces that institution's catalog. In the 1930's even such a university as Yale provided only a few courses on the Far East; today it lists well over forty in the fields of history, geography, economics, and the arts.

*Coordinated Programs*

Encouragingly enough, much of the improvement taking place in the language field is a result of initiative undertaken at the local and regional levels. Some of the programs are even state-wide. One of the boldest cases of voluntary action in modern language history is the recently announced ten-year Indiana

Language Program. This aims to make modern language instruction available by 1972 in all the public high schools of the state of Indiana, of which as many as possible are to offer a four-year sequence. At the same time every college-bound student will be counseled to study either an ancient or modern tongue for as long as possible.

The provisions of the Indiana plan would warm the heart of any linguist. Excellent teaching is to be recognized while friendly persuasion will be employed to induce mediocre instructors to improve their techniques. Outstanding high school language students will be encouraged through scholarships to continue this study in college with a view to becoming teachers of the subject. Moreover, they will be urged to undertake less commonly taught tongues while still undergraduates. A Council on Language Research and Experimentation will be appointed to promote effective methods and texts for both foreign language instruction and teacher training. This plan required a tremendous communications effort and coordination among foreign language teachers and their colleagues in other fields, members of the University of Indiana administration and that of other colleges within the state, the State Department of Instruction, as well as public school officials, parents, and students. A $650,000 Ford Foundation grant is helping to launch the program.

Beginning in 1965, California public schools will be required to teach a foreign tongue from the sixth through the twelfth grades. This, by the way, is a dramatic reversal of a state law passed previously forbidding a foreign language requirement for graduation from high school. In at least a half dozen communities throughout the United States ten-year sequences of language study from grade school through high school are either a reality or in the planning stage. All of these cases have a history of forward-looking parents, language instructors, and school administrators who have been willing to spearhead a dynamic program, alerting the public to linguistic needs and following up with a campaign to bring more and better language training to the community or state. At times, however, these community efforts fail, because of either poor planning or short-lived enthusiasm.

180

Last year the School Board and County Council of one of the most enlightened counties of Maryland, located just outside of the nation's capital, announced their intention to eliminate the FLES program as an economy measure. And this was a well-organized and sound effort, rather than one of the jerry-built programs that have in recent years been doing more harm than good to the language cause.

The best planned programs in the world, however, cannot succeed unless we have enough well-trained teachers and adequate teaching materials. This is being realized increasingly as efforts are being made in the language field, both at home and abroad, improve these areas. It would be impossible to list here all the projects and experiments which have been initiated since World War II, but a sampling of them will give an idea of these undertakings. Under Title VI of the NDEA a number of experiments are in progress at various universities intended to test out more effective methods of teaching both the spoken and written phases of language, with emphasis on the former. A beginning has been made in producing texts through the "team" approach in which linguists, classroom teachers, and psychologists pool their knowledge. The first of these to come out was *Modern Spanish,* produced with Modern Language Association funds and published by Harcourt Brace and Company. NDEA research funds enabled John Gumperz, Director of the South Asia Language and Area Center at the University of California, Berkeley, to go directly to India and Pakistan. There, together with several colleagues, he prepared sound films of people speaking in such typical situations as the bazaar, home and family, and at work. Research is also being carried on in the field of testing and in audio-visual devices.

At the same time, there is a growing tendency in the new approaches to language teaching to pay more attention to the culture and background of the people whose tongue is being taught. Speaking at the Washington Area chapter meeting of the American Association of Teachers of Slavic and East European Languages on October 10, 1962, Professor Hugo Mueller of American University aptly defined the study of a foreign idiom as the process of learning to "regard reality through another language." Thus, in the new approaches, the student learns not merely to parrot phrases but rather to understand the cultural elements involved in a given speech situation and the type of response that it would evoke from a native speaker. It is a fact, for example, that in the Hindi and other Eastern societies, one does not ask about the health of the members of the interlocutor's family. However, modern texts for Hindi alert students to this and supply the sort of conversational material which would be appropriate in a casual chat with a Hindi-speaking acquaintance.

## Developments Abroad

Aside from American attempts to step up the effectiveness of language instruction, there are also European efforts which are worth noting here. Much like the American teaching in the "new key," there is in most of these a reaction against bookish traditional approaches in which more time is spent talking about the language than in practicing it. Along with this, there is also a striving to utilize the findings of linguistic research and to find its applications in the classroom. In various countries of Western Europe, in the Soviet Union, Japan and many other parts of the world, there is growing dissatisfaction with the status of language teaching, and important reforms are taking place.

In France, the Centre de Recherche et d'Étude pour la Diffusion du Français of the École Normale Supérieure, located at St. Cloud, has been carrying on significant work. Their courses are based on what constitutes the most basic, frequently used, and culturally essential vocabulary and grammatical patterns of French. This study is explained in a book titled *L'Élaboration du Français Elémentaire: Étude sur l'établissement d'un vocabulaire et d'une grammaire de base (Development of Elementary French: Study of the Determinations of a Basic Vocabulary and Grammar)*. A team of scholars, consisting of Professors Georges Gougenheim, Paul Rivenc, René Michéa, and Aurélien Sauvageot determined the frequency of words and grammatical constructions in a broad sample of spoken French. One of the most novel aspects of the study was the emphasis on the quality (*disponibilité*) that some words have for readily coming to mind in discussions of a given topic. The basic vocabulary arrived at totaled 1,500 words.

The method elaborated at St. Cloud has been adopted by the General Office of Cultural and Technical Affairs of the Ministry of Foreign Affairs for the teaching of French as a second language. It has helped set up more than forty audiovisual teaching centers in over twenty countries. Their instructors have taken an orientation course at St. Cloud and are expected to employ the methods and materials developed at the École Normale Supérieure. The language material is recorded on magnetic tapes, which are coordinated with filmstrips designed to show the meaning of the taped phrase or of the cultural situation in which it would be used; the appropriate name given these materials is *Voix et Images de France*. The use of filmstrips in this manner is noteworthy since, by and large, these have been neglected by American language teachers.

The basic St. Cloud course consists of thirty-two lessons. In a typical lesson the essential material to be covered is learned in the dialogue; sentences involving grammatical manipulations of the same material are introduced in the second phase; a final segment is devoted to sentences picked to highlight certain French sounds. As each frame of the filmstrip is projected on the screen, the instructor clarifies the meaning through mimicry, gestures, and drawings. There is a constant endeavor to maintain, through speech and pictures, a "transposed reality" in which the new language comes to seem an integral part of the situation. Next comes the stage of active repetition and memorization, with close attention to the pronunciation of the students as they repeat. After this the lesson enters the phase of using sentences which illustrate certain grammatical alterations of variations of dialogue material. The immediate goal of these manipulations is to lead the student to the point where he can participate in conversation in the context of situations similar to that presented by the lesson.

In the United States St. Cloud is represented by the Center

for Curriculum Development in Audio-Visual Language Teaching in Philadelphia (525 Locust Street). Two-day orientation seminars, one-week workshops, and four-week institutes are conducted by the Center for American and Canadian teachers interested in applying the St. Cloud method at their schools. A certain number of scholarships are available to applicants. In the academic year 1962–63 some 850 teachers came to the Center for Curriculum Development either as students or in search of information about the St. Cloud approach. Similar materials have also been developed for German and Russian and a Spanish course is in process of being prepared.

A survey of all the attempts throughout the world to overhaul language instruction and sweep away the barnacles of ineffective traditionalism would fill several good-sized volumes. The direction of change is one in favor of teaching the spoken language rather than mere passive knowledge. As in Western Europe this current of reform is making itself felt today in many other parts of the globe. Behind the Iron Curtain there is a great deal of discussion of the need to emphasize oral-aural skills. On June 4, 1961, the Council of Ministers of the Soviet Union issued a special decree "Concerning the Improvement of Language Study," which called for a vigorous increase in the number of Soviet youngsters and adults studying foreign tongues and for more emphasis on the spoken skills. Aside from such measures taken, a growing number of schools have sought to revitalize second language teaching. An example is the Gor'kij Pedagogic Institute of Foreign Languages where the faculty held several stormy sessions protesting the slowness of improvement. Taking things into their own hands, they adopted a spoken approach, installed a language laboratory, and set up special re-training courses for teachers of the local city schools. Today the Gor'kij Institute has the reputation of being one of the most effective language teaching centers in the U.S.S.R. A similar face-lifting took place at the Riga Pedagogic Institute and other schools.

In Germany experimentation is being carried on by a group of linguists who are developing the concept of "Inhaltsbezogende Grammatik" or "Meaning-Oriented Grammar." These include Professors Leo Weisgerber of the University of Bonn, Hennig Brincktmann of the University of Heidelberg, and Hans Glinz of the Pädagogische Hochschule at Kettwig and the University of Zürich. Although largely accepting the basic tenets of Bloomfieldian linguistics, this school chooses to approach structure through meaning, and assigns a role to semantics which runs counter to the American school. In their pedagogical application, they insist on the necessity of the student's acquiring insight into a foreign language and mastering it not externally but internally by developing an intuitive grasp of its semantic system. The new Duden grammar, intended for German youngsters, embodies many of the ideas of these theoreticians, as does Heinz Griesbach and Dora Schultz's text for German as a second language, titled *Deutsche Sprachlehre für Ausländer,* Part I, new edition, published in 1962 in Munich.

All in all, therefore, there is reason for feeling that the new currents in the language field promise to bring about considerable improvement. The trend away from the passive grammar-translation procedures and toward active mastery of the spoken language is helping to revitalize the study, so long held in abhorrence by youngsters in America and elsewhere. It is certainly to be hoped that somewhat more cross-fertilization will occur through a better exchange of information among American and foreign researchers experimenting with more effective methods of language teaching.

# Chapter 14

# Blueprint for a
# Bilingual America

### The Direction

Not long ago, a "typical American mother" challenged, "Give me one good reason why my youngest son, about to enter high school, should waste his time studying a foreign language. Three of my children took foreign languages in high school and college—and not one of them can order so much as a cup of coffee in the language he studied. I'm in favor of learning languages, but not the way it's being done in most places."

Such opinions are standard fare for language teachers, who are constantly challenged to justify themselves and their subject on the American curriculum. If they are genuinely frank, as most instructors are, they will be inclined to agree with this "typical American mother," and also with Walter Pitkin, who said thirty years ago in *Life Begins at Forty* that language study is not worth the candle. In view of the evidence presented in the previous chapter, it must be admitted that it is impossible to teach the youngsters of the United States to read, write, and speak a foreign tongue in the traditional two-year, three-hours-a-week lock-step.

Our children will fare no better than their parents unless America scraps its present concept of too little, too late. Ours is the doubtful distinction of being the only civilized country where language study is postponed until the individual has passed the age when he is most receptive. Then he is given so light an exposure that it does little more than build up an antagonism toward everything connected with the subject.

There is no good reason why every normal American youngster cannot graduate from high school with a basic speaking, reading, and writing knowledge of a major world language. The old saw that Americans do not learn languages easily is simply absurd. Waclaw Lednicki of the University of California and Henri Peyre of Yale, both scholars reared in the European tradition, have expressed their admiration for the way our young men and women succeed with foreign tongues when they are highly motivated. The claim that there is simply no room on the curriculum for more language will not hold water. Throughout the country Americans are awakening from their language lethargy and taking steps to provide youngsters with lingual skills.

Two years ago in our desert state of Utah several high schools introduced Arabic, Chinese, and Japanese, mostly taught by Mormon missionaries with firsthand experience of the languages and areas. From all indications, the effort has been a successful one. It led to a project undertaken by the Arabic instructor in Bountiful, Utah, to produce a secondary level text, financed by NDEA funds. Thus it is that a tiny city at our very grass roots is making a unique contribution to our increased knowledge of an important tongue and is helping fill our need for high school texts in the Eastern languages. Inspired by this example one secondary school in Colorado has introduced Arabic, while several California schools are introducing Chinese and Japanese. Sometimes the initiative to bring in vital Eastern and African tongues comes from the pupils themselves—the very individuals who supposedly are so indifferent to languages. About a year ago students of a New Jersey high school petitioned for an after-hours course in Swahili. The school board liked the idea; an instructor was somehow located and this African idiom was introduced.

Realizing that Eastern tongues take a long time to master, more and more educators are trying to make them available at the pre-collegiate level. Columbia University orientalists, with the aid of a grant from the Carnegie Corporation, are planning to bring Chinese to New York City area high schools. This is expected to include a four-year sequence with an initial planning and trial period during the summer and fall of 1963. The University's Department of Chinese and Japanese is preparing special teaching materials and instructors.

It is also being recognized that if Russian youngsters of eight can tackle English, Hindi, Arabic, and even Chinese, there is no reason why our children cannot do likewise. At the University of Kentucky Foreign Language Conference on April 27, 1963, Nicholas Pahl of Kent State University described the successful teaching of Russian in grades four through seven in Ohio schools.

These few case studies have been noted to show that American youngsters are by no means indifferent to foreign language study, and to suggest the opportunities that now exist for language building. Moreover, if youngsters can be brought to cope successfully with such complex tongues as Chinese, Arabic, and Russian, it is clear that the possibilities for a rich learning yield in more closely related tongues such as German, French, and Spanish should be no less.

## A General Plan

At any rate, there is every reason to believe that the atmosphere in the United States is more favorable than it has ever been toward the study of foreign tongues. What is lacking is any sort of coordinated planning for building up our language facilities beyond their present stage. Below is a very simple outline of the sort of blueprint that could make of America a bilingual nation within one generation.

KINDERGARTEN AND GRADE SCHOOL
Begin instruction by grade 6.
Languages offered: French, Spanish, German, Italian, language of local interest (Polish, Hebrew, Ukrainian, Slovak, etc.).
*Total:* 1–6 years.

JUNIOR AND SENIOR HIGH SCHOOL

Continue instruction in same language begun in grade school, and/or begin a new language.

Languages offered: French, Spanish, German, Italian, Russian, Arabic, Chinese, Japanese, when instructors are available.

Optional subject: Latin or Greek (available from 7th grade for 4 years).

*Total:* 6 years (Combined total: 6–13 years of modern languages and 4 years of Greek or Latin).

(Plus compulsory course in "Languages and Linguistics in the World Today" to be taken in senior high.)

COLLEGE

*Option A:* Continue with language begun before college; specialize in language, literature, or area studies, 3–4 years.

*Option B:* Begin new language and study 3–4 years.

*Option C:* Study language two years for research-reading purposes.

*Option D:* Graduate study in particular language group, such as classical, Slavic, Romance, Germanic, Semitic, 1–5 years (also presupposes Option A or B).

*Total:* 2–9 years.

(Specialists and advanced students also pursue courses in area studies, linguistics, literature, pedagogy, depending on major interest.)

POST-COLLEGIATE

Adult education courses available as university or high school extension. These programs will not be of exclusively written nature, but will include at least one class a week, with stimulating extra-curricular activities (field trips, presentation of talks, skits, etc., supper meetings). Activities can be coordinated with or be conducted within the framework of adult community language clubs.

INTENSIVE SUMMER COURSES

Attempts should be made to set up full-time intensive summer courses of approximately 8-10 weeks duration, roughly equivalent to a year's non-intensive work. These would serve the double purpose of providing learners with opportunities to improve knowledge gained during the regular year. They also would make available facilities for those otherwise unable to pursue language study. Summer courses should exist at all levels from grade school through college.

*Total:* 1–70 or more years.

As can be seen, there is absolutely nothing mysterious about the requirements for the type of language training which twentieth-century living requires. These are not visionary, starry-eyed objectives and do not require a gigantic outlay of school funds.

If the "Ideal Plan" were adopted, it would mean that every normal high school child would graduate with a basic reading, writing, and speaking knowledge of some important world language. He would keep up his fluency and interest in the language through the adult education courses and language clubs. College graduates would come out with a minimum of two years of training and in many cases would take three or four years. The plan also provides for language specialists' training.

There are, of course, many variations possible within the framework of the plan. A few words of commentary regarding some of its provisions would not be amiss.

First of all, local conditions in a given community will have considerable importance in deciding whether language will be introduced in kindergarten, the first grade, the third or fifth or seventh grades. In foreign countries there is wide variation, but the subject is usually presented before adolescence.

The choice of languages to be taught also allows some room for debate since it is difficult to predict just what language young Americans are sure to find useful in the future. However, since the study of any language enriches the learner in terms of better understanding of other peoples, he cannot completely go wrong on any of them. In a private conversation with one of the authors, Charles A. Ferguson, Director of the Center for Applied Linguistics, suggested that for the non-specialists there are perhaps a dozen major "culture" idioms which provide the key to a rich written literature and which serve as mediums of communication for large segments of the world's population. While no two people would probably come up with the same list, it appears to us that the following tongues are strong candidates for inclusion as "Languages Most Likely to Be Useful to Young Americans": French, Spanish, Portuguese, Italian, German, Russian, Hindi-Urdu, Arabic, Persian, Indonesian, Chinese, Japanese, and Swahili.

Factors in the choice of a language include availability of instructors, languages already taught, and ethnic considerations. In areas with a concentration of persons of a particular national origin, there is sometimes interest in teaching the ancestral speech.

Many public schools in Hawaii prefer to offer Chinese and Japanese as the foreign tongue. In numerous parts of the mid-west and Pennsylvania, German and Scandinavian tongues are favored, while in the East, particularly in the industrial centers, Slavic tongues, Hungarian, and Italian are of interest. Certain cities have for one reason or another attracted particular groups. Boston has the largest colonies of Armenians and Albanians; Cleveland, Ohio, of Hungarians, Slovenes, and Croatians; New Bedford, Massachusetts, of Portuguese; Indianapolis of Bulgarians; while sheep-grazing areas in Nevada and California have drawn concentrations of Basques from Spain. Most of our large cities have scores of different ethnic groups. Too little has been done in encouraging the teaching of their tongues on a regional basis.

Curiously enough, however, the parents' support of ancestral idioms is often weak or non-existent, perhaps because of the fear that the child will remain too "foreign" or that the language in question is not of sufficient practical importance. In a recent conversation with Theodore Huebener, former supervisor of foreign language instruction in New York City, this was brought home to one of the writers. According to Dr. Huebener, although New York leads our cities in the number of varied ethnic backgrounds, neither the parents nor the younger generation appears to be much influenced by national origin in choosing a foreign tongue. Although there are easily three million Jewish people, only 4,000 high schoolers elected Hebrew; Brooklyn has a fairly large Norwegian community but only a handful elected Norwegian. At the University of Wisconsin, a state with a very high Polish population, enrollments in that tongue have never been high. To attract the Polish vote, a state legislator in the 1930's set up a chair of Polish. A visiting professor from Poland was hired, a collection of Polish books purchased, and excellent courses organized. In 1938 the annual enrollment for all courses amounted to about twenty (including one of the authors). Recent interest in the Slavic world, however, vindicates the Wisconsin politician, and the University's Polish facilities are among the best in the country.

What about Latin and Greek? The writers feel that there is no conflict between modern and classical tongues but that their roles are different. Latin and Greek bring insight into concepts basic to western civilization, and their study as optional subjects ought to be encouraged. Greek, taught in only a small number of private and public secondary schools, should be revived and expanded. It ought to be noted that in the academic (non-vocational) secondary schools of Italy, France, West and East Germany, Latin and/or Greek are required along with modern tongues.

Our blueprint also includes a course to be given sometime during high school on "Languages and Linguistics in the World Today." This would, in simple terms, introduce young people to the basic facts about sound systems and grammatical structure, would give a picture of the language families of the world, and some notions of socio-linguistic problems in international affairs. Such a course ought to help break down any myths the students have already absorbed, replacing them with more scientific notions of how languages work, and their place in society. Almost nothing of this sort exists today, which helps to explain why otherwise educated people display such abysmal ignorance of the subject. It is gratifying to learn that Pacific High School, a private institution in Palo Alto, California, recently introduced a three-month course on linguistics for its students.

According to our blueprint, students would graduate from high school with a six-year sequence in French, Spanish, German, Russian, or even Chinese or Japanese, and then move on to study one of fifty languages which large universities offer. Students will be able to become language and area specialists, majoring in the Far East, Middle East, South Asia, Soviet orbit, Latin America, Western Europe, Africa, and even North American studies, with special attention to French Canada, Mexico, and our Spanish Southwest.

The Soviet solution to the problem of training language specialists lies mainly in the five- or six-year pedagogic language institutes. In our own master plan we would rather encourage the present American trend of developing specialties by institution. Thus, in addition to such Slavic and East European centers as Harvard, Columbia, and Indiana, we have a Middle Eastern center at Wisconsin and Princeton, a South Asia center at Berkeley and Pennsylvania, and an African center at Howard University and the University of California at Los Angeles. Other centers can be built with the help of NDEA funds or with the sort of government backing that will in all likelihood be provided when the NDEA expires.

### Special Needs

In addition to training language and area experts as government analysts and desk and regional officers in the foreign service, and as university teachers, universities need to add training in several specialties that are now neglected by academic institutions. There are almost no courses in our universities in the art of translation and interpretation—Georgetown University's Institute of Languages and Linguistics being a notable exception.

Colleges must shed their anachronistic ivory tower attitudes toward languages and linguistics and introduce courses that stress twentieth-century advances. Such courses would cover translation, interpreting, mechanical translating, information retrieval, the teaching of English as a second language, literacy work, devising and reform of writing systems, language policies in established and emergent states, language studies for overseas work for government information and technical officers, and for journalists. Nor is this list exhaustive. There are many similar, related topics.

Although there are limits to the number of courses that one may take in an undergraduate or graduate program, language specialists should be expected to take a minimum number of units in linguistics, literature, area studies, and—if they intend to teach—pedagogy. Such training will give them not only greater versatility but security from the type of unemployment that may result if enthusiasm should subside.

It is advisable, too, for the young language specialist not to restrict himself too narrowly. If he wishes to become a Tibetan specialist, he ought also to take a larger Eastern tongue, such as Chinese or Japanese, as a minor and so on.

Our blueprint should not be allowed to become a plan for

language specialists only, since it is aimed at the average American citizen, at the language and area expert, and at the specialist who needs language as a tool. In the fall, 1961, issue of the *Journal of Geological Education,* Dorothy B. Vitaliano of the U.S. Geological Survey at Indiana University, presents a convincing case for more language power for scientists. She maintains that the researcher who cannot do his own reading in foreign literature is at a tremendous handicap since translations are often expensive, out of date, and inept. In one paper on the internal constitution of the earth, the Russian word *kora* (crust) was consistently mistranslated as "core," while the Russian equivalent for "barren strata" came out "unpregnant beds"! She concludes that, "Before dismissing as unrealistic the thought that the day might ever come when every American geologist—or every American scientist for that matter—will have a working knowledge of three other languages, remember that Europeans have long achieved it as a matter of course."

The acquisition of at least two languages for scientists is not difficult. If the student has French, German, or Russian in high school, about all he would need in college is a course in Scientific Russian or German, French such as is already available in many institutions. He can then also take one year or two semesters of another tongue which is exclusively devoted to reading. Courses like these are being offered by more and more schools.

Government and armed services schools of language would continue their activities, but would not, or should not, have to spend time on elementary instruction in common languages. They ought rather devote their efforts to teaching exotic tongues and specialties, such as military interrogation, technical translating, interpreting and the like.

As has been suggested several times throughout this work, there is need at all levels for an improvement of instructional methods. Although excellent instruction is carried on here and there, the over-all picture is not a favorable one, thanks to several generations of neglect and indifference.

Basic to the entire effort to revitalize language teaching in America is the need for increasing the exposure. There is no reason why the six-year sequence (which we follow the Modern

Language Association in recommending in our blueprint) should not be sufficient to give the learner an elementary to intermediate control of speaking, reading, and writing. This would mean a vocabulary of about 1,500–2,000 words and an ability to handle the main structural features of a language. Fluency would be gained by additional study in adult education courses or at college.

It is necessary to step up the healthy trend initiated during World War II of increasing the number of intensive and semi-intensive courses. Cornell's Division of Modern Languages insists on eight hours per week of class work plus a minimum amount of laboratory practice, and grants six hours of credit for this. Ohio State University and the University of New Hampshire require five hours of class time and give as many hours of credit. Other schools are following suit, but can find time to do little under the burden of other requirements. The number of hours required to achieve a given level in languages depends on so many factors that it is impossible to set down absolute norms—the learner's ability, his motivation and diligence, and the difficulty of the target tongue. Below is a chart devised by Henry Fenn, former Director of Yale's Institute of Oriental Languages, which suggests average learning time for various idioms:[1]

| PROGRAM | TOTAL HOURS | TIME REQUIRED FOR COMPETENCE | |
|---|---|---|---|
| | | In German: | In Chinese: |
| Traditional: | | | |
| 3 hpw. × 30 wks. × 4 yrs. . . . | 360 | 6.7 yrs. | 11.1 yrs. |
| Standard: | | | |
| 5 hpw. × 30 wks. × 4 yrs. . . . | 600 | 4.0 yrs. | 6.7 yrs. |
| Double Course: | | | |
| 10 hpw. × 30 wks. 1st yr. | | | |
| 5 hpw. × 30 wks. next 3 yrs.. . | 750 | 3.2 yrs. | 5.3 yrs. |
| The same plus 2 summers: | | | |
| 25 hpw. × 10 wks. × 2 . . . . . . . | 1250 | 1.9 yrs. | 3.2 yrs. |
| Full time: | | | |
| 30 hpw. × 48 wks. (1 yr.) . . . . | 1440 | 20 wks. | 33 wks. |

[1] Henry C. Fenn, "Training for Language Competence," *Proceedings of Neglected Language Conference* (March 27-31, 1961), Modern Languages Association, New York, 1961.

The implementation of our blueprint, or anything similar, is dependent more than anything upon the ability to secure a sufficient supply of highly qualified teachers. The instructor, not any "gimmick," no matter how well prepared, is the real touchstone of effective language power.

Up until now there was little reason, except love of the subject, to induce youngsters to go into the language field. As a result, a disturbingly large number of our language courses in the public schools are taught by persons mostly trained in other specialties, but with a minor of only ten to fifteen hours in a foreign tongue. Over a third have never been to the country whose language they "teach" and literally cannot carry on a simple conversation in it. This is in most cases not their fault but merely that of circumstances.

As in other fields one of the problems here is that of attracting gifted young people to the foreign language specialization. They are not to be blamed for shunning an occupation that requires much more training than it takes to become a lawyer, doctor, or dentist, but offers little in prestige and pecuniary rewards. In the 1957 graduating class of the University of Indiana only 1.7 per cent of the students had majored in a foreign tongue. Better salaries, travel-study opportunities and more recognition for this difficult and highly skilled type of work, plus emphasis by student advisors on the opportunities and challenges offered by this profession are the only apparent answer. There is a real shortage of persons trained in linguistic science. According to an estimate by the Center for Applied Linguistics, there are only 500 or 600 trained linguists in the land—far below the demand.

## Public Participation

Finally, our blueprint is one which does not limit the pursuit of language to formal academic auspices. The day is gone when knowledge of foreign languages was the privilege of the cultured only. Today, jet speeds and contracting borders create opportunities and needs for linguistic know-how for almost everyone. Never have there been so many exciting international exchanges of persons, never so much travel, and never have we been so underprepared linguistically for our opportunities.

This is why no viable blueprint for a bilingual America ought to concentrate exclusively on the utilitarian uses of language: as if languages were only useful for consular officers and import-export managers, with all due credit to the importance of both. It ought, instead, provide for opportunities and rewards for lifelong practice of language, both as a practical tool and as an effective instrument of communication between peoples.

Fortunately, in contrast with the apathy of the 1920's and 1930's, there is today growing evidence of spontaneous citizen interest in learning and promoting foreign tongues. Adult education classes, both at commercial schools like Berlitz and adult education centers, are booming. There is no way of knowing how many informal classes are at this moment meeting. A few years ago in New York City, for example, an Inter-American Cultural Association was formed, meeting at the Park Royal Hotel every Tuesday evening. Classes met in the ballroom, informally, at round tables. A few years ago retired professor of languages John M. Pittaro, together with a few other altruists, donated his services so that ordinary American citizens could refresh their knowledge of languages. Each member paid a nominal fee of $15.00 yearly for the privilege of meeting in this relaxed setting "intended to make the member feel that he is not in school again, but rather that he is learning or reviewing the language of his choice as a pleasant experience with a group of friends." The Association also organizes cultural lectures and dances and does its bit for person-to-person diplomacy by showing Latin-American newcomers around the area. Thus it is that housewives, stenographers, Civil Service workers, retail merchants, and others in this fast-moving twentieth century began to play a modest but important, informal role in our statesmanship.

It is not necessary to leave our shores to participate in Uncle Sam's diplomatic efforts. The United States Travel Service, set up by law in 1961, seeks out and maintains contact with volunteer citizen groups interested in showing hospitality and assistance to foreign travelers. For example, in Baltimore it is in touch with that city's "language bank," a novel venture which deserves to be emulated. Any foreign tourist who checks into a hotel receives a call within an hour from a local resident who speaks the visitor's tongue.

In a small Iowa city, a homemaker, cooperating with the local hotels and the Chamber of Commerce, holds a coffee klatch for foreign tourists who stop there. If a tourist with a language difficulty signs in at Washington's Statler-Hilton Hotel, a clerk hands him a card that says in thirty-two tongues, "I speak —————— and I require an interpreter." The hotel then provides an interpreter from its staff or furnishes the name, address, and telephone number of one. That Americans, once considered by many as provincial and aloof to foreigners, maintain a posture of great friendliness to people from other areas is attested by Mr. Voit Gilmore, Director of the U.S. Travel Service, who has remarked, "People want to do something for their country. They want to be hospitable." But most of us can do little more than exchange glances.

Volunteer efforts, no matter how praiseworthy, are not quite enough to insure the implementation of any blueprint. Teeth need to be put into any master plan for making America a nation of practicing bilinguals. All our efforts to build up a truly effective force of linguists for war or peace will be hamstrung unless provisions are made for some sort of follow-up training. At present, for example, as much as $15,000 may be spent by the armed services or government to train a man in an important tongue—let's say, Persian or Chinese. After leaving the government or military, the individual's skills in a few years become slight or lost entirely through disuse. This can be remedied by setting up a Language Reserve Corps, similar to the forces' reserves, which will provide monetary incentives and opportunities for refresher and advanced training for all those who can be induced to keep their skills functional for our national reservoir of tongues.

A network of "language practice centers" needs to be set up throughout the country where citizens at a minimal charge might have the opportunity of keeping their language knowledge functional and of gaining new language skills. Specified standards and tests would be set up whereby individuals could qualify for the National Language Reserve Corps. Since this is a cause of such common concern, funds for support would have to be solicited from government, industry, the foundations, and from citizen groups.

Finally, to give guidance and direction to the numerous and varied patchwork of linguistic efforts now in existence, it is suggested that a National Language Coordinating Council be created, responsible only to the White House itself. Made up of experts and leaders from the armed forces, other government agencies, industry, the schools and citizen organizations, such a body could add a dimension to the nation's language efforts which is sadly lacking today. It also could help implement a national blueprint for more language power. While nourishing no illusions about what committees can accomplish, a Coordinating Council might do a great deal of good. A similar body for science exists in the National Science Foundation. Why not a National Language Foundation?

An educational writer commented recently that perhaps our future will be assured, not on athletic fields or through physical fitness programs—however necessary these are—but in classrooms where science, mathematics, the humanities, and foreign languages are taught. Echoing this, we might paraphrase King Lear and say: "Let us mend our foreign speech, lest it may mar our national fortune."

# APPENDIX

## Reading List for Information about Linguistics

Two articles which are genuine popularizations of technical linguistics, the only ones to date, both appeared in *Astounding Science Fiction* (now called *Analog*):

"How to Talk to a Martian," by G. R. Shipman, Vol. LII, No. 2 (Oct. 1953), pp. 112-120.

"How to Learn Martian," by Charles F. Hockett, in 1955, reprinted in *Coming Attractions* edited by Martin Greenberg (New York: Gnome Press, 1957), pp. 39-51.

Something of the history of linguistics and the development of some of its important basic concepts can be found in Chapter II, "Linguistics: The Study of Language," in *Linguistics and Reading* by Charles C. Fries (New York: Holt, 1963), pp. 35-92.

A linguistic point of view and an insight into the tremendous variety possible in grammatical systems can both be found in:

"American Indian Grammatical Categories," by Edward Sapir and Morris Swadesh, *Word,* Vol. II, No. 2 (Aug. 1946), pp. 103-112.

A general explanation of what linguistics is about—from a point of view somewhat different from that of the authors of this volume—is given by André Martinet in "Structural Linguistics," appearing in *Anthropology Today* edited by A. L. Kroeber (Chicago: University of Chicago Press, 1953).

The books about linguistics written in a popular vein are scarce—and tend to be a bit one-sided.

*Learning a Foreign Language: A Handbook for Missionaries* by Eugene A. Nida (New York: National Council of the Churches of Christ in the U.S.A., 1950) certainly gives a picture of what linguistics is like, but most of the book is made up of instructions to people who must learn a language for which adequate textbooks or courses are not available.

The imaginary dialogs of a linguist defending his ideas occupy Nida in *Linguistic Interludes* (Norman, Oklahoma: Summer Institute of Linguistics, 1944). The book is not easy to find, but might be the next logical step for anyone whose interest has been engaged by the sections about linguistics in this present volume.

*The Science of Language: An Introduction to Linguistics* by John P. Hughes (New York: Random House, 1962) presents some topics well, but slights others that many linguists would consider important.

*Language: An Introduction to the Study of Speech* by Edward Sapir (1921, reprinted as a "Harvest Book" HB7 by Harcourt, Brace) still contains valuable insights and much food for thought, but the directions linguistic science has taken since have often not been along the lines of his major interests.

The most reliable and readily understandable general introduction to linguistics is definitely polemical in tone and, if you are at all committed to the views of language you are taught in high school, it might be best to take a tranquilizer before reading it:

*Linguistics and Your Language* by Robert A. Hall, Jr. (New York: Doubleday, 1960—an "Anchor Book").

Dr. Hall has also written—and in a less contentious vein— the only book in the field which can be called, without any qualification, an elementary textbook: *Introductory Linguistics* (Philadelphia: Chilton Books, 1964). The presentation is at the same time reasonably comprehensive and also reasonably simple and straightforward. Eighty lesson-length chapters introduce the major topics generally recognized at present as belonging in a beginning course in linguistics (except that he has deliberately not given any account of the history of linguistics or any survey of the world's languages). Major emphasis falls on acquainting the reader with the study of both the structure and the history of languages; these two areas receive approximately equal treatment.

There are, as yet, only three general books giving a picture of the whole field and considered basic for a serious understanding of it. These, which are all definitely technical, are listed here, starting with the least difficult:

*An Introduction to Descriptive Linguistics,* Revised edition, by H. A. Gleason, Jr. (New York: Holt, 1961).

*A Course in Modern Linguistics by* Charles F. Hockett (New York: Macmillan, 1958).

*Language* by Leonard Bloomfield (New York: Holt, 1933).

Observing what interests linguists when they are dealing with your own language can be one way of gaining more appreciation of linguistics. The two books we would recommend for this, in spite of their slight disadvantage of dealing with British English, are:

*Modern English Structure* by Barbara M. H. Strang (New York: St. Martin's Press, 1962).

*The Use of English* by Randolph Quirk (London: Longman's, 1962).

An excellent recent book, with some of the clearest presentations of linguistic topics that can be found, is:

*A Linguistic Introduction to the History of English* by Morton W. Bloomfield and Leonard Newmark (New York: Knopf, 1963). In a typical chapter one period in our language's history and a particular set of linguistic procedures are explained together. It includes an introduction to a generative approach to syntax.

# INDEX

**Date Due**